If Looks Could Kill

If Looks Could Kill

MICHAEL BLAIR

M&S

Cloth edition published in 2001
First paperback edition published in 2002

National Library of Canada Cataloguing in Publication Data

Blair, Michael, 1946–
If looks could kill

ISBN 0-7710-1128-8

I. Title.

PS8553.L3354I3 2002   C813'.6   C2001-903276-5
PR9199.4.B53I3 2002

We acknowledge the financial support of the Government of Canada
through the Book Publishing Industry Development Program
for our publishing activities. We further acknowledge the support
of the Canada Council for the Arts and the Ontario Arts Council
for our publishing program.

Cover design by K.T. Njo
Cover photo by Elizabeth Knox / Masterfile

Typeset in Bembo by M&S, Toronto
Printed and bound in Canada

McClelland & Stewart Ltd.
The Canadian Publishers
481 University Avenue
Toronto, Ontario
M5G 2E9
www.mcclelland.com

1 2 3 4 5   06 05 04 03 02

for Pamela

I

Saturday afternoon around the middle of June, Harvey and I were in the Vancouver airport domestic arrivals concourse, waiting for Hilly's flight from Toronto to unload and amusing ourselves watching the bright summertime bustle. Harvey sat beside me, resting on his elbows and leaning heavily against my leg, his big rectangular head swivelling slowly back and forth. I shoved him with my knee. "Sit up straight," I said. "And quit drooling on the terrazzo." He grinned stupidly up at me. Even when he was on his elbows, the top of his head reached almost to my waist.

Harvey was a hundred kilograms of Harlequin Great Dane that belonged to Maggie Urquhart, one of my neighbours. Because Maggie didn't drive, I had agreed to pick Harvey up from the vet on my way to the airport. I had brought him into the terminal with me because when I tried leaving him in the car he had raised such a ruckus I was afraid he'd rip off a door and bust out. I didn't know if dogs were allowed in the airport, but so far no one from airport security had tried to throw us out.

Harvey's weight against my leg slowly increased until I had to brace myself to prevent him from falling over. I shoved him with my knee again. He straightened up with an indignant grunt. A woman standing nearby glared at me and moved warily away.

"Daddy!"

My arms were suddenly full of twelve-year-old girl.

"Hey, scout." I kissed the top of her head. Her reddish-blond hair smelled of sweet apples and recycled air. I held her at arm's length. She seemed a foot taller than when I'd last seen her at Christmas, all elbows and knees and a smattering of freckles across the bridge of her nose. She'd also had her nose pierced and wore a tiny silver ring through her left nostril. I thought she was still a bit young for that sort of thing – hell, I knew she was a bit young for that sort of thing – but I kept my comments to myself. It wasn't easy, though.

"You've grown," I said.

"You've shrunk," she said.

"That must be it," I said. "All this damp West Coast weather."

I noticed a tall, stern-faced woman waiting impatiently for the reunion to end. She was wearing a flight attendant's uniform and holding a large carry-on. I looked at Hilly. She smiled innocently.

"What's going on?" I asked.

"My name is Eunice Hackett," the woman said. "Senior flight attendant. Are you this young lady's father?"

"Yes, I am." We didn't shake hands. "Is something wrong?"

As if noticing him for the first time, Hilly exclaimed, "Oh, he's darling!" and knelt beside Harvey. She petted his huge head. If he'd been a cat, he'd have purred.

It was a transparent ruse and brought a scowl to Ms. Hackett's face. The expression did not look good on her. She held out the carry-on. I took it.

Disconcertingly, it writhed, as if alive.

"I have a bad feeling about this," I said as I set it carefully on the floor and started to open the zipper.

"Be careful," Ms. Hackett warned. "It may be vicious."

"Oh, she is not!" Hilly said in a disgusted voice. "Let me. You'll only scare her."

Hilly unzipped the bag and a small black-and-tan and elegantly whiskered wedge-shaped face thrust out, pink nose twitching, black button eyes curious and intelligent. The rest of the creature followed, flowing into Hilly's arms, eighteen sinuous inches of silky fur.

"It's a weasel," Ms. Hackett said.

"Beatrix is not a weasel," Hilly said emphatically. "She's a ferret."

"Whatever it is," Ms. Hackett said, "it terrorized your daughter's seatmate. Fortunately, it didn't bite anyone."

"Beatrix only got upset because you tried to take her away from me," Hilly said. "She doesn't like being handled by strangers."

Realizing he was no longer the centre of attention, Harvey woofed loudly. Ms. Hackett jumped. Beatrix squeaked and disappeared into Hilly's bomber jacket.

"Shush, Harvey," I said. "Is Hilly under arrest or something?" I asked Ms. Hackett. "Or do you want me to buy Beatrix a ticket?"

Hilly giggled.

Ms. Hackett was not amused. "I don't make the rules. Animals are supposed to travel in the cargo hold, not first class."

"First class? I take back the offer to buy a ticket."

"Sir," Ms. Hackett said. "You don't seem to be taking this very seriously."

"I'm sorry," I said. "I disapprove of her actions, of course. Smuggling her pet onto the aircraft was irresponsible and dangerous, although likely more dangerous to Beatrix than to the other passengers. But what would you have me do, Ms. Hackett? What would you suggest as an appropriate punishment?"

"They'd never have caught us except Beatrix couldn't keep quiet. I don't think she likes flying."

"Hillary, pipe down."

"I suppose grounding her till she's sixteen would be too much to expect," Ms. Hackett said hopefully, almost wistfully.

"A little extreme, perhaps," I said, revising my opinion of her. Maybe she did have a sense of humour after all. "And not very practical, under the circumstances; my ex-wife has custody. I was thinking more along the lines of a couple of weeks of hard labour."

"Daddy!"

"That would be acceptable," Ms. Hackett agreed solemnly. Then she smiled. It looked good on her. "By the way," she added, "did you know that, ah, Beatrix is trained as an aid to the hearing impaired?"

"No, I didn't." I looked sternly at Hilly. She had worn hearing aids since she was four, tiny devices that fit into her ear canals and were almost − but not quite − invisible. "A hearing-ear ferret?"

"She is, you know," Hilly said. "At home she wakes me up when I sleep without my hearing aids. Well, most of the time," she amended.

I turned back to Ms. Hackett. "Ma[...]
hard labour *and* bread and water."

Hilly snorted, a not very ladylike sou[...]
she said. "You're a lousy cook anyway." [...]
Ms. Hackett. "The last time I visited he tr[...] [poi]son
me, I'm sure of it, but my mother wouldn't believe me.
I begged her not to send me this summer, but she
wouldn't listen. Do you know he's wanted by the police
in three states and at least one province? I'm adopted. I
must be. What else could explain it?"

"I warned the doctors not to leave your test tube
next to the microwave."

"Thank you for flying Air Canada," Ms. Hackett
said. "Perhaps you could take the train home."

"You flew first class?" I said to Hilly after Ms.
Hackett made good her escape.

"Mom insisted."

"Well, I hope she bought you a return ticket."

"Cheapskate. Don't worry, I've got it right here." She
patted the side of her carry-on.

"Do you have any more luggage?"

"Do bears –"

"Don't say it!"

"You say it all the time."

"Don't do as I do . . ."

". . . do as I say. I know. Hypocrite."

We found the appropriate carousel and watched as
luggage of every shape and size tumbled down the conveyor. We hadn't waited long when a huge black suitcase
plummeted down the conveyor and smashed a soft-
sided suit bag against the rim of the carousel. A beefy
man in a rumpled business suit jumped back in alarm.

s mine," Hilly said.

apologized to the man as I wrestled the massive suitcase off the carousel. "Good grief," I said. "Did you bring everything you own?"

"Mom packed for me."

"It's got wheels," I said. "Where's the engine?" Hilly did something and a handle popped out of one end. "Good thing I have a trailer hitch on my car."

As I grasped the handle and started towing the suitcase toward the exit, I caught sight of a dark-haired woman standing at the next carousel and my heart seemed to implode in my chest.

2

There was a roaring in my ears and I couldn't catch my breath, as if all the oxygen had suddenly gone out of the air. I wanted to run away, but I no longer had control of my legs. I just stood there, gulping air like a stranded fish and silently beseeching the bush-league gods in charge of this corner of the universe to be merciful. Maybe it wasn't her, I thought. Maybe it was simply someone who looked like her, a resemblance heightened by a trick of the lighting.

But it was her.

I moved toward her on rubbery knees.

"Vince, this is stupid," I heard her say to the man with her at the carousel. "Where is Sam? He should be doing this, not you. You'll only hurt your back again."

"How the fuck should I know where he is?" the man answered. "And watch who you call stupid." He was dark and hawk-featured, as squat and ugly as she was lithe and beautiful.

"I wasn't calling you stupid, Vince," she said. "What I said was –"

"Yeah, yeah, never mind," he said, waving away her reply.

Two years hadn't changed her much. Her face was a bit fuller, rounder perhaps, and her black hair was worn more simply now, more elegantly. But her wide-set, slightly almond-shaped eyes were the same deep indigo blue I remembered and her ivory skin still seemed to glow with an inner luminescence. I could feel cracks starting to form in the fragile emotional shell I'd grown since she'd left.

"Carla?" I said, my voice dry and brittle.

She stiffened at the sound of her name, turned and looked at me, her flawless features composed and her indigo eyes as hard as glass. She stared at me for so long I became irrationally certain she could not place me, didn't remember me. Then her expression thawed slightly and she bared her teeth in a smile.

"Why, Tommy McCall," she said brightly. "What a pleasant surprise. How long have you been standing there?" When she stepped close and kissed me on the cheek, I almost backed away. "Be cool, Tommy," she whispered close to my ear as she not-quite-touched her lips to my other cheek. "Don't weird out on me."

"Vince," she said, turning to her companion. "This is Tommy McCall. Tommy, Vince Ryan."

Ryan stuck his hand out toward me. "McCall," he said.

"Vince," I said.

His hand was square and strong and he shook hands as though it was a test of strength. I gave back as good as I got, which brought a slight smile to his face.

Vince Ryan wasn't really ugly, but no one would ever call him handsome. His square face looked as though it had been put together from parts no one else had wanted: small deep-set black eyes under heavy,

8

overhanging brows; a great hooked beak of a nose that had been broken more than once; thin, bloodless lips; and a wide, powerful jaw that bulged with muscle.

When he finally released my hand, I turned back to Carla. I had imagined this encounter many times in the months after she'd left, played and replayed what I would say to her in my mind, but all I could think to say now was, "You're looking well."

"I am well, thank you," she replied. "And you? Are you prospering?"

"Prospering?" I said. It wasn't the kind of word I expected from her. "I'm not sure I'd say prospering exactly."

"It's been, what, two years?"

"About that," I said. It had been two years and four months, but who was counting? I became conscious of Hilly standing slightly behind me. "You remember my daughter, don't you?" I said.

"Is this Hilly?" Carla said, surprising me by remembering Hilly's name. "No, it can't be. How are you, Hilly?"

"I'm okay," Hilly said.

"You're almost all grown up now."

"I'm only twelve," Hilly said.

Vince Ryan said, "Hiya, kiddo," but at least he didn't pat her on the head. Good thing. Hilly might have bitten him. "Hey, nice rat," he said as Beatrix poked her head out of Hilly's jacket to see what was going on. Bored, Harvey flopped down onto the floor with a grunt and a thud.

We all stood around in awkward silence. There were a million things I wanted to say to Carla, a million questions I wanted to ask, but my mind was a chaotic jumble of half-formed thoughts and feelings.

"What have you been up to?" I asked lamely. "Did you ever do any modelling?"

Carla shook her head and Vince Ryan laughed. It was a harsh, humourless sound, half bark, half cough. He placed his blunt, powerful hands on her shoulders, his thick fingers making deep impressions in the filmy fabric of her blouse, pressing into the soft flesh beneath. I bit back the urge to tell him to take his hands off her.

"Carla works for me," he said. "She's my Gal Friday. Not to mention all the other days of the week," he added with a broad wink. "What do you do, McCall?" he asked.

"Do?" I said, as if I didn't understand. I find the question annoying, on a par with "What sign are you?" or "What was your taxable income last year?"

"Yeah, do," Ryan said, his heavy brows descending in a scowl so that his eyes were mere dark slits.

"Tommy's a photographer," Carla said.

"Oh, that's right," I said. "Sometimes I forget."

"A photographer, eh? All those gizmos the Nips are putting in cameras these days, almost anyone can take pictures."

"Yes, indeed," I said. "Almost anyone." Had he really said "Nips"?

"Well, it's been a pleasure meeting you all," Ryan said, smiling with all the sincerity of a politician hustling votes in a suburban shopping mall, "but we're going to have to cut it short. We're on our way up to Whistler. If my bloody driver ever gets here," he added, looking around.

"A driver, no less?" I said, looking at Carla. She gave me a wry smile.

"You ever done any skiing on Blackcomb Glacier?" Ryan asked.

"Horstman," I said.

"What?"

"There's no summer skiing on Blackcomb Glacier," I said. "Only on Horstman Glacier."

He shrugged it off. "Whatever. It's not important. Probably won't have time anyway. I'm working on a deal that will really put the place on the map."

"Whistler seems to have done all right so far," I said.

Ryan laughed his unpleasant laugh. "All right may be enough for some people," he said, "but not for me."

A massive blond beach-boy type joined our little group, about doubling its size.

"Sam," Ryan said. "Where the fuck've you been?"

"Sorry, Mr. Ryan," Sam replied easily, offering no explanation.

"Those are ours," Ryan said, pointing to a stack of matching luggage beside the carousel. Sam loaded the bags onto a cart and headed toward the exit.

Ryan nodded curtly to me and took Carla's arm.

Carla, momentarily resisting, said, "It was good to see you again, Tommy."

"Wait," I said.

She stopped and turned, Ryan's hand still on her arm.

I had spoken impulsively, with no idea of what I was going to say. There wasn't anything to say, I realized. Not now. "Nice to see you too," I said.

Ryan pulled her almost roughly toward the exit.

I held my breath, bracing myself for the crush of disappointment, for the same profound loss I'd felt two years ago when she'd disappeared without a word. When it did not come, I let the air leak slowly out of my lungs. I felt a peculiar sense of relief, as if I'd just awakened from one of those vividly real dreams in which a tooth has fallen out or I'd started smoking again. Carla had messed up my life once, and once was quite enough, thank you. As interesting as the wrapping was, I didn't need the hassle that came with the rest of the package. Nevertheless, I could feel the spot on my cheek where she'd kissed me, and the heavy musk of her perfume still lingered in the air.

"Daddy?" Hilly said.

Mentally shaking myself, I said to Hilly, Beatrix, and Harvey, "All right, troops, let's hustle."

3

It took teamwork, but we finally managed to get Harvey into the back of my old long-bodied Land Rover, wedged between Hilly's suitcase and the heavy steel equipment case I'd had bolted into the rear cargo space. Harvey still didn't seem to be aware of Hilly's furry little pal, even though the ferret kept peering over Hilly's shoulder at the dog. I wondered if ferrets had multiple lives like cats.

"You should zip Beatrix into her bag," I told Hilly as we pulled out of the airport parking lot. "I don't want her getting underfoot while we're driving."

"But she likes looking out the window," Hilly said.

"At least put her on a leash," I said.

"I don't have one."

In the luggage space, Harvey sat up, his huge grey-and-black head looming in the rearview mirror. Beatrix beat a hasty retreat into Hilly's jacket as he laid his head on the back of the seat.

"Does your mother know you smuggled her onto the plane?" I asked.

"No. She thinks I left her with a friend. You won't tell her, will you?"

"No," I said. "I won't tell her. How did you manage it, anyway?"

"Inside my shirt."

"Is she housebroken?"

"Well, she kind of uses kitty litter, most of the time. She's still in training."

"Wonderful."

She reached into the side pocket of Beatrix's bag, took out a small hardcover book with a photograph of a very cute ferret on the cover, opened it, and started reading silently to herself.

The Saturday afternoon traffic was light and we made good time, aided by some luck with the lights on Granville. At 16th Avenue, I turned right off Granville, then left onto Hemlock. As we approached the lights at Hemlock and Broadway I spotted a pet store in the small shopping centre at the corner. Lucking into a parking space, we left Harvey in the Land Rover, barking and slobbering on the windows, while Hilly and I went into the store. Over Hilly's protests, I selected a cage large enough to give Beatrix some room to move around, a litter pan that fit inside, a bag of litter, a drinking bottle, and other paraphernalia to make Beatrix a home away from home. I also bought a harness and leash so Hilly could take Beatrix for walks, or whatever one did with a ferret.

"Beatrix doesn't like cages," Hilly said again as I loaded the cage into the back of the Land Rover.

"Neither do I," I said, "but until she's completely housebroken I'm damned if I'm going to give her free run of the house."

"That's not fair."

"Perhaps not," I agreed, "but that's the way it's going to be."

I opened the passenger door for her and she threw herself into the car, scowling darkly. She was still sulking a few minutes later when we swung under the six-lane span of the Granville Bridge approach and drove between the massive bridge piers onto Granville Island, a renovated industrial area in False Creek, the narrow inlet that separates the southern sections of Vancouver from the downtown core. I lived in Sea Village, a community of a dozen or so floating homes moored two-deep along the embankment between the Granville Island Hotel marina and the Emily Carr Institute of Art and Design. My house was a registered vessel called *Enterprise*, of all things, owned by Howie Silverman, an old friend and real-estate developer (and *Star Trek* fan) who'd retired to Israel, to the frustration of Revenue Canada. It resembled a New England two-storey wood-frame cottage transported west and installed on a reinforced concrete hull, except that the clapboard was forest green and the roof was flat and surrounded by a cedar railing. I paid a nominal rent, plus the taxes, mooring fees, utilities, insurance, and maintenance. I might have been able to live more economically else-where, but Granville Island was a lively and interesting place, although in the summer sometimes a bit too lively. And it was a three-minute ferry ride across False Creek to the dock at the foot of Hornby Street, from where it was an easy walk to my studio at Granville and Davie.

I parked the Land Rover in my reserved slot next to the boardwalk and unloaded Harvey and Hilly's luggage. The tide was out and Sea Village's main floating dock, which runs parallel to the embankment, was fifteen feet below the level of the boardwalk atop the embankment. Harvey looked uncertain as I led him down the steeply sloped ramp onto the dock, which I was sure sank slightly under his weight. I wondered if dogs were susceptible to motion sickness. Some people, my mother among them, find the constant slow movement of the docks and the floating homes disturbing, although my father insists it's all in her head. But Harvey seemed to relax as soon as he was surrounded by the walls of Maggie Urquhart's house.

"Was he any trouble?" Maggie asked as she unclipped the leash from his collar.

"None at all," I said.

Maggie was about fifty, petite and slim, with quick dark eyes, thick grey-blond hair cut boyishly short, fine bone structure, and a firm, flawless complexion. A professor of anthropology at UBC who had written an international bestseller a few years ago about urban spiritualism or something that had made her comfortably well-off, she and Harvey had moved into Sea Village about six months ago. She was taking a sabbatical to write another book and had offered to keep an eye on Hilly from time to time.

"I really appreciate your picking him up," she said.

"It's the least I can do," I said.

"Still," she said, opening a fat red nylon wallet. I thought for a moment that she was going to try to give me money, but she unzipped a compartment and took out a purple-and-black business card. "Maybe I can do your chart."

"My chart?" I said. She indicated the card. There was a complex wheel symbol in the corner, and the text read MAGGIE URQUHART, ASTROLOGER. "Ah," I said. "My chart."

"Hilly, don't give me a hard time about this," I said as we unloaded Beatrix's new cage from the Land Rover. I put it into the communal wheelbarrow the residents of Sea Village use to transport groceries and such down the ramp onto the docks. "I'll bet your mother doesn't give her free reign in her house."

"She makes her live in a cage in the basement," Hilly answered resentfully.

"I'm surprised she even let you keep her."

"The school shrink said it would be good for me to have a pet, teach me responsibility and all that dreck." Hilly made a face. "Mom wanted me to get fish. Fish aren't pets, they're pet food."

"What about a cat? Cats are nice. Or a dog."

"Boring. Besides, the jerk's allergic to dogs."

"The jerk?"

"Mom's husband," she said with a disparaging sneer. "My ugly stepfather. The Fat Food King."

"Ah, Jack." Jack Flynn was my ex-wife's husband. He owned a chain of fast-food franchises around Toronto and made buckets of money. I suppressed a guilty thrill of satisfaction that Hilly didn't like him. I had met him only once and he had seemed to be an okay guy, but he was, after all, married to my ex-wife, and for the last five years had played a larger part in my daughter's life than I had. "And he's not allergic to Beatrix?"

"She's hypno-allergic."

"That's hypoallergenic, I think."

"Whatever."

"I'll make a deal with you," I said. "Until Beatrix gets used to the place, she lives in the cage with her litter pan. Once she's proved she's trained to the litter, she can come out. But only when you're around to watch out for her. And," I added, "the ferret on the cover of your book has a bell on its collar. I think that's a good idea. Keep her from getting stepped on."

"I have a collar like that, but she doesn't like it."

"She'll get used to it. Do we have a deal?"

"I suppose," she agreed grudgingly.

"Good," I said. "All right, let's get this stuff put away. Your grandparents will be here soon."

Hilly's huge suitcase almost got away from me on the ramp. It was probably waterproof, but I was relieved I didn't have to fish it out of the harbour. Daniel Wu was out on his roof deck, tending his forest of plants. Daniel was an architect, sixty-odd, about five feet tall, and owned the biggest house in Sea Village, directly across the dock from mine. Hilly adored him.

"Daniel," Hilly called, waving. Daniel waved back. "Daddy, can I go introduce Beatrix to Daniel?"

"Sure," I said. "But put this on her first." I helped her fit Beatrix with the harness we'd bought, and attached the leash. Beatrix twisted herself double and bit at the harness.

"She doesn't like it," Hilly said.

"She'll get used to it," I said.

"Daniel, can I come up?" Hilly called up to Daniel.

"You certainly may," he called down. "The door's open."

Hilly went to visit with Daniel while I lugged her suitcase, the cage, and the rest of the stuff into my more modest dwelling. My parents would be arriving within the hour and I had to get dinner started, so I just left everything in the hall and went into the kitchen. Yes, I know, boats have galleys, not kitchens, and some of the residents of Sea Village insist on calling their kitchens galleys, but as far as I'm concerned, floating homes are houses, not boats, notwithstanding that they must be registered as such. Some people call them houseboats, but they aren't. A houseboat is an actual boat, in form and function, with a motor and a pilothouse, and you can unhook it from the utilities and a-sailing go. My house, on the other hand, wouldn't have looked out of place in any mainland neighbourhood, except maybe for Maggie Urquhart's eighteen-foot Boston Whaler parked in the slip between her house and mine.

I started laying things out on the stainless-steel countertop. I'd planned the menu days earlier, had got in everything I'd need – normally my cupboards made Old Mother Hubbard look like a hoarder. I liked to cook, even liked to think I wasn't half bad at it – at least I hadn't killed anyone – but I didn't get much joy out of cooking for myself, so when I got a chance to display my stuff, I tended to go all out. Hanging on a hook on the inside of the pantry door was the funny apron Carla had given me. It was the only gift I'd ever got from her. On a whim, I put it on. I'd never used it and it was stiff with starch and newness. On the front was an enlarged replica of an Emergency Poison Control sticker.

For a long time after Carla left, whenever I closed my eyes I saw her face, felt the smooth silken touch of her against my palms, remembered the taste of her, the delicate scent of her skin and her hair. I got over her slowly, but I got over her. At least I thought I had.

I had a little time to spare so, feeling masochistic, I went upstairs to the small room I used as a TV room and home office. I opened the bottom drawer of the file cabinet and took out a brown manila folder. The folder contained a dozen eight-by-ten black-and-white photographs and an equal number of three-by-five colour prints I had taken of Carla. The black-and-whites were studio shots, stark lighting accentuating her moonlight-pale skin against the light-absorbing seamless black backdrop, so that she appeared to float weightless in a starless space. Even though it had been her idea, she'd been nervous at first, uncomfortable about posing nude (but not half as nervous or uncomfortable as I'd been) and her earlier poses had been artlessly immodest and wouldn't have looked out of place in *Penthouse* magazine. Soon she'd begun to relax, though, to forget about the camera, about me; she'd begun focussing inwardly. And I'd cooled down enough to think about lighting and composition, contour and texture and contrast.

The colour photos had been taken on a summer's day in Stanley Park, by the big freshwater pond called Lost Lagoon, and on Prospect Point, with the dark arc of the Lions Gate suspension bridge in the background. They were just casual snaps, but as I flipped through them, my chest filled with an icy white heat that made breathing difficult. In the colour prints she was real, a flesh and blood and bone human being, not the unearthly creature in the black-and-whites, cool and soulless and distant.

She was radiantly, exquisitely, breathtakingly beautiful and it had been a source of constant wonderment that she'd loved me.

But she hadn't, of course.

I tossed the photographs back into the drawer and went downstairs to shell shrimp.

4

"I don't know why you insist on living here," my father said, stirring his Scotch-rocks with his finger. "For what it costs you to live here you could buy a condo in Kitsilano or Point Grey. You're not building any equity, either. You should think about your future." Dad was sixty-three and had worked for the same engineering firm since graduating from Queen's University at age twenty-four. Three years ago he'd taken early retirement to devote himself full time to managing the modest stock portfolio he'd built.

"Forty," I said as I went on shelling shrimp.

"Eh?"

"I'll start thinking about my future when I turn forty," I said. Truth be known, however, I'd been thinking about my future since I'd turned thirty. I just hadn't done much about it, except quit my job at the *Vancouver Sun* to start my own photography business, a decision I occasionally but only mildly regretted. I'm not the entrepreneurial type, don't really have the hustle. I liked the freedom, though, so it was a worthwhile trade-off.

"You're what?" Dad said. "Thirty-eight?"

"Seven."

"When I was thirty-seven I'd already paid off the mortgage on our house."

"Which you probably immediately re-mortgaged to invest in some crazy scheme —"

"I never took chances with the roof over our heads," he said. "I had a responsibility to your mother and you kids." He sipped his drink. "With careful management your mother and I won't become a burden on our children in our later years."

"I thought you always intended to be a burden on your children," I said. "We owed you, you said."

"You do," he agreed. "But at the rate you're going, you'll never be able to afford it."

"How about Mary-Alice? She's got plenty of money. Or David has, at least."

"Christ, my son-in-law the proctologist," Dad said with a snort of disgust. "She could at least have married a real doctor. It's bad enough he's damned near as old as I am."

And damned near as stuffy, I added to myself. Of course, what could you expect from a man who'd spent the best part of his adult life peering at people's nether regions? When I'd told Linda, to whom I was still married at the time, that my little sister was going to marry a proctologist almost twice her age, her only comment had been a dry, "Bummer."

I finished shelling the shrimp, put them in the refrigerator, and wiped my hands on paper towel. "Refill?" I asked, pointing to Dad's drink.

"Uh?" He seemed surprised his glass was empty. "Sure." He handed me the glass.

My mother came into the kitchen and Dad's expression turned stony.

"Is Hillary still next door with that man?" my mother asked.

"Yes, she is," I replied. I heard the edge of irritation in my voice, but if my mother noticed it, she chose to ignore it. I handed my father his drink and punched a button on the kitchen phone. It dialled Daniel's number. When his machine picked up, I hit the pound-sign button to bypass his outgoing message and said, "Daniel, would you send Hilly home, please? Her grandparents are here. Thanks." I hung up.

"I don't know how you can let her stay alone with that man," my mother said.

My father said, "His name is Daniel, for god's sake."

Mother ignored him. He took his drink into the other room.

In the early fifties, before meeting and marrying my father, my mother had been a runway model and B-movie actress. I'd seen photographs of her and she had been a very lovely woman, cool and elegant and grace-ful. While it's difficult for a son to be objective about his mother without twinges of Oedipal guilt, she was still attractive, although sometimes it was hard to tell through the pancake, rouge, and eyeliner. Time and gravity, though, as well as two children, had taken a toll. She wasn't obese, but she wasn't exactly slim either. And she dressed as though she still weighed a hundred and ten pounds, in close-fitting garments that empha-sized her plumpness and severely strained the contain-ment limits of Lycra.

"Do you have any Gravol?" she asked as I started on the salad dressing.

"In the downstairs bathroom," I said. "Mother, I don't see how my house can make you seasick when

24

you manage the ferry trip from Victoria without any problems."

"That's different," she said. "The ferry's a boat, which is supposed to rock. This is a house, which isn't."

I couldn't dispute her logic.

"I don't know why we couldn't have had dinner at Susan's restaurant," she said with a martyred sigh.

"It's not Susan's restaurant," I said. "She just manages it."

"You know what I mean." She dipped a finger into the salad dressing and tasted it. "Mmm," she said. "I don't know how you turned out be such a good cook. I can't even boil water."

"You know that's not true," I said. "You're a very good cook."

"No, I'm not," she insisted. "I was never any good at those kinds of things, like cooking and sewing and managing a household budget. Just ask your father. I never had time to learn, I was always too busy with my career."

I sighed. Her career had been over for forty years. I was saved from the consequences of an impolitic remark to that effect by the slamming of the front door.

"Grumps!" Hilly shouted.

"Stinkpot!" my father replied.

Mother scowled disapprovingly.

"Whatcha got there?" I heard my father ask.

I went into the living room. Beatrix was perched on my father's shoulder, snuffling his hair.

"Careful, Dad," I said. "She probably thinks it's a relative."

"Watch your tongue, junior," Dad replied. "I noticed you're starting to get a little thin on top."

"What *is* it?" Mother asked, a look of horror on her plump, powdered face.

"It's a ferret," Hilly replied. "Her name is Beatrix."

Beatrix, satisfied that Dad's hairpiece wasn't competition for the local food supply, jumped into Hilly's arms. Hilly started toward her grandmother.

"Please," Mother said, raising her hands and backing away.

"Hilly," I said, "put Beatrix in her cage."

"I'll take her," Dad said.

Hilly handed Beatrix to her grandfather then came and hugged her grandmother.

"My, how you've grown," Mother said, not quite kissing Hilly's cheek.

"It's very nice to see you again, Grandma," Hilly said politely.

"Please, darling, call me Eleanor."

Hilly stammered, "Well, I dunno . . ." She looked at me in consternation.

"Mother," I said, "I don't think Hilly's comfortable with that."

"Well, fine," Mother said. Her voice was brittle. "It's up to her, I won't insist."

"Oh, for god's sake, Eleanor," my father said.

My mother glared at him. I recognized the look. I had seen it too often in the final years of my marriage.

"What is this?" she said. "Pick-on-Eleanor day or something?"

"No one's picking on you," I said.

"It certainly feels like it."

"For heaven's sake, El," my father said. "Relax. Don't spoil the evening."

"See," Mother said. "Now I'm ruining the evening. I can't do anything right."

"Are we going to eat soon?" Hilly asked, a hint of desperation in her voice.

"We're waiting for one more guest."

"Who?" Hilly asked.

"A friend," I said.

"A girlfriend?"

"You could say that," I answered. To forestall more questions, I said, "Hilly, why don't you go and set up Beatrix's cage. I put everything in your room. I'll call you when supper's ready."

"I'll help," Dad said. "C'mon, Stinkpot."

"Gordon," Mother said. "I wish you wouldn't insist on using that childish nickname."

He ignored her and he and Hilly took Beatrix upstairs.

"Old fool," Mother said, half under her breath.

I went to the small bar in the living room and poured myself a much-needed drink.

"Are you going to change?" Mother asked.

"No," I said. I was perfectly respectable, I thought, dressed in freshly laundered jeans, a mite faded perhaps, but with plenty of mileage left in them, a forest-green cotton shirt, a red-and-black silk tie, and creased but recently polished Boulet cowboy boots, handmade in Quebec, of all places.

"You should try to set a better example for Hillary," my mother said.

"I know," I said. "But I tried setting a good example for Mary-Alice and look what happened."

"What do you mean? What's wrong with Mary-Alice?"

"Never mind," I said, looking at my watch and wondering where Susan had got to. She was supposed to have been here by six and it was now almost seven.

"I wish you'd reconsider letting us take Hillary back to Victoria with us now," Mother said, "instead of at the end of the summer."

"We've been through that," I said. "I haven't spent much time with her since the divorce. I want to get to know her before she's all grown up."

"What are you going to do with her when you're at work?"

"I've got a couple of interesting shoots coming up."

"Do you really think she'll enjoy that?"

"One's a movie location. She'll get to meet George Clooney."

"How thrilling for her. But what about the rest of the time? She can't just hang around your office all day."

"The community centre has a excellent summer program," I said. "I've also arranged with Maggie Urquhart, my next-door neighbour, to keep an eye on her. And in a pinch there's always Daniel."

I knew it was a mistake as soon as I said it.

"You aren't going to leave her alone with that man, are you? Why, he's . . . he's . . ."

"Chinese?" I prompted.

"You know what I mean."

"No, what do you mean?"

"He's a *homosexual*," she said.

"Then Hilly's safer with him than with a lot of straight men I know," I said.

The gate buzzer rang. Thank god, I thought. I went into the kitchen and pressed the button by the phone that released the gate.

"We'll talk later," Mother said as I went to the front door to let Susan in.

Susan Shore and I had been seeing each other for about eight months. She managed a restaurant on Granville Island called Chez François, very chic and upscale. I hated it and she knew it, but we were adult about it. Sort of. My mother loved it and, with some cautiously expressed reservations about Susan's religious "persuasion," she also approved of Susan.

I liked Susan. She was attractive, intelligent, and independent-minded, with a healthy attitude toward the physical side of a relationship. I could certainly do worse, and had done. Perhaps I even loved her, but I had recently come to the realization that I wasn't ready to consider a permanent, even if informal, arrangement. I had been divorced for only five years, after all.

"Sorry I'm late," she said as I closed the door behind her. She kissed me quickly, handed me a bottle of California Chardonnay, already chilled, then went to my mother and hugged her. "How are you, Eleanor?" she said. "I hope I haven't kept you waiting. Saturday night is a busy time."

"That's all right, dear," Mother said. "*I* understand." From the emphasis and the glance in my direction, I inferred that my mother felt that I, on the other hand, did not.

"Where's your daughter?" Susan asked me. "I can't wait to meet her." She hadn't met Hilly last Christmas, had spent Hanukkah with her parents in Florida.

"Upstairs with my father," I said.

I went into the kitchen and put the wine in the refrigerator.

"I tried to convince him that we should eat at Chez François," I heard my mother say, "but he insisted on cooking."

"He's a good cook," Susan said. "Even if I haven't been able to train him to devein shrimp," she added, raising her voice a little for my benefit.

Hilly came stamping down the stairs, a dark scowl on her face, Beatrix draped around her neck like a living stole. "She hates it," she declared. "I knew she would."

"We'll discuss it later," I said, hearing my mother's voice in my head. "Hilly, this is my friend Susan Shore. Susan, my daughter, Hilly. Short for Hillary."

Susan thrust out her hand. "How do you do, Hilly," she said.

Hilly looked uncertain, tentatively took Susan's hand. "Hi," she said.

"And who's this?" Susan asked.

"Beatrix."

"May I pet her?"

"Sure," Hilly said. "She won't bite."

Susan gently stroked between Beatrix's small, teddy-bear ears. "She's sweet."

Dad came down the stairs.

"Gordon, your hair," Mother cried.

"Oops." He laid his hand atop his head. "Beatrix liked it so much I gave it to her to play with. Think I'll let her keep it. I hate the bloody thing anyway."

Mother opened and closed her mouth two or three times, finally made a very unladylike sound, and went to the bar and poured herself a large glass of white wine.

My father ignored her. "Hi, Suzy."

"Hello, Gordon." She'd given up trying to get him to stop calling her Suzy.

"Has this insensitive lout of a son of mine offered to make an honest woman of you yet?"

"Not so far," Susan said.

"I think I'll start dinner," I said, heading toward the kitchen.

5

"I don't like Susan," Hilly said.

It was Monday morning. We were standing on the Aquabus dock by the Public Market waiting for one of the tubby little ferries that ply between Granville Island and the north shore of False Creek. The weather was fair, but it was early in the day and there was still a slight chill in the air.

"Why not?" I asked.

Hilly shrugged. "She's too much like Mom."

"She is not," I said, just a little horrified by the thought.

"Oh, c'mon, Daddy."

"All right," I conceded. "Maybe a little." I suppose, like most men, I'm attracted to certain types of women, although I'd prefer to think I was more flexible. Both Susan and Linda were slim, dark-haired, and dark-eyed, but that was where any real resemblance ended.

"I like Carla," Hilly said. "She's way cool."

"Way cool, eh? The last time you saw her you were ten. I'm not sure ten-year-olds are very good judges of character."

"How many ten-year-olds have you known, Daddy?"

"Point taken," I replied. "But you saw Carla — what? — two or three times."

"I guess."

"Besides," I added, "she was on her best behaviour. Just give Susan a chance, okay?" This despite my own feelings of ambivalence.

"Sure, Daddy," Hilly said as the brightly painted little ferry bumped gently against the dock.

The Aquabus was about twenty feet long and shaped vaguely like a sea-going caboose, except that it was rounded at both ends. It was piloted by a sturdy young woman in jeans and a sweatshirt with the sleeves cut off.

"Hi, Tom," she said.

"Morning, Heidi."

Hilly and I waited while Heidi helped a pair of elderly tourists disembark, then we climbed aboard and ducked into the aft passenger cabin. I paid Hilly's fare. I was a regular, had a monthly pass, which I seldom bothered to show. Heidi climbed onto her high seat in the cupola-like wheelhouse, pushed the throttle forward, and the tiny boat bobbed and burbled away from the dock toward the far side of False Creek.

"This is neat," Hilly said.

She hadn't been keen on coming to the studio with me, especially after I'd told her she'd have to leave Beatrix at home. I didn't think the ferret would get along very well with Bodger, the old tabby cat that lived in the studio and allegedly earned his catnip by keeping the mice properly deferential. She'd come around, though, when I'd told her that a local rock band named The Scum or The Scabs or some such thing was coming in to select shots for the liner notes of their second self-produced CD.

Heidi let us off at the dock at the foot of Hornby Street and we walked up the hill to Granville and Davie. My studio was on the third floor of a small commercial building on Davie just around the corner from Granville, but before going up I bought half a dozen sweet rolls at the Chinese bakery across the street, trying to order them in Chinese from the girl behind the counter. Her name was Xuan, pronounced Swan, and she giggled as she tried in vain to correct my pronunciation.

As Hilly and I crossed to my building I saw that the chubby teenaged whore was hanging around the entrance again. Her face was garishly painted and her hair was dyed orange and black, the colours of Halloween candy. She wore a thin white Lycra halter top stretched across plump immature breasts, a shiny black vinyl micro-skirt, fishnet pantyhose, and absurdly high spiked heels, despite which she was barely a fraction of an inch taller than Hilly.

"It's eight-thirty in the morning, for god's sake," I said to her.

"Fuck you, pops," was her reply. Those were the only words she'd ever spoken to me. It wasn't a business proposition.

The phone-booth-sized lobby was dimly lit and stale-smelling. It was early yet and Dingy Bill was probably still sleeping it off in the stairwell, so we took the elevator to the third floor. I figured Hilly had seen enough local colour for one morning. I know I had.

The elevator was key-operated. As the only tenant on the third floor, I had exclusive use of it; for some reason the doors on the second floor, where the tenants were a one-man insurance agency, a driving school, and an escort service run by twin sisters named Meg and Peg,

34

had been sealed up. The ground floor housed a Mexican restaurant/bar called Zapata's and an occult bookstore run by a middle-aged woman who called herself Raven and claimed to be a professional witch.

In the elevator Hilly said, "Was that girl a hooker?"

"Yes, she's a hooker."

"Why'd she tell you to fuck off?"

"I guess she doesn't like me," I said. "And, listen, I'd just as soon you didn't use that kind of language, all right? I know you probably hear it all the time at school and likely use it yourself when you're with your friends, but give your old dad a break. Okay?"

"Sure," she said in a bored voice.

The elevator door clanked open and Hilly and I stepped out into the reception area of the studio. Ron Church, my lab tech, was at the reception desk, heels up and flipping through a *Penthouse* magazine. When he saw us he closed the magazine and put his feet down.

"Is the West Coast Hotels job ready?" I asked him.

"Not yet," he replied.

"They're expecting it this morning. And be careful. I don't want another screw-up like last time."

"Hey, man, that wasn't my fault."

"I didn't say it was."

He folded his magazine, got up slowly, and went into the lab at the back of the studio.

Ron had worked for me for a little over two years, but I knew sooner or later I was going to have to let him go. More likely sooner than later. I didn't much like him, but it wasn't something I felt any pleasure about. He knew his way around a lab and, when he took the trouble, could be a very good technician. But he'd been surlier than usual of late, on top of which I'd had to speak to him three or four times in as many weeks about his carelessness, most recently as a result of an incident that had cost us three days' work and quite possibly the client as well. I couldn't prove that the foul-up had been his fault – it may not have been – but his explanation that Bobbi, my assistant, had forgotten to change the program card in the film processor had been pretty lame. The lab was his responsibility, after all. Or perhaps I was simply more inclined to side with Bobbi. Either way, West Coast Hotels was one of our most important clients, if not our most important, so we'd reshot everything at our own expense. At considerable inconvenience to them, however.

The door from the stairway banged open and Bobbi stamped in.

"Goddamnit," she said.

"Good morning," I said.

"Oh. G'morning, boss," she said. She saw Hilly. "Oops. Hey, Hilly."

"Hi, Bobbi."

Roberta "Bobbi" Brooks was twenty-eight, almost as tall as I was, a wholesome, girl-next-door type with big brown eyes and long chestnut hair worn in a ponytail. She filled out jeans very nicely, but was as flat-chested as a boy, as evidenced by the drape of the T-shirts she habitually wore under her faded jean jacket.

"I gotta call the super," she said to Hilly. "Then we can visit."

"What's wrong?" I asked.

"Dingy Bill, uh, defecated on the landing again."

"Shit," I said. Hilly giggled. "I guess we're going to have to do something about him."

"Such as?" Bobbi wanted to know. "Last time we gave him money for a flop, he drank it. And when the super let him use the room in the basement, he damned near burned the place down."

Maybe we should move, I thought, find a nice new space in a better neighbourhood, get away from foul-mouthed teenage hookers and incontinent street people. But until things picked up a little, moving was out of the question; it was tough enough making the rent on this place.

I left Hilly and Bobbi to get reacquainted while I went into the main studio and started coffee. Bodger was asleep in my office, curled up in the fancy ergonomic executive chair that had been a parting gift from my co-workers at the *Sun*. He hissed at me when I tried to roust him, so I rolled the chair to the window and dragged another over to the desk. I stared out the window for a moment, at the blank wall of the old Hotel California across Davie. The building now housed a Howard Johnson's and the mural of the fifty-foot blue-jean-clad blonde that had adorned the wall had been painted over. I missed her and made a mental note to print up some of the shots I had taken of her over the years since I had moved into the studio. Then I woke up my computer and started working on the bid to do the photography for Garibaldi Air Services' annual report.

Half an hour later Bobbi knocked on the door frame. Without waiting for an answer, she came in, picked Bodger up, and sat in my chair, cuddling him in her lap. He purred loudly as she stroked his chewed-up ears.

"Bloody cat," I said. "Why do I tolerate him? He hates my guts and he hasn't caught a mouse in I don't know how long. You feed him too much. Look, he's getting fat as a pig."

"Boss," Bobbi said, "I've seen you feeding him those treats you keep in your drawer."

"Bribery is the only way I can get him out of my chair. And quit calling me boss." Although she'd been with me since I'd started the business six years ago and was now more friend and partner than employee, I couldn't get her to stop calling me "boss."

"Sorry. Can we talk?"

"Sure. What's up?"

"It's about the West Coast Hotels thing. I feel awful about it. I was certain I put the E6 card back in the processor after I used it."

The Wing-Lynch film processing machine I had bought second-hand when I had started the business had two program control cards: an E6 card for processing colour transparencies – that is, slide film – and a C41 card for processing negative film for colour prints. The cards fit into a single slot in the front of the processor, which was about the size of a small refrigerator. To switch between negative and transparency film processing, you had to pull out the C41 card and replace it with the E6 card. Mostly we worked in transparency, but for some of our smaller clients and most portrait work we shot colour print film. Someone, either Ron or Bobbi, had forgotten to change cards when we processed the West Coast Hotels job, which we had shot on transparency. If you use the right film, the right exposure settings, and avoid certain subject-matter colours, you can achieve some interesting creative effects developing slide film using the C41 process, but for our purposes the films had been ruined.

"Don't beat yourself up about it," I said, with perhaps more charity than I felt. "These things happened. Is the new stuff ready yet?"

"I just sent it down to be scanned."

More and more, both existing and prospective clients were demanding electronic files rather than film. I knew if I wanted to stay in business much longer, I was going to have to bite the bullet and go into hock to switch to digital; however, I intended to put it off as long as possible. So far we were managing by having transparencies scanned to CD-ROM disc by a service bureau, although it was eating into our already slim margins. But why had Bobbi sent the work out? That was Ron's job. I asked her.

"He said he was too busy," she said.

"With what?" I wondered aloud.

She shrugged.

"Right." Bodger jumped down from her lap, stretched, and sauntered out of the office. Maybe I should let Hilly bring Beatrix to the studio, I thought. Teach the bugger some respect. I had to start somewhere. "When are your rock 'n' rollers coming in?" I asked.

"About three."

"What are they called again? The Scum?"

"The Sluts," she said. "Nice girls. It was a fun shoot."

"I bet."

"I'm not sure if I'd call the stuff they play music," she said, "but the kids like it. Their first CD sold pretty well wherever they played. Hilly's listening to it now."

"If she dyes her hair green and red and starts wearing black combat boots," I said, "I'll know who to blame."

"Not me," Bobbi said with a laugh. "These girls dress more like that little hooker who hangs around downstairs."

"Oh, swell."

The phone in the reception area rang. Mrs. Szymkowiak, my part-time receptionist/bookkeeper wasn't in yet, so I intercepted it from my extension.

"Tom McCall," I said.

"Tommy? It's me. Carla. I need to see you."

6

I wanted to say no. I really did. My brain even sent the signal to my mouth, but what came out was, "Where are you?" Perhaps some other organ had taken control.

"I'm downtown," she said. "Around the corner from the place you bought me breakfast that first time."

"I have an appointment with a client near there at ten. I could meet you later, I suppose, say around eleven."

"I was hoping to see you sooner than that," she said.

"Come here then," I said.

"No, that wouldn't be a good idea. Could you meet me before your appointment? It won't take long."

"What won't take long?" I asked.

"I'd rather explain in person."

"Not even a hint," I said. "Should I check my insurance coverage?"

"Tommy, please."

"All right," I said. "I'll meet you in the coffee shop of the Pacific Palisades Hotel at Robson and Jervis in half an hour."

"Thanks, Tommy," she said, and hung up.

I arranged with Bobbi to courier the CD of scanned images to Pat Jirasek, West Coast Hotels' head of public relations and advertising, as soon as it was back from the service bureau, with a note that I'd talk to him later. Since I didn't have enough time to go home to pick up the Land Rover, I asked her if I could borrow her VW Golf, but she told me it was in the shop. I took a cab.

All the way downtown I berated myself for not having the good sense to say no to Carla. Since running into her at the airport I'd taken out my memories of her, held them up to the light, and examined them carefully. Even after two years it still made me squirm with embarrassment to remember what a complete idiot I'd been. But everyone was entitled to make mistakes. It was history now, though, time to close the book on that chapter of my life. Maybe I could do that today, over coffee.

When I first met Carla Bergman she was working as a singer with a cheesy lounge act called The Seven Ups, even though there were nine of them, if you counted the two girl singers. Music for every occasion – weddings, bar mitzvahs, grads, coming-out parties (I hadn't known people still had coming-out parties). They weren't very good. In fact, they made Lawrence Welk sound like the London Philharmonic. Remarkably, though, they'd grossed a couple of hundred thousand the year before and were prepared to spend some of it to upgrade their image. Who was I to argue? They set up in the studio, donned their lounge-lizard outfits, their manager loaded some tapes into my sound system – to help put them in the right mood, she said – and I began shooting. After a while I asked if I could turn the music off; I found it distracting.

The music wasn't half as distracting as one of the two girl singers in the group. A study in contrasts, both had probably been hired for looks rather than singing ability. One was bubbly and blonde and under any other circumstances I would have found her quite attractive. But the other literally took my breath away. She was lean and lithe as a dancer. Her coal-black hair was silken and slightly curled and her pale, flawless skin had a subtle yellowish cast, like antique ivory. But it was her eyes – indigo, almond-shaped and tilted and set almost too far apart – that I noticed first. They bewitched me and I wasted a dozen shots because of them, unable to resist the compulsion to capture them on film.

During a break I collected my nerve and asked her name.

"Carla Bergman," she said in a soft husky voice that made my pulse race.

I asked if she'd ever done any modelling, trying to build up the courage to ask for her telephone number. She smiled, and said, no, she hadn't, but it sounded interesting. Singing wasn't exactly her thing.

I kept my opinion to myself. When she'd sung along with the tapes, her voice had had a thin, reedy sound and she'd had trouble making the higher notes. The other girl might not have been able to compete in the looks department, but she was the better singer, hands down.

When the shoot was over, the manager wanted to talk about doing the same thing for another group she handled, and by the time I was finished with her, The Seven Ups, Carla included, had packed up and gone. I quietly obsessed for about a week, thought about calling The Seven Ups' manager and asking for Carla's telephone number but never did, then I more or less forgot about her.

Until one morning about three weeks later when she walked into the studio, told me she'd been fired and asked me if I'd been serious about the modelling. I told her that she certainly had the looks and the figure, but that modelling wasn't something you could just take up, like pottery or scuba diving, that she needed to put together a comp and register with an agency if she really wanted to work. But, I added, if she wanted to discuss it I'd be glad to buy her lunch.

She accepted. Since I had an appointment downtown, I took her to brunch at Benny & Dick's, a tiny breakfast place occupying what had once been the front porch of an old house on Jervis, just above Pender.

"Why were you fired?" I asked her after we'd placed our orders.

She shrugged and said, "I suppose I could tell you it was because I wouldn't go down on Jimmy, the band leader, but that would be only partly true. Let's put it this way, if I had been willing to go down on him, he might've been willing to overlook the fact that I can't sing. Not that I have anything in particular against oral sex, but besides not needing the job that badly, the guy's a pig and a girl can't be too careful these days."

"You might have a case for a sexual harassment complaint," I said.

"Except that he would just claim he fired me because I can't sing, which is true."

"You aren't that bad," I said.

She laughed. "Thanks, but I'm not that good, either," she said with a shrug. She wasn't wearing a bra under the thin cotton T-shirt and the gesture made interesting things happen. "Let's face it, neither of us was hired for singing ability alone. At least April can

44

carry a tune. I was thinking about moving on anyway. Did you mean what you said? Do you really think I could get work as a model? Or were you just bullshitting me? It wasn't just a line, was it?"

"Not entirely," I said.

"But still a line?"

"Well, yes," I admitted. "It was an excuse to talk to you."

"You didn't need an excuse to talk to me," she said. "I was hoping you would."

My pulse quickened and I could feel the heat on my face. "But it wasn't entirely a come-on," I said quickly. "You're very attractive, you probably wouldn't have too much trouble finding work, but there's a lot of competition and looking good isn't all there is to it. As I said, you've got to be represented by an agency and you need a comp. It helps to have a good portfolio too."

"What's a comp?"

"A brochure with sample photographs of yourself, showing different styles and moods. Plus your specs: measurements, sizes, and so on. Advertising."

"And the portfolio?"

"Examples of work you've done."

"How do I go about getting a comp?"

"If an agency agrees to represent you, they might do it for you. Some will deduct the cost from your first few jobs, others will charge you. If you can afford it, you could hire a photographer and do it yourself. Design-wise, they're fairly straightforward, but it would probably be a good idea to have a graphic artist lay it out for you."

"Could you do it?"

"Me?"

"You're a photographer."

"Yes, I know. But I don't do much fashion work. I don't do *any* fashion work, actually."

"You hire models, don't you?"

"Yes, but the models we use are more like extras in a movie. Bodies. People standing around hotel lobbies or riding chair-lifts on a ski hill. What you want is someone who can make you look like a *Vogue* model, not a guest in a hotel or a diner in a restaurant."

"Is it expensive?"

"It can be," I said. "I wouldn't advise you to do it on the cheap, though," I added. "You get what you pay for."

She said, "I don't have much money."

The food arrived, ham and eggs and home fries for her, one of Benny & Dick's huge blueberry pancakes for me. She attacked her food as if she hadn't eaten in a week.

"How long has it been since you've eaten?" I asked.

She swallowed. "About a day and a half, I guess. Sorry. I hope I'm not embarrassing you."

"Don't worry about it," I said.

We ate in silence, until she'd finished her meal, plus what was left of mine. This time I wouldn't be making my usual contribution to the local food bank – the penalty exacted by Benny and Dick for leaving food on your plate.

I got us more coffee from the thermos on the counter by the kitchen. Sitting down, I asked, "Do you have any money at all?"

"No," she said, holding her fingertips over her mouth as she belched inaudibly. "I spent my last thirty dollars on a room last night."

"So you don't have a place to stay."

"No," she said. "But I'll be all right."

Before I realized what I was saying, I said, "I have a spare room you could borrow."

She looked at me for a long time before speaking. "I don't know," she said.

"If you're worried, there's a lock on the door," I said. "You'd be perfectly safe. Besides, I'm not the dangerous type."

"It's not that," she said. "I can take care of myself. But I wouldn't want to put you out. You probably have a wife or a girlfriend. How would she feel about me camping out in the spare room?"

"No wife," I said. "No girlfriend either, so there's no problem."

"You're sure?"

"Yes, I'm sure."

"Well, all right, if you're sure. But only for a little while," she added. "A couple of weeks at most, until I find a job or something."

"That's fine," I said.

So she moved in with me.

And for about a week she actually slept in the spare room.

7

I'd been waiting for almost half an hour, had drunk two cups of insipid coffee and turned down a third, and was within seconds of leaving, when she finally made her entrance. There was no artifice, no pausing, adjusting, looking around, spotting her target, and waving. It was more subtle than that, and less. It was as if the room suddenly filled with an electrical charge. Zap. It turned the head of every man in the room, and the heads of a few of the women. And she'd dressed for effect, in a slightly flared wrap-around skirt that came to mid-thigh and white raw-silk blouse that drifted across her breasts like smoke. She carried a large shoulder bag.

My stomach knotted. I didn't know if it was with apprehension or desire. Perhaps it was both. I stood and she kissed me on the cheek. Her lips were cool and waxy with lipstick, but they left a spot of heat on my cheek, like a gentle brand. I resisted the urge to rub it.

"Thanks for coming, Tommy," she said as she sat down.

I hated being called Tommy, but I didn't say anything. It had never done any good anyway. No matter how many times I'd told her I preferred Tom or Thomas, she'd persisted in calling me Tommy.

"What was so important it couldn't wait an hour or so?" I asked.

"Would you order me a cup of tea?"

I signalled the waitress and placed the order.

"So, what is it you need to see me about?" I asked. I winced inwardly at the adolescent whine in my voice.

"Can't we take a few minutes to get acquainted again?" she said.

I shook my head. "You're unbelievable," I said. "More than two years and not a word. Nothing. For all I knew you were dead. I even thought about hiring a detective, but I couldn't afford it. And now you want to get acquainted again. Jesus. Do you have any idea how angry I was with you? Angry is an understatement. I was in love with you, for god's sake. I'd have given you anything you wanted." Her blue eyes were steady. "What happened? Why did you leave like that?"

"There were just too many strings attached," she said. "I've never liked strings."

"Don't give me that," I said. "If there were strings, they were yours, not mine."

"I couldn't live up to your expectations," she said.

"Where are you getting this stuff? Strings. Expectations. C'mon, Carla. I never put any conditions on our relationship."

"You seriously expect me to believe you did all those things, spent all that money on the comps and the modelling classes, without expecting something in return?"

"No, of course not," I said. "I'm no saint. I didn't expect to get stabbed in the back, though."

"I'm sorry I let you down."

"You didn't have to steal from me," I said in a voice that sounded petty and aggrieved even to me. When she'd left she'd taken my stereo — an NAD receiver and CD player with Mission speakers — a new Macintosh laptop computer, and a Hasselblad camera with motor drive and portrait lens. "The camera alone was worth five thousand dollars."

"It was broken," she said. "I didn't get anywhere near that much for it. Besides, you were insured, weren't you?"

"Of course, but I had a hell of a time collecting. It's a good thing for you the insurance agent was a friend of mine, otherwise I'd've had to report you to the police or the insurance wouldn't have paid off."

"Why didn't you report me?"

I thought about that for a few seconds before answering. "Because I hoped you'd come back."

"Would you have taken me back, after what I did?"

"Yes," I said. I didn't have to think about that one.

"Poor Tommy," she said. "You shouldn't care so much."

"I guess it's my nature," I said.

"Do you still care?" she asked, reaching out and placing her hand on mine.

I jerked my hand away from her touch. Her eyes clouded and a pale flush highlighted her cheekbones.

"Sorry," she said in a small, hurt voice.

I felt something inside me break. I took her hand. An alarm went off in my head, but I ignored it. Her hand was soft and warm and yielding.

"Are you back?" I asked, looking into her deep blue eyes, pulse throbbing in my throat. What would I do if she said yes?

"I don't know," she said quietly. She squeezed my hand quickly and let go.

"Why did you want to see me?"

She took a long time answering. "I need your help," she said at last.

"What kind of help?" I asked, wary in spite of myself. "Do you need money? Your friend Ryan looked loaded to me."

"No, I don't need money. But I do need a place to stay for a couple of days."

"You've got to be joking."

"It doesn't have to be your place," she said. "Actually, I'd prefer if it wasn't your place. Vince might look for me there. Your friend Daniel, does he still have his house up the coast? Maybe you could arrange for me to stay there for a while."

Daniel had a house in Halfmoon Bay, near the town of Sechelt, about two hours up the Sunshine Coast. With two bathrooms and a hot tub it wasn't exactly a cabin in the woods, but it was fairly isolated. He'd let me use it from time to time, when I needed to get away. I'd taken Carla there once.

"What's going on, Carla? Why do you need to hide from your boss? Exactly what do you do for him anyway? I don't recall that you demonstrated much in the way of business skills."

"There's a lot you don't know about me."

"I'm sure that's true," I agreed. "All right, I apologize for stereotyping you as a brainless gold-digging bimbo getting by on her looks, but you can hardly blame me, can you? You still haven't answered my question. Why do you need to hide from your boss?" I hit my forehead with the heel of my hand. "Of course. How stupid of me. You stole something from him too, didn't you?"

"Jesus, Tommy, let it go, all right? They were just things. I never realized you were so materialistic."

"Materialism has nothing to do with it. With the exception of the stereo, they were the things I used to earn my living."

She started to speak, but I put up my hand.

"You're right," I said. "They were just things. It wasn't the loss of them that hurt me, it was that you stole them."

"Look, I'm sorry. Okay. I —"

I raised my hand again. "Forget it, all right? Forget it. So, if you didn't take anything from him, why do you have to hide from him?"

"He is more than just my boss," she said.

"No kidding." She scowled at me. "Sorry," I said. "Go on."

"After I left you I realized that I had to get myself together and do something with my life. After all, the big three-oh was creeping up on me. I decided to go back to school and finish my business degree. Don't look so surprised. But I needed a job so I answered an ad on the school bulletin board. Companies are always looking for business students to do scut work and Vince's office wanted someone to work a few hours a day cleaning up files and entering data. After a few weeks Vince offered me a full-time job as his executive assistant."

"Impressed by your superior typing skills no doubt," I said.

"At first I thought it was a come-on too," she said, "but he travels a lot and needs someone to look after airline bookings, car rentals, hotel reservations, caterers for business meetings, that sort of thing. I don't think I would have got the job if I didn't speak French, though."

"You speak French?" I said.

"*Bien sûr*," she said. "I grew up north of Montreal and hardly spoke any English until I was ten or eleven. God, you don't know how hard it was to get rid of my accent. Anyway, Vince heard me speaking French to the guy who delivered spring water to the office and asked me if I wanted the job. He told me French wasn't essential but helped in Europe and Asia. I jumped at it."

"So he started out as your boss," I said. "When did that change?"

"About a year ago," she said. "We were in Germany when the office called and told him his wife had been killed by a hit and run. They'd been separated for a couple of months but were in the process of getting back together and he was really broken up about it. When we got back there were a lot of loose ends to take care of and we were together quite a bit and, well, things led to things. I guess it just happened."

"Like it 'just happened' between us," I said.

"You have a right to be angry with me, I suppose," she said. "But I never meant to hurt you."

"Never mind," I said. "Go on about Ryan. It's over now, right?"

She nodded. "But he doesn't want it to be over."

"Neither did I," I said. "Did you hide out after you left me?"

"I left town."

"What's stopping you from leaving town now?"

"There are some things I have to take care of," she said. "Nothing to do with Vince. Please, Tommy, it'll only be for a few days. A week at most. Vince isn't like you, Tommy. He frightens me. He has to have total

53

control of things. Our relationship isn't over until he says it is."

"He doesn't own you."

"Don't be naïve. Most of us are owned one way or another, we just aren't aware of it, any more than that old cat that hangs around your studio knows you own it."

"I'm not sure that I do own him," I said. "But people aren't cats or dogs, Carla. What's Ryan going to do? Send his burly blond beach boy to drag you kicking and screaming home again?"

"Sam? That's a laugh. No, Vince has other people he uses for that kind of thing."

"You're serious? You really believe he'd try to keep you against your will."

"Damn right I do."

I shook my head. "Sorry, Carla. I don't buy it. If Vince Ryan has that kind of hold on you, it's because you let him. Look, you're here now, aren't you? You're obviously not being held prisoner. You're free to come and go as you please. You want my advice, forget whatever you think you have to do and get on a plane. You said you didn't need money, but if you do I suppose I can let you have enough for the airfare home at least. If you fly standby. But that's as far as I'm willing to go."

"I don't need your money," she said. "I have money. Or I will, once I've taken care of my business here. That's why I need the time. Just a few days, Tommy. That's all. Then you'll never see me again. I promise. I'll be out of your life completely. If that's what you want."

I knew as she spoke the words that that wasn't what I wanted at all. There was something unresolved

54

between us and maybe this was an opportunity to put whatever it was to rest once and for all. Or perhaps a part of me believed we could put the past behind us and try again.

"All right," I said. "I guess I can speak to Daniel."

"Thanks, Tommy. I knew I could count on you. You aren't the type to nurse a grudge or turn your back on a friend."

"Don't make me regret this," I said.

"I won't," she said. "Look, I've got a couple of things to take care of. Can I come by your place later? You haven't moved, have you?"

"No."

"I've got to use the ladies' room," she said, standing up. "I'll see you around supper time, all right?"

"Fine," I said and she left.

I paid the bill and took another cab back to the studio, wondering all the way what I was getting myself into.

8

"Maybe you should consider yourself lucky," Daniel said. "I know I do."

It was early Tuesday evening, thirty-odd hours since I'd agreed to help Carla hide out from Vince Ryan. Daniel had agreed, readily but without any great enthusiasm, to let her use his house in Halfmoon Bay. But she still hadn't shown up.

"I really shouldn't care," I said. "If Vince Ryan wants to lock her in a cellar and feed her cold Kraft Dinner once a day, let him. She probably deserves it. But . . ." I shrugged.

"You do care."

"Stupid, huh?"

"Not stupid," Daniel said. "Unwise."

"I try to tell myself it's not personal," I said. "That I care about her the way I care that there are too many homeless people on the streets, too many teenage whores, too many drunk drivers, too much violence on television, and that you can't buy a decent bottle of wine for under ten bucks any more. But it doesn't work."

"Of course not."

"Fuck it," I said.

"That's a little bitter, Thomas," he said.

"I think I've earned the right to be a little bitter, after what she did."

"What did she do? She screwed you silly for six months then swiped a few trinkets."

"Have a little sympathy, please," I said. "She broke my heart."

"Think of it as a learning experience. You haven't suffered any permanent damage, have you?"

"No," I conceded. "Except for slightly elevated insurance rates. A Hasselblad and a Macintosh laptop are hardly trinkets."

"While she isn't exactly my type," he said, "many men might think it was worth it."

"Well . . ."

Hilly was off somewhere. Daniel and I were sitting on his roof deck amid a forest of potted trees and shrubs and ferns and flowering vines. All that was missing was the sound of jungle birds.

Daniel stood up. "Do you want another?" he asked, indicating my drink.

"Gee, I dunno. Two club sodas is about my limit. Oh, what the heck. Why not?" I handed him my glass. Daniel didn't keep anything stronger than tea in the house. He went to the little mobile bar parked under the awning at the rear of the deck.

"Has it occurred to you that she might have been less than truthful with you?" he said as he fussed with lime twists and ice.

"She does have a tendency to, ah, dissemble," I said.

"Dissemble," he said. He shook his head, refusing the challenge. "Not today, Thomas." He handed me my drink.

"Two lime twists," I said. "I can barely control my excitement."

"Oh, shut up." He returned to his seat. "So you think that she stole something from her employer-cum-boyfriend and came to you because she needs a place to hide out till the heat's off, so to speak."

"I'd say it was a safe bet." Nor had she actually denied it in so many words.

"Why did you agree to help her then?"

"Because she might be telling the truth."

"And you're still a little in love with her."

I saluted him with my drink. "Unwise, huh?"

"No," he said. "Stupid."

"Thank you."

"How are things going between you and Hilly?" he asked, changing the subject.

"Oh, you know," I said with a shrug.

"Actually, I don't."

"I'm beginning to wonder if I made a mistake, agreeing to take her for the whole summer. She tries hard, but it's pretty obvious she's bored out of her mind at the studio. There isn't a whole lot to do, especially when we get busy, which isn't often enough lately, but does happen occasionally. The community centre has a day-camp program, she could meet kids her own age, but when I suggested it, she said that those places were for geeks and dweebs. I never knew there was a difference. We got into a bit of a row over it this morning."

"Give her some slack, Thomas. She's a good kid."

"She's a great kid," I agreed.

"She needs some time to adjust," Daniel said. "She's likely just homesick. She misses her friends, her own room, her things, her mother. Don't take it too seriously if, when she's upset, she tells you she wants to go home."

"I worry about her," I admitted. "She did something during our row this morning that she's never done before, at least with me. She turned off her hearing aids."

"Did you never stick your fingers in your ears when you were a kid?" Daniel asked. Of course I had. "Just give her a chance," Daniel said. "Yourself as well."

"Yeah, but it ain't easy. It doesn't help that I've missed so much of her life. Damned near half. It's like having a stranger in my house." I drained my glass of club soda, chewed on a sliver a lime. "Have you heard the music she listens to? It sounds like the inmates of a lunatic asylum destroying musical instruments with hockey sticks. Groups with names like Tossed Cookies, Toe Jam, and On the Rag. And that bloody ferret. It's cute as hell, but it gets into everything. The other day I left my sock drawer open and it ripped up a whole box of condoms."

"You keep condoms in your sock drawer."

"Of course. Where else?"

He shrugged. "I suppose it serves you right for leaving your sock drawer open."

"And it smells."

"Your sock drawer?"

"The ferret, damnit. A little like a skunk."

"Maybe you could leave the cage out on your deck, under the awning."

"I thought of that, but Hilly would have a fit."

"Ah, parenthood," he said. "I'm grateful I was spared the experience. Most of the time I am, anyway."

"You mean sometimes you aren't?"

"Not too often, but yes, I sometimes regret not having children. Today it's possible for same-sex couples to adopt." He shuddered. "God, I hate that expression. But when I was younger, homosexuality was still illegal in many places, which made it difficult to have a family. Ah, at the risk of opening a rather nasty can of worms, the police busted some kids dealing dope around the market. Have you talked to Hilly about drugs?"

"Yes. Some. I don't think I have too much to worry about in that department. She's a pretty sensible kid. But who knows?"

"How about sex?"

"Christ, Daniel, she's only twelve."

"Age isn't relevant, physical and emotional development is. And she's starting to develop physically, or hadn't you noticed."

I admitted I had. "The last thing I need is to have to talk to Hilly about the birds and the bees," I said.

"I'd offer my services," Daniel said, "but —" He shrugged. "Speaking of parenting, I spoke to your father briefly on the weekend. How is your mother?"

"Hasn't changed," I said.

"I wouldn't wait," he said. "Your father seemed somewhat down in the dumps."

"Hilly thinks they're getting a divorce. She told me they're acting just like Linda and I did before our divorce."

"Unfortunately it happens," Daniel said.

"If they do," I said, "my sister will go absolutely ballistic." I pitched my voice an octave higher. "'Tom, my god, this is awful. We can't let them do this. There must be something we can do.' Mary-Alice is pathologically incapable of minding her own business."

"How do you feel about it?"

"I'm not sure," I said. "What are your views on astrology?"

"Pardon me?"

"Astrology. Y'know, birth signs, zodiacs?"

"I had a Zodiac once, but it sank."

"Not that kind of zodiac. The Age of Aquarius kind of zodiac."

"Yes, of course. Personally, I don't have much use for it. Why do you ask?"

"Did you know that Maggie Urquhart was studying to become an astrologer?"

"No, I didn't."

"She came over for lunch on Sunday to meet Hilly. My father could barely contain himself. He was actually charming. It was embarrassing."

"Embarrassing? Why were you embarrassed, Thomas?"

"He was making a fool of himself."

"And you've never made a fool of yourself over a woman."

"Of course I have. But it's not the same thing. He's my father and he's being disloyal to my mother." I sighed heavily. "I guess we always tend to relate to our parents as if we were still children. It's difficult, maybe even impossible, to see them as ordinary people."

"Try, Thomas."

I looked at my watch and stood up. It was five-thirty and I was supposed to be at Susan's at six. "You're sure you don't mind looking after Hilly? I shouldn't be late."

"No, of course not," he said. He walked me downstairs.

At the front door I said, "If Carla shows up, would you mind entertaining her until I get back?"

"Not at all. It will give me an opportunity to practise my sleight of hand. By the way, is Susan thinking about moving out of her condo?"

"Not to my knowledge," I said. "Why?"

"It may be nothing," he said, "but I ran into her the other day in front of the Island Realty office. She was looking through listings of bungalows."

9

"Planet Earth to Mr. Tom," Susan said, tapping me gently on the side of the head. "Is anybody in there?"

"Uh, sorry," I said.

"You could at least pretend to be interested," she said.

"Sorry," I said again.

We were sitting in the gathering dark on the balcony of her Kitsilano Point condo, watching the lights of the freighters anchored on English Bay. Debussy drifted through the open door from the stereo in the living room. I knew it was Debussy because Debussy was Susan's favourite composer.

"If you'd rather be somewhere else," Susan said, "don't let me keep you."

"I'm just a little preoccupied," I said. "I guess I've got a lot on my mind."

"You guess?"

"I do have a lot on my mind," I amended.

"Do you want to talk about it?"

"There's really nothing to talk about."

"Does it have anything to do with us?"

"No," I said.

"Are you sure?"

"Yes, I'm sure." Lying to her made me feel like a bastard, but if I told her where I really wanted to be was at home in case Carla called, I didn't think she'd understand. In fact, I was certain she wouldn't understand. I didn't. Not really.

"Why did you come here if you didn't want to be with me?" she said.

"I didn't say I didn't want to be with you."

"Not in so many words," she said.

"I'm sorry," I said. "I'm just not very good company tonight."

"Maybe you should go."

"Maybe you're right."

"You don't have to be so bloody accommodating."

I almost said, "Sorry," but bit it back. I was sick of hearing myself say that word.

"I think we have to talk," she said.

"About what?" I asked, pouring myself another glass of wine from the bottle on the deck of the balcony.

"We've been seeing each other for almost a year now," she said. "I think it's time we made some plans."

"What kinds of plans?" I asked, playing stupid, which for me wasn't at all difficult sometimes.

"You know what I'm talking about," she said.

"Marriage," I said, drinking some wine.

"Well, yes," she said. "Eventually, but not right now. I was thinking more along the lines of an engagement."

"Like with a ring and all that."

"All that?"

"Figure of speech."

"I see. Yes, I would expect a ring."

"Um. How long would this engagement be for?"

"A year is not uncommon."

"And then we'd get married."

"That's generally the idea."

I emptied my wine glass, refilled it, and drank half. "Commitment," I said.

"Pardon me?"

"You want some kind of commitment from me."

"Is that expecting too much?"

"No, I guess not."

"After all, neither of us is getting any younger."

"God, Susan, you're only thirty-two," I said. "And I'm only thirty-seven. Not exactly ready for retirement."

"You know what I mean."

"You keep saying that."

"Well, you do, don't you?"

"Children," I ventured.

"Yes, I want children," she said. "You do want more children, don't you?"

"I hadn't really thought about it," I lied.

"What's to think about?"

"Lots," I said. "Plenty," I added. "Lots of plenty. Hilly's a good kid, but I think the human gene pool can get along without further contributions from me."

"You aren't taking this very seriously," she said, voice frigid.

"On the contrary," I said. "I'm taking it very seriously."

"What is it? Children? Being married? Being married to me?"

"I was married once," I said. "It didn't work out well at all."

"I'm not your ex-wife."

I almost said, "Not yet," but my instinct for survival was strong. "No," I said. "You're not. But that's not the problem."

"What is the problem then?"

"I'm not ready to get married again," I said. "Or engaged."

"I see." She stood up and walked to the railing. When she turned around to face me there were tears on her cheeks and when she spoke her voice was thick. "I don't think you're being entirely honest with yourself," she said. "I think you're just making excuses."

"You may be right," I granted. "But I'm happy with my life right now, the way it is. It's taken me a long time to feel comfortable with myself. I want to enjoy it for a while longer."

"I think you're just afraid you're going to get hurt again so you won't let yourself get emotionally involved with anyone."

"Well, what's wrong with that?" I said. "Look, maybe we're after different things here. You want commitment, marriage, a family. I'm not sure I do. Not yet, anyway. And it isn't going to help if you start pressuring me."

"I'm not pressuring you," she said.

"It sure feels like it."

"I just want to make sure you understand how I feel."

"I understand."

"No, I don't think you do."

"I wish you'd stop telling me what I think or feel. How can you be so certain? You're not a mind-reader. Maybe you want me to be afraid of commitment."

66

"That's ridiculous."

"Is it? I can get over fear of commitment, but I can't get over not wanting to commit to you."

"I thought you loved me."

So there it was. The cards were on the table. Place your bets, ladies and gentlemen. Who's going to be the next big loser?

"Well?"

Say something, you idiot. Don't just sit there with your brain hanging out. Tell her the truth. You don't love her, not the way she needs to be loved.

"I guess I was wrong," she said, voice soft and full of hurt.

I felt like an absolute shit, unworthy to breathe the same air she did, walk the same planet. On the other hand, I'd never told her I loved her, never said the words. I stood up.

"There's someone else, isn't there?"

"What?"

"You're in love with someone else."

"No, I'm not in love with anyone else."

"You were a little too quick to answer. I think there is someone else." She turned her back. "Goodbye, Tom."

Susan's condo was a fifteen-minute walk from Granville Island. The last couple of glasses of wine had given me a headache, but the cool night air cleared my head. It was a beautiful evening, the air clear and sweet, but I was in no mood to appreciate it. If the Big One hit tonight, swallowed me up and buried me under a million tonnes of rock and a hundred metres of sea-water, I was ready. I deserved it. I had committed the single unpardonable sin in my personal rulebook: I had hurt someone I cared about. Perhaps it had been unavoidable, but that didn't change the way I felt. To make matters worse, I was already beginning to wonder if I'd made a mistake. Bertrand Russell said that the stupid are cocksure and the intelligent full of doubt, but he didn't know me. I was both stupid and full of doubt.

I was so wrapped up in my self-pity that I didn't notice the long dark limo parked by the ramp down to Sea Village until the back door swung open, the interior lights went on, and a man said, "McCall."

I jerked around and almost lost my balance.

The man climbed out of the car. "Hey," he said. "Didn't mean to startle you." But I could see the gleam of teeth in the dark face.

It was Vincent Ryan.

The driver's window whined down and the blond beach-boy type who'd picked Carla and Ryan up at the airport said, "Should I wait?"

"Yeah," Ryan said. "This shouldn't take long." He turned to me. "Where's Carla?"

"What?"

"You heard me," he said, large head thrust aggressively forward on his thick, powerful neck, hands balled into grapefruit-sized fists at his sides. "Where is she?"

"How the hell should I know?" I said, unsettled by his belligerent manner. I had four inches on him, and a slightly longer reach, but he outweighed me by a good twenty pounds, and not an ounce of it looked like fat. He also looked as if he knew how to handle himself in a fight, whereas I hadn't been in a fist fight since high school, and I'd lost that one.

"Don't fuck with me," he said. "I know she came to see you yesterday."

Did he, or was he just guessing? "Yes," I said. "But I haven't seen her since."

"I know all about you and Carla," he said.

"Is that right?" I said. "What do you know?"

"Enough. I'm no chump, McCall. I'm not going to fall for any two-bit hustle."

"If you're being hustled," I said, "it isn't by me."

"I'm supposed to believe you?"

"Believe what you want," I said. "I'm not interested."

"Maybe you ought to get interested," he said. The implied threat was left to my imagination.

"I'm not helping her hustle you," I said.

"Why'd she come to see you then?"

"It was a personal matter."

"I want to look through your house."

"Forget it," I said.

Predictably, he said, "She's in there, isn't she?"

"No, she isn't."

"Then you won't mind if I look around."

"Damned right I mind. My daughter will be in bed."

"Bullshit," Ryan said. "She's next door with the little Chink."

What was with this guy? Hadn't he heard that it wasn't politically correct to use terms like "Chinks" and "Nips"? Not to mention distasteful. "You're still not searching my house," I said.

"And who's going to stop us?"

"Us?"

"Sam," Ryan said. "Get out of the car."

69

"Leave me out of this, Mr. Ryan," Sam said. "You pay me to drive, not beat up on people or break into their homes and scare their kids."

"Fuck you, asshole. You're fired."

"Fine." Sam started the car.

"You son of a bitch. Turn off the engine. I'm paying a hundred-and-a-half a day for that heap."

"Take a cab," Sam said. "I'll leave the car at the hotel." The car lurched as he put it in gear.

"All right already," Ryan said. "Shut off the god-damned engine. You're not fired. Shit. You know I can't drive the fucking thing."

Sam turned the engine off and got out of the car. I backed up a little. He looked even bigger and beefier than he had at the airport.

"I'm going to take a walk," he said. "Maybe get a beer at that pub we passed. You two sort this thing out between yourselves." He started to cross the parking lot, then turned to me. "He can be a complete pain in the ass sometimes, man, but help him out if you can." To Ryan he said, "You might attract more flies with shit than with honey, but no one will love you for stinking up the place."

Ryan and I both stared at his broad back as he walked away from us.

Ryan turned to me. "He's a vegetarian," he said, as if it explained Sam's behaviour. "All right, look, he's right, I shouldn't have come on so heavy." He stuck out a blunt hand.

"No problem," I said, disconcerted by the sudden shift in mood. Tentatively, I took his hand, readying myself for his crushing grip, but he just gave my hand a brief squeeze and let go.

"You have no idea where she might be?" he said.

"None. But if it'll make you feel any better, she did the same thing to me a couple of years ago. I suggest you go home and count the cutlery."

He slumped against the fender of the car. "You wouldn't have a cigarette, would you?"

"I don't smoke," I said. I realized I felt sorry for him. Maybe he wasn't such a bad guy after all. "You can come inside for a drink if you like, as long as you promise not to insist on searching through the place."

"I can't promise not to sneak a look through any open doorways."

"Fair enough."

Inside, I fixed him a double vodka over ice. I had club soda.

"Nice place," he said, looking around the sunken living room. "Not very big, though. How many bed-rooms?"

"Three," I said. "Go ahead," I added with a sigh. "Look around if you like."

"Naw, it's all right. She isn't here."

"How do you know?"

"I'd've smelled her perfume." I must have looked sceptical. He said, "Someone here uses some kind of floral scented stuff, probably your daughter. It's popular with the kids."

I had no idea what sort of perfume Hilly used. I was not aware that she used any at all. Perhaps Ryan smelled my mother's perfume.

"You've got a pet skunk or something."

"You smell my daughter's ferret."

"The rat thing I saw at the airport?"

I nodded. "It's a domesticated weasel."

He breathed in slowly through his nose, said, "You've had salmon within the last few days . . ."

"Last night."

". . . and you're using some kind of musk deodorant, not an antiperspirant."

"Oops."

"I've got a hyper-sensitive olfactory system," he added.

"I'll bet that's unpleasant sometimes."

"Damned right. I hate Paris." He tossed back his drink. "Mind if I have another? I'm not driving. Can't. Tunnel vision. You may have noticed that I swivel my head a lot."

I hadn't noticed. Nor did he seem to. I fixed him another drink.

"Can I ask you a favour?" he said as I handed him his drink. He sat down on the sofa and crossed his legs. He immediately uncrossed them.

"You can ask," I said.

"Would you help me find her?"

"No, I don't think I can do that."

"Well, at least give it some thought."

"I don't need to," I said. "I don't want anything to do with it. I'm sorry she ran out on you, but you're probably better off without her anyway."

"I disagree, but that's not your problem. So, what was this personal matter she came to see you about?"

I looked at him and he looked back. His eyes were very dark and hard and he had undoubtedly lost very few eye-contact contests. But I'd long ago lost any self-consciousness about staring at people. He finally shrugged and looked away, probably not so much

72

because I'd won the contest but because he'd realized it was a waste of time.

"All right, fine. Don't tell me. How much do you want to help me find her?"

"I told you," I said. "I'm not going to help you. Besides, I wouldn't know where to look."

"She still has friends here," he said. "You could just ask around."

I shook my head. "Talk to them yourself."

"I don't know who they are."

"That's going to make it difficult," I said.

"You're not being very co-operative," he said. His voice was smooth and level, but his face was tight and his hard, dark eyes were narrowed to slits. "That's not smart. You got a nice set-up here, McCall. Nice house. Nice kid. Nice life. Things happen, though. You never know."

My pulse raced and my chest was tight with anger. I was suddenly very conscious of the physical presence of this man, the powerful width of his shoulders and chest, the bulge of muscle beneath the fabric of his shirt sleeves, the thickness of his wrists. He frightened me a little, perhaps more than a little, but I was damned if I was going to let it show.

"It's been nice talking to you," I said, going to the front door and opening it. "Don't bother finishing your drink."

"You're stupider than I thought," he said, casually downing the rest of his drink and placing the empty glass on the table in the hall.

"Take out replacement-value insurance next time."

"What?"

"Never mind. Good night."

He reached into his shirt pocket and handed me a business card. "In case you change your mind," he said.

I dropped it onto the coffee table. "Don't hold your breath," I said.

"I'll be seeing you," he said.

"Not if I have anything to say about it."

"You don't," he said as I closed the door on him.

10

"**D**o I have to?" Hilly said at breakfast the next morning. "It's boring. Anyway, I thought Susan was supposed to take me to the science centre today?"

"Something, uh, came up," I said. "You'll have to come to the studio, I'm sorry. I don't feel right about leaving you alone all day."

"Mom does it all the time," Hilly said, feeding Beatrix a shred of toast.

"I wish you wouldn't do that," I said.

"Why not?"

Why not indeed? What harm did it do? So what if Beatrix learned to expect to be fed at the table? I recalled my mother telling me not to feed Ginger, her standard poodle, at the table. Ginger hadn't whined or begged or pawed, he just sat hopefully beside my chair, waiting with doggish patience. If it had bothered her so much to have him hanging around the dinner table, why hadn't she just banished him to the other room? But it had nothing to do with feeding Ginger at the table. My mother had been simply exercising parental authority for the sake of exercising parental authority, because she had it. As I was now.

"Forget it," I said. Returning to the subject, I said, "Does your mother really leave you alone all day?"

"Well, maybe not all day, but a lot. Like when she goes shopping or does her volunteer work at the hospital. And usually Mattie is there."

"Mattie? Who's Mattie?"

"The maid."

"Your mother has a maid?"

"Sure."

I wondered how much of my child-support payments went to help pay for the maid. "Well, I don't have a maid," I said.

"No kidding."

"And, besides, I don't really care what your mother does. I don't feel right about it. You're too young to be left alone all day and I can't impose on Daniel or Maggie all the time. You're sure you won't change your mind about the community centre? The day camp sounds like fun. They do all kinds of interesting things."

"Sure," she said. "Like visit museums and take nature hikes."

"You were looking forward to visiting Science World with Susan."

"Did you break up with her?"

"Quit trying to change the subject."

"Well, did you?"

"My social life is not open to discussion."

"You did, didn't you?"

I sighed. "Look, I think I'm going to insist you give the day camp a try."

"I won't like it."

"I'm sure they won't mind if you bring Beatrix along."

"You think so?"

"As long as she stays out of trouble."

"Well, I suppose . . ."

What's so hard about raising children? You just have to know how to handle them.

I took Hilly to the community centre, insisting that Beatrix wear her harness and leash. While I signed Hilly up and explained to the young woman behind the counter that the only time Hilly's hearing aids were likely to be a problem was when she was swimming – she had to take them out – Hilly examined the notices pinned to the bulletin board, Beatrix perched on her shoulder.

"About the ferret," I said.

"No problem," the young woman said. "Lots of kids like to bring their pets. We have a cage we can use if we have to. We also have a couple of hearing impaired kids in the group. Does your daughter sign?"

"No."

"Do you think she'd like to learn?"

"I don't know," I said.

I kissed Hilly, wished her a good day and told her that if I was not home for dinner, she should go to Maggie's. As I said goodbye a couple of boys came into the centre, signing to each other, fingers furiously flashing. They looked enough alike to be brothers. One was about Hilly's age. The other was older, maybe seventeen. A pair of Walkman headphones dangled around his neck. The older one kept making emphatic gestures to the younger one, repeatedly slapping the back of his right hand into his left palm. I had no idea what was going on, but it was clear they were arguing about something. I left Hilly watching them.

When I got to the studio, Bobbi had the Land Rover loaded and was waiting for me, a little impatiently. I apologized and we drove downtown. We were scheduled to take executive portraits for Northwest Trust's annual shareholders' report. The company's board of directors had insisted we come to them, believing, perhaps not unreasonably, that their time was more valuable than ours. So we went to them, with our cameras and tripods, flash units, cables and lights, reflectors and backdrops. It took us a couple of hours to set up in the boardroom, take light readings and Polaroid test shots. It turned what would normally be a half-day job into a day, even a day and a half, but I had no objection to billing them the extra time. I was going to need all the billing I could generate if West Coast Hotels followed through with their threat to find another photographer.

Bobbi was very good on these kinds of assignments. She had endless patience with subjects who regarded the whole thing as an utter waste of time. She could get the most self-important executive or the most obstreperous child to jump naked through flaming hoops. Maybe it was her big brown eyes or her big sweet smile. Whatever it was, I didn't have it. From my newspaper days I'd learned to just get in their faces and shoot. It didn't bother shopping malls or helicopters, but people tended not to like it.

But today Bobbi was distracted and careless. During the set-up I had to remind her to adjust reflectors, take light readings, change camera backs, things she normally did automatically. And during the morning shoot she was short with a vice president who kept telling us that he had more important things to do and would we please hurry it up.

Over lunch, I asked her what was bothering her.

"It's nothing important," she said. "I'm sorry. I'll try to get back on track this afternoon."

I'd known Bobbi for six years, saw her almost every day, considered her a friend even though we rarely got together outside of work. She was an only child, her mother a nurse at Vancouver General Hospital, her father a cop in Richmond, divorced for some time. She had a boyfriend, Tony Chan, with whom she'd lived for a year or so, but I'd met him only a couple of times. He claimed to be a painter. He painted, so I suppose he was a painter. In my opinion, he wasn't a very good painter, but some people thought he was and even paid money for his paintings, quite a bit, as such things go. But I knew very little else about her private life.

"Look," I said. "Your personal life is none of my business, except how it affects your work. Everything okay at home? With your parents?"

"Yes, Mom's fine. And Pop, well, he's fine too, but I don't see very much of him."

"Everything okay between you and Tony?"

"Yeah, sure."

"If you need some time off," I said, "all you have to do is ask, you know that."

"I'm okay."

"C'mon, Bobbi, I've never had to remind you to reload cameras. Does this have anything to do with the West Coast Hotels thing?"

"Maybe."

"Bobbi, help me out here. I'm not very good at this kind of thing. I'm not cut out to be a boss, but I'm stuck with it and you're going to have to bear with me." She nodded and smiled meekly. "I'm not trying to pry into your life. I'm your friend and I respect your privacy. But I'm also your employer and your personal life becomes my business, so to speak, if it affects your work. Our work."

"I'll try not to let it," she said.

"Good," I said. "But I want you to know that if there's anything I can do to help, you just have to ask."

"I know," she said. "Thanks."

I looked at my watch. It was a few minutes before one. "Back to work," I said, standing, collecting both Bobbi's tray and mine.

The afternoon sessions went better, except for one minor incident involving a senior vice president who was very sensitive about his male pattern baldness and had brought with him an aerosol can of hair enhancer. I had to bite my cheek to keep from snickering and about halfway through the session Bobbi excused herself from the room to make an emergency pit stop. She came back a couple of minutes later and we finished the sitting. After the VP left we both dissolved into fits of giggles. Through tears, Bobbi told me she'd had to leave the room or wet her pants with the effort to keep from laughing.

I got home around seven-thirty. Hilly was upstairs watching TV. "How was your day?" I asked, straightening a photograph of the Lions Gate Bridge I'd taken from a helicopter.

"What?"

"How was your day?" I asked again, a little louder and facing her so she could read my lips. She doesn't do it consciously, she says, but she has less difficulty understanding if she can see your lips when you speak to her.

"Okay," she said.

The photograph didn't want to stay straight. Because of the movement caused by tides and the wash of passing boats, hanging pictures were always going out of true. For that reason, most of the works on the walls, like mirrors, were fixed at both the top and bottom.

"Your house is tilted," Hilly said.

"What?"

She pointed to a glass of soda on the end table. Sure enough, the liquid in the glass did not seem level.

I went downstairs, stood in the middle of the hall, and listened carefully. I heard the distant thrum of the bilge pump. Normally it runs for a few minutes, then shuts off, perhaps three or four times a day. I'm hardly ever aware of it, never notice it unless I listen for it. I waited for it to stop. It didn't. I jerry-rigged a plumb bob with a six-foot length of string and a bit from an electric screwdriver and thumbtacked it to the inside of the kitchen door jamb. The screwdriver bit hung almost two inches from the base of the door jamb.

I went outside, knelt on the dock near the corner of the house, and looked at the side of the hull. Floating homes don't have Plimsoll marks, those lines on the sides of ships that show how much water they are drawing, but the more or less constant draft causes a line of salty, oily crud to form just above the waterline. I could not see the crud line.

My house was sinking.

11

I had no idea how fast the house was taking water. Was it in any real danger of sinking? The hull was ferroconcrete but the rest of the structure was mainly wood. Wood floats, doesn't it? But wooden ships sank, didn't they? Otherwise how did all those old Spanish galleons end up on the bottom of the Caribbean? Okay, so they were filled with Aztec gold and bedecked with cannon and cannonballs. My house was neither filled with gold nor equipped with cannon. Nevertheless, I was worried.

My first impulse, of course, was to panic, run in circles shouting, "My house is sinking! My house is sinking! Abandon ship – er – house. Women and children first." I wasn't even certain how deep the harbour was at low tide, but I knew it was a damned sight deeper at high tide.

It occurred to me that perhaps Vince Ryan was behind it, that he had somehow sabotaged my house because I had refused to help him. The idea seemed a little paranoid, even to my fevered imagination, but I couldn't shake the cold feeling that this was what he had meant when he'd said, "Things happen."

Hilly was largely unconcerned. "It's not like it's a long swim to shore," she said.

I called Daniel. "I suggest pumps," he said.

"This is hardly the time to talk fashion," I said.

"Not those kinds of pumps. Water pumps. Just in case your bilge pump can't handle it."

"Right. I'll call Budget Rent-a-Pump."

"Are you all right?"

"No, of course not. My house is sinking."

"May I remind you," Daniel said, "that it's really Howard's house and he's not going to be very happy to learn that you have sunk it."

"I didn't sink it," I said. "I mean, I didn't run it aground or hit an iceberg. But ownership is beside the point," I added. "It's sinking and I'm living in it. Ergo, my house is sinking."

"Point taken."

"Purple Tools," I said. "They might rent pumps."

"Indeed, they might," Daniel agreed. "Purple pumps."

"I'll call them," I said.

"Do that," Daniel said.

I looked up the number for the Purple Tool rental outlet at 3rd and Pine and called them. It was after eight P.M., so naturally a machine answered.

"Sorry," a pleasant female voice said. "We're closed. Please call again after eight in the morning. But if it's an emergency, you can reach us at 555-TOOL. That's five-five-five-eight-six-six-five."

I called the number, and after a couple of rings, the same pleasant female voice answered. For a second I thought I'd got another tape, but the voice added, "How can I help you?"

"Do you rent pumps?"

"Yes, we do," she said. "Purple ones, naturally."

"My house is sinking."

"Excuse me."

"My house is sinking and I need a pump. I really don't care if it's purple."

"Who is this? Hal, is that you? Did those idiots at Grumpy's put you up to this?"

"Look," I said. "This isn't Hal and I don't know anyone named Grumpy. My house really is sinking."

"Sorry. You must live on one of those houseboat things on Granville Island. I didn't think they could sink."

"Trust me," I said. "It's sinking."

"You need a pump."

"Yes, indeed."

"Gas or electric?"

"Electric will be okay, I think."

"How big?"

"I really don't care how big it is. You can park it on the boardwalk."

"No, I mean, what capacity?"

"Sufficient to keep the Pacific Ocean out of my bilge," I said.

The purple pump arrived twenty minutes later, on its own little purple trailer towed behind a little purple pickup and accompanied by a young woman in well-stuffed stretch jeans and an oversized sweatshirt. With her was a towering old man in twill coveralls.

"Mr. McCall?" the woman said in the familiar pleasant voice. "I'm Gwen. We spoke on the phone."

"Thanks for coming," I said.

"No problem. Which is yours?"

"That one," I said, pointing.

"All right, then, let's get to it. Would you mind giving me a hand? Pa's not supposed to do any heavy work."

"Sure," I said.

I helped her unload the purple pump from its purple trailer and skid it down the ramp and through the gate to a point on the finger dock near my house. Pa watched. It took about twenty minutes to get the intake hose through a vent into the bilge, Gwen doing most of the work, Pa providing helpful suggestions in heavily accented English, suggestions she more or less ignored. She then ran a heavy-duty extension to the outside outlet, plugged the pump into the extension, and started it up. It whirred and thumped and then settled into a steady thrum as it spewed water into the harbour.

"This thing'll handle about thirty gallons a minute," Gwen said. "I doubt you're taking water that fast. Your house'd be probably on the bottom of the harbour by now if you were. It's got an automatic shut-off if it starts pumping air, but you have to start it yourself." She pressed a switch and the pump thumped to a stop. "Give it a try."

I pressed a big button labelled START. The pump thumped and whirred and I released the button. The pump stopped.

"You've got to hold the button down until the pump gets going," Gwen said. She waited expectantly while Pa stood behind her, eyes half closed, shaking his head slowly from side to side.

Feeling like a first grader learning how to flush a urinal, I pressed the START button again and held it until the pump settled into a steady thrum. Then I released it. To my relief it continued to thrum and spew water into the harbour.

"That's better," Gwen said, beaming at me.

Pa grunted and muttered something in what sounded like Russian but was more clipped.

"My father doesn't approve of my instructional methods," Gwen said. "He thinks I'm too patronizing. I don't mean to be. Do you think I'm being patronizing?"

I didn't want to hurt her feelings, so I said, "It's better than getting a call in the middle of the night because someone can't start the pump."

"Exactly."

"I think I can handle it," I added.

"Good. See, Pa."

Pa looked unconvinced.

"It might help if you attached a tag or plate with starting instructions," I said. "'Hold START button until pump operates steadily.' Save yourself a lot of trouble."

I signed a one-week rental agreement, at fifteen bucks a day, hopeful that the insurance would cover it, then Gwen and Pa climbed into the little purple pickup and were off. After they left I watched the pump for a few minutes – not particularly exciting – then went inside. The jury-rigged plumb bob was still hanging at an angle to the door frame.

"I guess I won't have to wear a life jacket to bed after all," Hilly said when I told her about the pump.

"Very funny," I said and went back downstairs to fix myself a drink.

I putzed around for a couple of hours, listening to music, trying to catch up on my reading but mostly thinking about my sinking house, my relationship with Susan, Carla and my refusal to help Ryan find her, my sinking house, what was bugging Bobbi, what the loss of West Coast Hotels would do to my bottom line, my house, Susan, Carla, the unhappy client, my – well, you get the idea. At eleven I went out to check the pump and found that it had stopped. I pressed and held the START button, but the pump spit air and shut itself off after a couple of seconds. Back inside, I made myself another drink, turned off the stereo and the lights, and sat in the dark with a drink I didn't want, wondering how my life had suddenly become so crowded with complications. When no answer was forthcoming I dumped the drink down the sink, went upstairs, brushed, flossed and rinsed, and climbed into bed.

I got up almost immediately and went to look in on Hilly. She was fast asleep, Beatrix curled up on the pillow by her head. The ferret raised her head and regarded me suspiciously as I approached the bed.

"Is it all right if I kiss her goodnight?" I asked her in a whisper. She did not answer. Nor did she object when I leaned over and kissed Hilly on the cheek. Some complications, I told myself as I returned to my room, were easier to live with than others.

I woke up at seven-thirty, feeling as though I'd slept on a pile of rocks. I hobbled into the bathroom and stood in the shower for a long time, just letting the heat soak into me, before dressing and dragging myself down-stairs, limp and lifeless. Hilly was up and dressed and annoyingly cheerful. As I was working on my second cup of coffee, still not fully conscious, Hilly told me she wanted to get to the day camp early.

"Does this mean you like it?"

"It's okay," she said.

From her, okay was a shining endorsement.

It's impossible to get lost on Granville Island. Just look for the massive span of the Granville Bridge over the north end of the island or the tall mixing towers of the Ocean Cement plant, a holdover from Granville Island's industrial heritage. But the narrow streets and irregular layout can be confusing to newcomers, so I walked Hilly and Beatrix to the community centre. When I got back to the house, I checked the pump. I'd been up three times during the night: at one o'clock, at three-thirty, and again at five-thirty. At one the pump had started up properly, but two and a half hours later it had spit air for a few seconds then shut off. I'd started it again at five-thirty, but now, at eight, it spit air again when I tried it.

After checking the pump I drove to the studio, left a note for Bobbi explaining that I would be in after lunch and that I was leaving the Land Rover in case she needed it, then took the ferry back home. I reheated breakfast coffee in the microwave (about all the damned things are good for, besides making popcorn), called my insurance agent and left a message on his machine to call me at home or at the studio. I called Daniel to ask him if he knew the name of a contractor who could repair the hull, and he gave me a number for Simpson Marine & Salvage. I called and left a message on another machine. As I hung up I wondered if anyone started work before nine A.M. any more.

Vince Ryan's business card was still on the coffee table, testimony to my less-than-exemplary house-keeping habits. I picked it up and for a moment thought about calling him and asking him if he was responsible for my house springing a leak. I didn't call him, though; I figured that if he was responsible I would be hearing from him sooner or later.

At ten-fifteen, tired of waiting for the insurance agent and the salvage contractor to return my calls, and reasonably confident that my house wasn't going to end up at the bottom of the harbour if I left it alone for a couple of hours, I walked over to the boat yard and got the Porsche out of the lock-up I rent there.

The Porsche was a fire-engine-red 1984 Carrera 911 that sounded like a sewing machine on anabolic steroids. I'd acquired it a couple of years earlier in lieu of payment from a client whose "previously owned" luxury car dealership had fallen on hard times. I didn't use it much; it wasn't really very practical for work and, frankly, I felt a little silly whenever I drove it. But it was a hell of a lot of fun to drive, especially on the Sea to Sky Highway to Whistler, thriving on the curves and thumbing its blunt snout at the steepest of grades. Unfortunately, it tended to attract speed cops like picnics attracted ants.

Because I hadn't had it out in a while, it ran rough for a few minutes. By the time I got to Gastown, the original site of what was eventually to become the City of Vancouver, it had smoothed out. I found a parking space on Water Street, not far from Ray Saunders' steam clock, locked up, and walked a block to Virginia Gregory's gallery at the corner of Water and Abbot.

Ginny Gregory's gallery carried Northwest Native art. Haida, Tlingit, Salish, and Nishga paintings, carvings, and crafts, both traditional and contemporary. I liked aboriginal art, but the distinctive styles had become a cliché of the Pacific Northwest. Most of

Ginny's customers were tourists and wanted something they could take back to Montreal or Tokyo or Sydney and show their friends and relatives. Something that would fit in their suitcase, the equivalent of a replica of the Eiffel Tower or the Great Pyramid. They didn't want art, they wanted mementoes.

But Ginny also sold to collectors of contemporary West Coast art and, like much contemporary art, some of the works in Ginny's gallery were totally incomprehensible to anyone but an expert. I was examining just such a piece, a weird artefact carved from a chunk of black soapstone, when a voice behind me said, "That's a Paul White. Like it?"

I turned to face a slim raven-haired woman with almost-black eyes and sharp cheekbones. "I don't know," I said.

Ginny Gregory could have passed for a Native North American, but had in fact been born in Scotland (which did not, I suppose, preclude Amerindian blood) and still bore a slight trace of accent when she said, "Oh, it's you."

"Nice to see you again too, Ginny."

12

A deep flush highlighted her high sharp cheekbones and she would not look me in the eyes, focussing instead somewhere in the vicinity of my chin. "I'm sorry," she said. "You caught me by surprise."

"You're not going to call the police this time, are you?"

"No." Her flush deepened and spread down her slim neck. She put her hand to her throat. "Oh, god. I can't believe I did that."

"Don't worry about it. I might have done the same thing in your position. I wasn't exactly in the best of shape the last time you saw me."

"No," she agreed. "You weren't. But still, I over-reacted."

"A little, maybe."

"A lot," she said. "For what it's worth, I am truly sorry. It was such a silly damned *female* thing to do. Of course, I didn't think so at time. You really did frighten me."

"I'm sorry. I didn't mean to, but, as I said, I wasn't exactly myself."

"I understand that now."

"Do you?"

"Yes, I do."

"Sorry," I said. "I didn't mean to sound bitter."

"I really do understand," she said. "I hope —" She stopped, shook her head, and said, "I was going to say I hope you can forgive me, but I didn't do anything that needs to be forgiven."

"No. You didn't. She was your friend. You were just protecting her. You didn't know me."

"It was more than that," she said. "I loved her too."

"I know. It took me a little while, but I finally figured that out."

"I guess it gives us something in common," she said. "You may not believe this, but I tried to call you a couple of times. To apologize. But I kept getting your answering machine or your service and I couldn't bring myself to leave my name."

"I thought about calling you too," I said, "but after a while, well, there didn't seem to be much point."

She put out her hand. I took it. "I'm glad we got that out of the way," she said. "And I'm happy to see you looking well." She gestured at a display of gaudy masks. "What can I show you?"

"I'm not here to buy, I'm afraid."

She smiled and shrugged. "No, I didn't think you were."

"Carla came to see me the other day," I said.

Her eyes closed for a moment and an expression of pain flashed across her face. "Yes," she said, opening her eyes. "I knew she had to be the reason you were here."

"Have you heard from her?"

"No. I haven't seen her since, well, shortly after she left you. But —" Her voice caught and she touched her lips with her fingertips and coughed, as if something were caught in her throat. "I wouldn't expect to," she said, a little hoarsely. "It's a long sad story," she added after clearing her throat. "Not so long, really, but certainly sad. Actually, pathetic might be a better word. Yes, pathetic is definitely the word. Not to mention banal."

I knew the feeling. I'd been there myself. And there was nothing to be gained from talking about it.

"How is she?" Ginny asked.

"She seems fine," I said. "Although I only spoke with her for a few minutes. She called me up more or less out of the blue on Monday and asked if I would put her up for a few days. She'd left her boyfriend, a hotshot entrepreneurial type named Vince Ryan, and needed a place to stay for a couple of days while she took care of some business. She was supposed to come to my place Monday evening, but she never showed up. I thought she'd probably changed her mind and gone back to him, but the next day he came looking for her."

"What is it with you guys?" Ginny said. "Rhetorical question," she added quickly. "I don't think I really want to know. Go on."

"I doubt I could tell you," I said. "Anyway, Carla was afraid that Ryan would come after her and try to take her back by force, that he was very possessive of her, but I think there's more to it than that. Although he denies it, I think she may have stolen something from him."

"Oh?"

"When she left me," I explained, "she took some stuff, including a laptop computer and a very expensive camera."

"We have more in common than I thought," Ginny said.

"She stole from you too."

"A little under two thousand dollars in cash."

"I'm sorry."

"Don't apologize for her, for god's sake." She shook her head. "But that wasn't why you came looking for her, was it? To get back what she took from you."

"No, of course not."

"But you think that's why this Vince Ryan wants to find her?"

"He doesn't strike me as the romantic type."

"I feel pretty much that way about all men."

"I'll try not to take that personally," I said.

"I must say, though," she said, "I'm surprised Carla got in touch with you at all. She made it pretty clear that if she never saw you again, it would be too soon. In fact, she told me that she'd, ah, rather turn gay than have anything to do with a man like you ever again."

"Ouch."

"She could be a little insensitive sometimes. Of course, there was little chance of her turning gay."

"You should consider yourself lucky," I said.

"Perhaps I do," she said. "In retrospect anyway."

"What kind of man did she tell you I was?"

"Does it matter?"

"That depends on what it was," I said.

"Ah, the male ego. It wasn't very flattering," she said. "But it didn't take me long to realize it wasn't true. When Carla first brought you around I thought you were nice. A bit shell-shocked perhaps, but harmless. I was happy for her, despite my own feelings. And when she left you I told her I thought she was making a mistake. But she thought that because I was gay I hated men and I'd be willing to believe anything about you so long as it was bad. She was wrong, though. I don't hate men, I'm just not sexually attracted to them. Nor do I think that you're all adolescent jerks who, if you think at all, do it with your penises." Her mouth twisted in a wry smile. "In fact, some of my closest friends are straight males."

I laughed. "I don't believe you said that."

I flinched as a nerve-jarring buzzer sounded through the room. The front door banged open and a squadron of Japanese tourists trooped in. There was an even dozen of them, six middle-aged couples, attired in shorts and bright Hawaiian shirts. A couple of them held little video cameras up to their eyes as they panned around the gallery. A beaming rotund lady accompanied them, only slightly less garishly dressed than they, but also sporting a camera. The tour guide, I supposed.

Ginny said, "Excuse me," and exchanged bows with the tour guide. I retreated to a back corner and watched as she escorted the group around the gallery and explained the works on display, pausing frequently while the tour guide translated.

With the exception of Bobbi and Daniel and The Seven Ups – the last I'd heard, they were in Japan – Ginny was the only person I knew in Vancouver who also knew Carla. Carla had brought me to the gallery one day. I'd even bought a small Haida sculpture as a birthday gift for my sister. A week or so after Carla had disappeared, I'd come to see Ginny, to ask her if she knew where Carla had gone, but she'd refused to speak to me, ordered me to leave. Teetering on the edge of control from worry and lack of sleep, I'd lost it, refused to leave and angrily demanded that she tell me where Carla was. She'd called the police. I left before they arrived and hadn't spoken to her since.

Although I'd told Ryan I wasn't interested in helping him, I'd decided it couldn't hurt to check with Ginny to see if Carla had been in touch with her. It hadn't been a conscious decision to come here. I'd just got in the car and come. I wasn't doing it for Ryan, though. I wasn't sure why I was doing it. Perhaps just to warn her that Ryan was indeed looking for her. There may have been another reason, of course. Whenever I thought about her my palms got sweaty and I felt as though my chest had been hollowed out and filled with dry ice.

In less than fifteen minutes Ginny sold eight or nine small sculptures at a hundred to two hundred dollars apiece, give or take a couple of dollars. Then the beaming tour guide herded her happy charges back out into the sunny street and into a waiting minibus.

"Whew," I said. "Does that happen often?"

"Not often enough," Ginny said. "But don't be deceived by appearances. The tour guide gets five percent of the sale price. Commission. Then anywhere from forty to sixty percent goes to the artist, depending on his or her popularity. And the overhead here is killing me."

She filled a couple of heavy ceramic mugs from a coffee maker behind her desk. I shook my head when she offered milk, accepted a sachet of sugar.

"So," she said. "Where were we?"

"How did you meet Carla?" I asked.

"About four years ago she came in with −" she paused, then went on "− with a man who said he was building a house in West Vancouver. He claimed to be a collector, but what he really wanted was something to decorate the entrance hall. What the hell, I've got to live, so I showed him the most expensive thing I had. He looked like he could afford it. When I told him it was fifteen thousand dollars I expected him to try to beat me down, but he just said, 'I'll take it,' and pulled out a cheque book.

"While he was making out the cheque I noticed Carla looking at a couple of nice little pieces and went over to talk to her. I don't like to hover over customers when they're writing cheques. We chatted for a few minutes, then he bought her one of the pieces she'd been admiring and they left.

"She came back a few weeks later and bought another small piece. She hung around for a while and we had coffee and talked. After that she started dropping by now and again to say hello or talk. In spite of the differences between us, we became friends. I had hoped for a while that we would become more than just friends, but she was strictly heterosexual. She told me she didn't have very many friends and it felt good to just relax and talk girl talk, so I kept my feelings to myself. And I was glad to have a straight female friend who didn't seem to care I was gay. At first she wasn't very good at it. Gradually, though, she stopped trying to impress me and we started talking about regular things: growing up, relationships, movies, that sort of thing. She was from Quebec, did you know that?"

"Yes, I did." I didn't add that I'd learned it just the other day. During the six months we'd lived together, I'd learned next to nothing about Carla's background. Carla had rarely, if ever, talked about her past. And whenever I had showed interest and asked, she had been evasive, deflecting the conversation away from herself.

"I don't think she had a very easy life," Ginny said. "She told me her mother was very strict, almost to the point of abuse, and that her brother was in jail for accidentally killing a man in a bar fight."

"What about other friends?" I asked. "Did she ever bring anyone else around besides me?"

"No."

"Do you think she might get in touch with the man who bought the sculpture?"

"She might."

"Could you give me his name?"

"I don't know if I should."

"I won't tell him where I got it, if that's what you're worried about."

"You never know," she said. "He might want to build another house." She shrugged. "His name was Brian MacIlroy."

"Brian MacIlroy? Why does it sound familiar?"

"I think he's a lawyer," she said, as if that would explain it.

"Do you have an address?"

"In my file." She went to a cluttered desk at the back of the gallery, came back and handed me a slip of paper on which she'd written Brian MacIlroy's name, a West Vancouver address and a telephone number. I folded it once and put it in my shirt pocket. I thanked her and turned to go.

"Tom?"

I turned back. "Yes?"

"If you speak to her, would you ask her to call me?"

"Yes," I said. "I will."

13

After tucking the Porsche away at the boat yard, I restarted the purple pump, checked my answering machine for messages – there weren't any – then took the ferry across False Creek and walked to the studio, stopping on the way at the Chinese bakery to pick up a couple of barbecued-pork buns for lunch. Bobbi was out, Ron was in the lab, and Mrs. Szymkowiak was busy with the books, so I poured myself a cup of coffee and took my lunch into my office.

Bodger was sunning himself on the windowsill. As I unwrapped the pork buns, he raised his blunt wedge-shaped head, nose twitching. Slowly, feigning disinterest, he roused himself, stretched, and leapt four feet from the sill to my desktop.

"Bugger off," I said as he sniffed at a bun. "Go catch yourself a mouse, you useless bag of fur." I tore off a chunk of bun and meat and fed it to him. He took it daintily from my fingers and gobbled it down.

Bodger and I shared one bun and I put the second in the little refrigerator under the coffee machine. Bodger returned to the windowsill and I put my heels up on my desk and wondered what I was going to do for the rest of the afternoon. I suppose I could have called Pat

Jirasek at West Coast Hotels, but there wasn't much I could say that I hadn't already said. I briefly considered sending him a bottle of good Scotch until I remembered he was a Mormon. He didn't even drink coffee.

I took the piece of notepaper Ginny had given me out of my shirt pocket and unfolded it. Brian MacIlroy. The name had a decidedly familiar ring, and not simply because it bore a resemblance to that of a former Canadian prime minister. I'd seen it in the papers or heard it on the news recently, but I couldn't remember the context. I dragged the phone over, propped it in my lap, and punched in a number I knew almost as well as my own name. Kevin Ferguson answered on the second ring.

"*Vancouver Sun* city desk. Ferguson."

"Kev, this is Tom McCall."

"Tom McCall? I knew a Tom McCall once, but he died. Must've done; no one's heard from him in years."

"How are you, Kev?"

"Content I am in the knowledge that I have not been a complete disappointment to myself, my friends, or my family, not necessarily in that order. And you, Flash? You're still wasting film, I trust."

"It's a living."

"Glad to hear it. What can I do for you?"

"Brian MacIlroy?" I said.

"What about him?"

"You know him?"

"Never met the man. Heard of him, though. Who hasn't?"

"I hasn't," I said. "The name sounds familiar, though."

"That's right," Kev said. "You've been dead."

"Not dead, Kev, just – well – busy."

"Don't tell me you've gone and got yourself married again."

"No, nothing like that. Why?"

"MacIlroy's a lawyer."

"A divorce lawyer?"

"Not just a divorce lawyer, m'son. The divorce lawyer from Hell. Made headlines last year when the unhappy ex of one of his clients, a building contractor by trade, tried to send him back the long way by planting ten pounds of dynamite under the seat of his Mercedes. When it didn't go off, the poor schmuck rammed MacIlroy's car with his Pathfinder. When that didn't work, he tried to dispatch MacIlroy with a three iron. Prob'ly explains why MacIlroy's decided to go into politics. Safer."

"I remember him now," I said. "A couple of years ago, didn't he win a huge settlement for the ex-wife of some computer billionaire?"

"T'other way round," Kev said. "MacIlroy represented the husband, one Parker O'Connor. Not worth quite as much as God or Bill Gates, but close. He holds the patent on some doodad that virtually every computer in the world needs to make it work right. The ex–Mrs. O'Connor was demanding a truly indecent sum of money, but settled for considerably less. When last seen, she was flogging cosmetics on late-night TV. Why the interest in this particular shyster, may I ask?"

"I'm hoping he'll be able to shed some light on the whereabouts of an old friend."

"Good luck," Kev said.

I hung up after promising to get together soon for a drink, and dialled the number Ginny had given me. I didn't know whether it was his home number or his office number. A woman with a thick Eastern European accent answered.

"May I speak to Mr. MacIlroy, please?"

"No," she said. "At office."

"Can you give me the number, please?"

"No. You leave name, number. He call." She paused, then added, "Maybe."

"Can you tell me the name of his firm?"

"Firm?"

"His office?"

"You leave name, number. He call." She paused.

"I know. 'Maybe.' Thank you."

The phone clicked loudly in my ear as she hung up.

There was a listing for MacIlroy & Raymond, Attorneys at Law, in the white pages. I dialled the number. A woman answered. This one had an Australian accent. "May I to speak to Mr. Brian MacIlroy, please?"

"Whom shall I say is calling?"

"My name is Thomas McCall."

Pause, no doubt while she checked my name against the list of acceptable callers. Then: "Mr. MacIlroy isn't taking any new clients, Mr. McCall."

"I'm not a client," I said. "This is a personal matter. It concerns a mutual friend, Carla Bergman."

"Hold the line, please. I'll see if Mr. MacIlroy will speak to you."

The phone clicked as I was put on hold. Every five or so seconds the line beeped to remind me I was still on hold, annoying but less so than canned music. I didn't really think MacIlroy would agree to speak to me, but after about a minute the line clicked again and a deep, oily voice said, "Mr. McCall? Brian MacIlroy.

Deirdre said you had a personal matter to discuss regarding a Carla Bergman. I don't believe I know a Carla Bergman."

If he didn't know her, why was he talking to me? I asked myself. Aloud I said, "It was four or five years ago. Black hair, pale skin, dark blue eyes."

"I'm sorry, I don't recall."

"She remembers you," I said, figuring it was probably true. "She was with you when you purchased a fifteen-thousand-dollar Haida sculpture from a gallery in Gastown."

"I've purchased many pieces of Northwest Native art, sir. It's a particular passion of mine, but I don't — wait a moment. Carla Bergman. Yes, I do recall meeting someone by that name a few years ago. I believe it was at my tennis club. Charming girl. But I would hardly call her a friend, Mr. Thomas."

"McCall," I said.

"Excuse me. Mr. McCall."

"Carla told me you were quite close," I said.

"I see. Let's not waste valuable time, shall we, Mr. McCall. What is the purpose of your call?"

"Has Carla been in touch with you recently?"

There was a long silence. Finally, he said, "Are you representing Miss Bergman?"

"No."

Another pause, even longer. A good habit, think before you speak. I made a mental note to try it. I resisted the impulse to break the silence, waited him out. "What is your interest in Miss Bergman?" he asked at last.

"Uh, I'm a friend. I'm trying to find her."

"Does she wish to be found?" he asked.

That was an odd question, I thought. In his place, I probably would have asked, "Why?" But MacIlroy was a lawyer, after all. "She was supposed to come to my home on Monday evening," I said, "but she never arrived."

Another pause. It was unnerving, which was likely his intention. Probably a very effective courtroom tactic. I was about to ask him if he was still there, when he spoke.

"I'm sorry, I can't help you, Mr. McCall. I haven't seen Miss Bergman in years."

And the phone went dead.

It had been naïve of me to think that I could just call up a man like Brian MacIlroy and expect him to answer questions about an old lover, if, in fact, that's what Carla was. People in MacIlroy's socio-economic class made a fetish of privacy. You needed leverage. Unfortunately, I didn't have any, nor did I know where to find any.

I have a rotten memory and I've developed the habit of doodling and jotting notes in a steno pad whenever I talk to clients. It's an unconscious activity, half the time I'm not even aware I'm doing it, which frequently makes the doodles difficult to interpret later. While talking to Brian MacIlroy, I'd drawn a crude totem pole, then added stubby legs and sneakers and written the word LOVE below it. No problem. MacIlroy had said he'd met Carla at his tennis club. I wasn't sure it was useful information, but it was something.

There was a sudden muffled crash from the outer office, which rattled the glass in my office door. Bodger's head snapped up, tattered ears cocked. I got up and went into the other room.

"What the hell was that?" I asked Mrs. Szymkowiak.

"It sounded like it came from the lab," she said.

Bobbi came storming out of the lab, shoulders hunched and face livid.

"Bobbi, what the . . ."

"Not *now*," she said through clenched teeth, and slammed out of the studio.

14

After dinner Hilly and Beatrix and I checked the purple pump then went for a walk. The season was in full swing and there were the inevitable tourists on the boardwalk gawking at the funny floating houses, hoping to catch a glimpse of the strange people who lived in them. A middle-aged man in a yellow polo shirt and a Toronto Blue Jays baseball cap aimed a video camera at us as we walked up the ramp. There was something odd about the way he held the little camera, then I noticed he was missing the two middle fingers of his right hand. I glared at him and he aimed the camera elsewhere.

The cobbled streets were busy, thronging with tourists from Des Moines and Kyoto, locals from Kitsilano and the West End on the other side of False Creek, mummers, mimes, and the occasional mendicant. The gulls were making their last noisy forays before retiring for the evening (to wherever it was gulls retired) and soon the thousands of grackles or starlings or whatever they were would be returning en masse to their roosts under the Granville Bridge, an event that was spectacular, albeit somewhat hazardous, to behold.

Beatrix didn't like walking and rode Hilly's shoulder instead, her small head constantly swivelling back and forth on her sinuous neck as she tried to take in everything going on around her. Our progress was slowed by the people who kept stopping us to admire Beatrix and I began to think that owning a ferret or some equally exotic pet might be a great way to meet people. The female variety, of course. Oh, what a darling little thing, what is it? It's my pet wombat, Elvis. Sit still for the nice lady, Elvis.

A group of teenagers — a "hormone," a curmudgeonly friend calls it — loitered around the entrance to the arcade next to the Kids' Market. The boys had a cloned look, hair shorn unevenly, dressed in baggy shorts, oversized T-shirts, and heavy-soled black shoes or paratrooper boots or sneakers that looked as though they'd been designed by NASA. The girls were dressed more individualistically, but only somewhat.

The arcade was a new addition to the attractions on Granville Island, not an altogether welcome one to some. An unpleasant electronic racket issued from the garishly lighted interior, a cacophony of synthesized gunfire, screaming tires, roaring engines, shrieks, grunts, pows, thuds, whirs, buzzes, boings, and bongs.

As we passed, one of the boys waved and called Hilly's name.

"Who's that?" I asked.

"A boy from the day camp," she said. "Can I, Dad?"

"All right," I said reluctantly. I looked at my watch. It was a little before eight. "Be home by nine."

She said "Thanks," and ran to join them.

I continued my leisurely circuit around the island. Unencumbered by a minor, I dropped into Bridges

Pub for a quick beer. It was a mistake. Susan was sitting by herself on the terrace. Unfortunately, I didn't see her until she'd seen me. By then I'd already picked up a beer at the bar and it was too late to duck out with dignity intact.

"Tom," she said.

"Susan," I said. "How are you?"

"Fine," she said.

"Are you alone?" I asked before I noticed there was another glass on the table. It was a stupid question anyway; Susan never went to bars alone.

"No," she said.

"Ah," I said. "Well . . ."

Just then her companion returned, a blandly handsome forty-something fellow named Colin Applegate. When he saw me he looked for a moment as though he were going to run, and probably would have if I hadn't smiled my most disarming smile.

"Tom," he said.

"Colin," I said, remembering just in time to pronounce his name properly.

Applegate was a suit, vice president of marketing or something. He lived in a condo in the West End, drove a BMW 735i, and kept a forty-five foot Hunter sloop at one of the marinas on the other side of False Creek. If Susan were husband hunting she could do worse, financially speaking, but I was disappointed in her; she could do a hell of a lot better than Colon Applejerk, as one of the waitresses at The Keg had dubbed him.

"Well, enjoy your evening," I said lamely.

I took my beer back to the bar, where I found a stool and wedged myself between a bulky gent who seemed to be coated in a thin patina of grey dust – I guessed he worked at the Ocean Cement plant – and a broad-shouldered, muscular woman in frayed cut-offs and sleeveless denim shirt knotted below her breasts. I'd seen her around, but didn't know her name. She was deeply tanned, but burnt on the tops of her shoulders, and her short hair was sun-bleached almost white. Her features were strong, nearly masculine, but not quite.

"How you doing?" she said. She was drinking a Granville Island lager from the bottle. Her hands looked capable of crushing rocks.

"Can't complain," I replied.

"That'll be a refreshing change," she said. "I hate men who whine."

"Well, you don't have to be so brutally honest about it," I whined.

She saluted me with her beer bottle, drained it, and held up the empty for the bartender to see. "You live in one of those floating homes, don't you?"

"Yes, I do," I replied.

The bartender placed a fresh bottle of beer in front of her. I thought about offering to pay for it, but that's all. She wasn't unattractive, not by a long shot, but the muscular development intimidated me a little. Hell, it intimidated me a lot.

"I heard one of 'em's sinking," she said. "Not that one, I hope."

"The very one," I said.

"Then I'd say you have something to complain about."

"What good would it do?"

"True. Well," she added, raising her bottle, "here's to Archimedes' principle." She knocked her bottle against my glass and we drank. "I'm Francine Janes," she said, offering her hand. "I know it's an awful name, but it's better than Frankie. I'll tolerate Fran, but prefer Francine. No one calls me Franny."

"Tom McCall," I said, shaking her hand. As powerful as her hands looked, her handshake was gentle, almost timid. "People call me all kinds of things." She smiled. She had very nice, very white teeth. "Do you work around here?" I asked.

"At the dive shop," she said. "I'm a general dogsbody and sometimes scuba instructor."

"That explains your knowledge of Archimedes' principle."

"Actually, no," she said. "That would be my degree in marine engineering."

"What's a marine engineer doing working as a general dogsbody and sometime scuba instructor?"

"I tried the nine-to-five routine," she said. "But it didn't suit my nature. Cousteau wasn't hiring," she added with a shrug, "so here I am."

"Jacques's loss," I said. We drank to his memory; he'd died just a couple of years earlier.

Colin Applegate's bland image hove into view in the mirror behind the bar.

"Oh-oh," Francine said.

"Can I have a word with you, Tom?" he said.

"Sure, Colin," I said, turning around. "What's up?" Surely he didn't want talk about Susan.

"I want to talk to you about Susan," he said.

Francine said, "Maybe you boys ought to take this outside."

I leaned back against the bar and waited. When Colin realized I wasn't going to say anything, nor suggest a change of venue, he said, "You aren't going to be difficult about this, are you, old man?"

"What do you mean?" I said. "Difficult about what?"

"I know that you and Susan have been seeing each other for some time," he said, "but she assures me that it's now pretty much over between you."

I had more or less arrived at the same conclusion when she hadn't returned any of my calls, but hearing it from Colin made me want to throw myself at her feet and beg for forgiveness. I restrained myself.

"I mean," Colin went on, "I wouldn't want you to think that I – that is, I wouldn't want to be the cause of – come between – well, I think you know what I mean."

"Susan's an adult," I said. "Who she goes out with is her business."

"I wasn't asking your permission to go out with her," he said. "I just want to be sure you understand."

"Understand what?" I said, refusing to let him off the hook.

He stared at me for a few seconds, then went away.

When he was out of earshot, Francine said, "Did he really say 'old man'? What did he think this was, an episode of *Masterpiece Theatre*?"

I swivelled around. "I almost feel sorry for him," I said.

"Why's that?"

"Susan isn't the type to suffer fools. I'm surprised she put up with me for as long as she did."

"Are you a fool?"

"Sometimes I wonder." I looked at my watch. It was almost nine. "I've got to go," I said. "I told my daughter to be home by nine."

"Mind if I tag along?" Francine said. "My car's parked in the lot near Sea Village and my three hours are almost up."

There is a three-hour limit on free parking on Granville Island and they are strict about enforcing it.

"Glad of the company," I said.

We were standing on the boardwalk at the top of the ramp down to the docks. My house was easy to identify from the purple pump on the dock.

"Still afloat, at least," she said.

"So far," I said.

"Are they built on pontoons or what?"

"Reinforced concrete hulls," I said.

"And it's leaking?"

"So it would seem. Would you like the twenty-five-cent tour? Maybe I could scare up a beer." Smooth, I thought. Very smooth.

"I wouldn't turn down a cup of tea," she replied. "Let me flip my car."

Her car was a battered Jeep Renegade with oversized off-road tires. The free parking lot was full, as usual in the summer, so she scrubbed the chalk mark off the tire with the sole of her sneaker, then backed the Jeep out of its slot and re-parked it, tail first.

I checked the pump – it was still running – and the answering machine, to see if my insurance agent or the salvage contractor had called – neither had – then put on a kettle. While we waited for the water to boil, I gave Francine the twenty-five-cent tour, during which she used the downstairs bathroom. It was not quite nine and Hilly wasn't home yet. When the water was ready, I made a pot of herbal tea and we took it up to the roof deck. The tide was in and the deck was above the level of the boardwalk.

"You aren't worried about being alone with a strange man?" I asked when we'd settled into deck chairs.

She laughed and said, "Are you strange?"

"A little, but I'm not dangerous."

"I'm pretty strong," she said.

"Yes, you look it. Do you lift weights?" I asked.

"Some," she said, "but mainly I row."

"Row?"

"Sculls. I was on the Olympic rowing team a few years ago. Almost took the bronze medal in '84, but I blew a muscle in my back."

I revised her age upward. If she'd competed in the 1984 Olympics she'd be my age at least, perhaps a year or two older. Rowing isn't a sport for kids.

"And now," I said, "you're a general dogsbody and sometime scuba instructor with a degree in marine engineering."

"That about sums it up. What do you do?"

"I'm a commercial photographer."

"What's a commercial photographer?"

"One who takes pictures of damned near anything for money, corporate vice presidents or helicopters."

"You must do all right," she said, "to have a place like this."

"The house belongs to a friend who lives in Israel. I'm a sort of a full-time permanent house-sitter. I pay the expenses."

"And it's sinking? Poor you."

"Yes, it surely is. I'm hopeful, however, that the insurance will cover it."

In the dim light of the string of ten-watt bulbs around the perimeter of the roof deck, I became acutely conscious of the pale glow of her sun-bleached hair, the unfathomable depth of her eyes, the sculpted curves and angles of her cheekbones and slightly square jaw, the swell of her breasts beneath her shirt, the powerful length of thigh and calf. The breeze shifted momentarily and carried to me the salty musk of her. It hit me like pheromones must hit a male luna moth, taking my breath away and producing a rush of desire that was almost overwhelming in its intensity. Adrenaline raced through me like an electric current.

I took a deep, unsteady breath and looked at my watch: nine-twenty. Where the hell was Hilly?

Francine stood and said, "I guess I should go."

I stood also, thankful for the poor lighting. "My daughter was supposed to be back from the arcade at nine."

I walked Francine to her car, where she said, "See you around."

I said, "You bet." She smiled and drove off.

I walked to the arcade and went into the bright, noisy glitter. I found Hilly at one of the machines with a different group of kids. These looked older, fifteen or sixteen, although sometimes it's hard to tell, especially with the girls; they try so hard to look older. Hilly half-heartedly apologized for losing track of the time and we walked home with Beatrix asleep inside her shirt.

After Hilly went to bed I sat on the roof deck, lights out, and thought about man's (do not read "humankind"; I have a limited perspective on the needs and motives of the female of the species) need for companionship, sex, intimacy, not necessarily in that order.

Susan was good company, a solid and reliable friend, someone with whom you spend a quiet evening at home, take to a concert or a play, who makes you chicken soup when you have the flu and soothes your brow when life gets you down. In short, the mother substitute every man is supposed to secretly desire (a theory to which I've never subscribed).

What I had felt for the muscular Francine, on the other hand, had been lust, pure and simple, unadulterated by any honourable motives. Well, not much, anyway; I was, after all, a hopeless romantic. Francine was the kind of woman with whom one climbed mountains, rode the white water, sailed the blue oceans and explored the dark jungles. She was an equal partner, maybe slightly more than equal, who relieved the male of the species of the heavy responsibility of being the so-called stronger half.

Which brought me to Carla. Two and a half years ago, bushwhacked by the sheer heart-stopping beauty of her, unable – or unwilling – to see the danger, I'd fallen in love with her. Since my divorce from Linda, despite the show I'd put on for my friends and family so they would stay off my case and leave me alone, I'd been running on inertia, just going through the motions as the flywheel slowly spun down, waiting for the energy to be dissipated so I could stop and lie down. Life simply wasn't worth the effort. Not that I ever considered doing anything about it. I simply wasn't going to work very hard at living. Then I met Carla. Suddenly I felt really and truly alive for the first time since the break-up of my marriage, and it was wonderful. Life was wonderful. The world was a wonderful place to live. I must have been insufferable.

And then, as suddenly as she had come into my life, she was gone (along with my stereo, computer, et cetera). I crashed in flames. For a few weeks the aching emptiness was overwhelming, the pain seeming worse by an order of magnitude than what I'd felt after my divorce. However, one morning not long afterward, I woke up, looked around and realized, with some amazement, that I was still alive and, remarkably, it didn't hurt any more. It was that simple. Of course, the world didn't look quite the same as it had. At first I thought it was the world that was different, but I soon realized that the difference was in me, that I'd changed. It was as though my internal camera was now properly focussed. Maybe I'd grown up. A little, at least. But I knew that I was definitely not the same person I'd been before Carla. And I'd learned something crucial. That I was in control. Over some aspects of my life at least. Me. No one else.

And for that I was indebted to Carla. For that I still loved her. In a way. But I wasn't bewitched by her now. I knew she was trouble. I'd stuck my finger into the bright blue flame and I knew it was hot. I wasn't fireproof, not by a long shot. Was the debt I owed her reason enough to risk getting burned again? A damned good question for which I had no reasonable answer. Or even an unreasonable one. Notwithstanding the lack of answers, reasonable or otherwise, it was probable, however, that I would continue to look for her, even though I hadn't a clue what to do next.

But I had other things to think about, and not just my incredible sinking house or my plummeting bottom line. A few minutes earlier I'd found a tampon applicator in the upstairs bathroom wastebasket. At first I thought it might have been Francine's, but she'd used the downstairs bathroom. It had to be Hilly's. Wonderful. Great. Just what I needed. It was little consolation that at least she evidently knew how to use one.

15

I woke at seven-thirty on Friday morning and went out to check on the pump. I found it still thrumming away, discharging a steady stream of scummy water into the harbour. It had stopped stopping, which meant that the leak had worsened and that the house was taking water faster than the little purple pump could suck it out. I knelt on the dock and looked at the side of the hull to see if the crud line was still visible. It was, but just.

"Everything okay?" Daniel called down from his roof garden.

"Oh, yes, fine," I said, standing, looking up at him. "I'll just paint the fucking thing yellow and rename it the *Titanic*."

"You're mixing metaphors again," Daniel said.

"Simpson Marine & Salvage," I said. "You're sure they're still in business? I called yesterday morning, but haven't heard from them yet."

"As far as I know they're still, ahem, above water."

"Very funny."

I fixed Hilly pancakes for breakfast, breaking out the last of my genuine Quebec maple syrup. I thought it would be a nice treat for her, but coming from the east she was blasé about such luxuries. When she finished she carried her dishes to the dishwasher, then said, "Do you think Beatrix will be okay if I leave her home today? We're going to Science World."

"Sure," I said. "I'll keep an eye on her."

The phone rang and Hilly picked it up. "Hello?" She listened for a moment, then said, "It's for you."

It was Wally Hoag, my insurance agent. "Hang on a sec, Wally," I said. "This won't take long," I said to Hilly. "Then I'll walk you to the community centre."

"I can find my own way," she said.

"You sure?"

"Yeah."

I kissed her goodbye, saw her out the door, then went back to the phone. After I explained the situation to Wally, he told me I didn't have anything to worry about, he was certain the policy covered me against sinking, but he'd get back to me later in the day with the details. I'd no sooner hung up when the phone rang again.

"Hello."

"Thomas McCall?" a gruff voice said.

"Yes. I'm Thomas McCall. Who's this?"

"Bernard Simpson." Said as though it was supposed to mean something to me.

"I'm afraid – did you say Simpson? Of Simpson Marine & Salvage?"

"That's me. Sorry 'bout takin' so long t' get back t' ya, but the machine's bin actin' up."

"The machine?"

"The answerin' machine. Since the wife passed away I haven't had anyone t'answer the phone. My son gave me this machine, but lately the consarned thing ain't bin recording properly or somethin'. I git only parts of messages. I was finally able to make out yer name, but hadda look you up in the book. Lucky there ain't too many T. McCalls. Yer house is sinkin', you say? Live in one o' them floatin' houses on Granville Island, do ya? I kin be there 'round eleven. That okay with you?"

"Fine. I'll be here."

I pressed the switch hook then dialled the studio number and left a message with the answering service that I'd be late. Pouring myself another cup of coffee, I got out the Yellow Pages and looked up tennis clubs. It was a long shot — Carla may have been a guest when MacIlroy met her at the tennis club — but it was the only lead I had. There were a dozen private clubs listed, as many public. I figured I could ignore the latter for now; MacIlroy would probably belong to a private club. I focussed on the clubs in West Vancouver, reasoning that he would choose a club close to home. That narrowed the list down to three. I started with the West Vancouver Tennis Club.

I took a couple of deep breaths and dialled.

"Pro shop, please. . . . Hello. My name is Dennis O'Toole of *Law Today* magazine. Are you familiar with our publication? You're not? Understandable, I suppose. Our readers are almost all legal professionals. The reason I'm calling is that we're doing a profile of a prominent local attorney named Brian MacIlroy for our October issue and we understand he's a very good tennis player. He once considered turning pro — pardon me? You don't know him? He's not a member there? I see. Well, our research department screwed up again. Sorry to bother you."

I hung up. Strike one. I dialled the number of the Hollyburn Tennis Club, but he wasn't a member there either. Perhaps it wasn't yet time to consider a career change.

The last number on the short list was the Capilano Canyon Tennis Club.

"Yeah, hi," I said after asking for the pro shop. "I'm Dennis O'Toole of *Law Today* magazine. We're doing a profile of prominent local attorney Brian MacIlroy for our October issue and we understand he's a very good tennis player. He once considered turning pro – excuse me? Oh, he's not that good? Middlin' fair for a recreational player? I see. I guess we won't include it in the profile, then. Sorry to trouble you. Thanks."

I hung up.

"Well," I said to Beatrix, who was wrestling with an old rolled-up sock, "that was easier than I expected."

The telephone rang. I jumped, startling Beatrix, who scampered under the sofa.

"Hello?"

"Tom, we need to talk." It was Mary-Alice.

"We do? What about?"

"Mother thinks Dad is having an affair."

"Pardon me?"

"You heard me. Dad is having an affair."

"You said, and I quote, 'Mother *thinks* Dad is having an affair.' What makes *you* certain he is?"

"What are you going on about? Of course I'm not certain."

"All right, what makes Mom think Dad is having an affair?"

"I don't know," Mary-Alice said. "When she called last night she was crying, so it was a little hard to make out what she was saying, but she told me she's sure Dad is having an affair."

"With whom?" I asked.

"Your next-door neighbour."

"What? That's absurd. She thinks Dad's having an affair with *Daniel*?"

"Not Daniel, goddamnit. Some woman he met last weekend."

"Maggie Urquhart? Don't be silly, Mary-Alice. They spoke for all of three minutes." Despite what I'd told Daniel about my father's reaction to Maggie Urquhart, I did not for one minute believe there was anything to my mother's suspicions.

"Thomas," Mary-Alice said in her sternest schoolmarm voice. "Do you want to talk about this or don't you?"

"No," I said. "I don't."

"They're our parents. Doesn't it matter to you that they might be getting a divorce?"

"Mary-Alice, just because Mom thinks Dad is having an affair doesn't mean they're going to get a divorce. Even if Dad *is* having an affair, which I seriously doubt, that doesn't necessarily automatically lead to divorce either." At least not right away, I added to myself. "Hey, M.-A. Relax, all right?"

"Easy for you to say," Mary-Alice said. "She doesn't call you up every other day and go on and on about Dad and how much she gave up for him."

"Better you than me," I said. "Look, they're going through a rough time. You'll just have to endure."

"Right, sure. Endure. Thanks heaps."

"I'm fine, by the way, thanks for asking."

"What? Oh, sorry. How are you? Hilly arrived safely, I guess. How is she?"

"She's fine too."

"I'm looking forward to seeing her. Why don't you bring her to dinner tomorrow? And Susan, of course."

"Ah, well, I guess Hilly and I could make it. But Susan and I are – we broke up."

"Oh, Tom. I really thought you and Susan – I'm sorry."

"Thanks, M.-A."

We chatted for a few more minutes, then Mary-Alice said, "Look, why don't I take Hilly shopping on Saturday? Do you think she'd like that?"

"She's female, isn't she?"

"I'll ignore that," Mary-Alice said. "I'll pick her up at ten. Then we'll have dinner here. Say around six. David will barbecue some salmon. How's that sound?"

"Sounds great," I said.

At ten forty-five I was outside on the dock watching the little purple pump. It was working very hard, valiantly but vainly trying to keep the hydrosphere where it belonged, rattling and rasping and sounding as though it was about to suffer an infarction of some kind. Perhaps I should call Gwen the Purple Tool Lady and get a bigger one, I thought. Just then a bright electric-blue step van pulled up to the boardwalk on the embankment. The driver's-side door slid open and Frodo Baggins stepped out.

"You McCall?" he called down to me.

It wasn't Frodo Baggins, of course. It was Bernard Simpson, of Simpson Marine & Salvage.

After I'd explained the problem to Mr. Simpson and he'd assured me that I needn't worry, I was in good hands, I got out the Porsche. Twenty minutes later, I turned the Porsche onto Taylor Way in the Municipality of West Vancouver and began the winding climb up Cypress Mountain toward the Capilano Canyon Tennis Club.

According to the CAA street map, the Capilano Canyon Tennis Club wasn't far from the Capilano Golf and Country Club, smack in the middle of the residential area known as the British Properties, perhaps some of the most expensive and exclusive real estate in the country, despite the fact that most of it is damned near vertical. I had worried that I might find it hard to talk my way in, but I just gave the uniformed flunky at the gate my name and address then drove through and parked in the visitor's parking lot. Driving a classic Porsche probably didn't do my credibility any harm. And I'd dressed for the occasion, in a sports jacket, shirt and tie, and pressed tan Dockers in lieu of jeans.

I asked directions to the pro shop from a middle-aged woman wearing a tennis skirt that went almost to her knees. I'd given what I'd say some thought during the drive out here, finally arriving at the conclusion that a more or less straightforward approach was best. Despite my success on the telephone, I didn't have much faith in my abilities as an actor or confidence man. I'd also decided to stick with the winning formula. The pro-shop staff was likely to be less suspicious of inquiries into the social lives of the club's prominent members than the front office.

In the pro shop I asked a well-tanned pre-cancerous chap, who looked like Troy Donahue gone to seed, if the club pro was available. He told me that the pro was on vacation, but that the assistant pro was around. "She's on the courts right now, though, giving a lesson. Nancy Petersen, with an 'e.'"

There were a dozen courts and all were in use. Two-thirds of the players were women but most of them were either too old, too young, too fat, or simply not good enough to be a professional. I finally narrowed the choices down to two: a lean and angular woman in her mid-to-late thirties who served with savage intensity, face contorting and grunting explosively as she blew ace after ace by her hopelessly outclassed opponent; and a compact brunette about thirty who bounded around the court as if her legs were made of spring steel beneath a thin layer of mahogany-coloured rubber, returning impossible volleys from a more powerful male opponent.

I asked a distinguished grey-haired gentleman in white slacks and a blue blazer with the club crest emblazoned on the breast pocket (looking more like he belonged at the Royal Vancouver Yacht Club) which of them was Nancy Petersen.

He said, "Neither one. That's her over there." He pointed toward a court on which a somewhat severe-looking woman with a dark, flying ponytail exchanged slow volleys with a gnarly old woman with pink hair that clashed with her forest-green sun visor and pale-blue tennis outfit. Finding a table from which I could watch Nancy Petersen and her septuagenarian opponent, I waved to a white-jacketed waiter and asked if it was possible to get a drink without being a member.

"Certainly, sir. We have a cash bar."

I ordered a club soda with a twist of lime. It set me back five bucks, not including tip.

The pro and the old lady rallied back and forth for a while longer, then knocked it off. As I stood up to intercept Nancy Petersen on her way to the clubhouse, the woman with the spring-steel legs called out to her.

"Nance, how 'bout it?"

Nancy Petersen said, "Sure, Liz," and they went at it.

Looking at them, I would have placed my money on Liz of the Spring-Steel Legs, but Petersen blew her off the court. Not that she had an easy time of it. Liz was inhumanly fast and her smashes damned near caused a sonic boom. However, Petersen played with a greater economy of style and more focus, forcing her opponent to chase the ball, and giving her little opportunity to use her smash. After Liz lost the sixth straight game, she flipped her racket end over end into the air and cried, "Uncle! Uncle!"

They shook hands and as they left the court I heard Nancy Petersen say, "You shouldn't give up so easily, Liz." Both women looked at me warily as I approached.

"Ms. Petersen," I said. "Do you have a minute?"

She nodded and said to the other woman, "I'll see you later, Liz." Turning to me, she said, "Are you a member? You'll have to talk to the pro-shop manager if you want to sign up for lessons." She was dripping with sweat, ponytail limp and damp, and she kept plucking her shirt away from her midriff.

"I'm not a member," I said. "My name is Tom McCall. I'm a photographer." I handed her a card. "I'm trying to locate this woman." I showed her the photograph, one of the nudes, cropped to show only her head and shoulders. "Her name is —"

"That's Carla Bergman," Nancy Petersen said.

"You know her?"

Nancy Petersen's green eyes narrowed. "I know her," she said. "May I see that?" I handed her the photograph. She studied it for a moment, then handed it back to me. "Did you take it?"

"Yes," I said. I slipped the photograph into my inside jacket pocket. "Was she a member here?" I asked.

Nancy Petersen shook her head and said, "No, she worked here."

"When was that?" I asked.

"Four or five years ago. May I ask why you're looking for her?"

As part of my more or less straightforward approach I'd concocted a ridiculous cover story about a fictional client who'd seen a picture of Carla and wouldn't settle for anyone else to represent his line of cosmetics or such, but I couldn't bring myself to use it.

"She's a friend," I said. "She's dropped out of sight and I'm trying to track down anyone she may have been in touch with."

"I see," Nancy Petersen said. "Listen, can you give me a few minutes to shower and change?"

"Of course," I said.

While I waited for her I watched a noisy foursome of teenage girls playing doubles. They seemed to be all tanned leg and sun-bleached hair and limitless energy.

They made me feel old. I was beginning to wonder if Nancy Petersen had had second thoughts about talking to me when an attractive red-haired woman dropped into a chair facing me.

"I hope I didn't keep you waiting too long."

"Not at all," I said.

I hardly recognized her. Dry, her hair was lighter, the colour of rusted iron, and wearing it loose took five years off her age. She no longer looked the least bit severe. She was what most men would call cute: dimples, high cheekbones, a wash of freckles across her nose, and a voice that was light and sweet and almost childlike. Her wide guileless eyes weren't green, as I'd first thought, but two-toned, pale luminescent green near the pupil, darkening to brown at the edges.

"Who's Bobbi?" she asked.

"Huh? She's my assistant, partner really. How . . . ? Ah, you called to check my credentials."

"Can't be too careful these days," she said. "So, I didn't think Carla had any friends. Especially of the male persuasion. Just victims. Are you one of those? Sorry," she added quickly, a pink flush highlighting her cheekbones. "None of my business."

"It's all right. Yes, you could say I'm one of her victims."

"I'm not going to be much help, I'm afraid. I haven't seen her since she worked here."

"What did she do?"

"She worked as a waitress for a few months, in the main dining room, then she was promoted to assistant to the club president."

"How long was she here?"

"Six months, maybe eight." She flagged the white-coated waiter. "Would you like something?" she said.

"No, thank you."

She ordered orange juice.

"How well did you know her?"

"Not well. She took some lessons, could have been quite good if she'd started young enough, but beyond that we didn't spend very much time together. I guess I was intimidated by her. She was so exotically beautiful and I'm – well, I'm not beautiful, that's for sure."

I thought she was very attractive, but I kept my thoughts to myself.

"Did Carla make any other friends while she was here?" I asked.

"Not that I'm aware of. She didn't mix much with the other staff, especially after moving up to the front office. Of course, every male who came within twenty feet of her tried his luck, but most crashed on takeoff."

"Can you think of anyone she might get in touch with?"

"I don't think anyone around here would be very happy to see her. She had her own version of the scorched-earth policy and that included burning most of her bridges behind her. She left rather suddenly, as I recall, and I heard a rumour that some cash was missing."

The waiter brought her orange juice in a big goblet. It was undoubtedly freshly squeezed and I shuddered to think what it cost, given the price of club soda. She sipped the juice and licked bits of pulp from her lips.

"Do you know Brian MacIlroy?" I asked.

Her two-tone eyes narrowed. "After a fashion. Why?"

"Did he try his luck?" I asked.

"Whoa, now," she said. "You wouldn't want me to get fired, would you?"

"Absolutely not," I said with as much earnestness as I could muster.

"Actually, there's really not much chance of that," she said. "But neither is there a lot I can tell you. Yes, he and Carla had something going. It didn't last long, though. Three months maybe. And Bri, as he insists his friends call him, was very discreet. No tawdry groping in the hallways or quickies in the laundry closet. And he was between wives at the time. Image is everything to our Bri. There have been rumours, of course, which I won't repeat, but –" she shrugged "– he's Teflon Man."

She looked at me over the rim of her glass, eyes bright with mischief. "Larry told me someone called the pro shop earlier today claiming to be from a law magazine and asking about MacIlroy." I could feel the heat rise in my face. "That was you, wasn't it?"

"'Fraid so."

"Sneaky," she said with an impish grin. "But if you're going to play detective, you better learn how not to blush."

"I'll keep it in mind," I replied. "Did Carla ever mention what she was doing before she started working here?"

"As a matter of fact, she did. It sounded like a great job, too. I don't know why she gave it up to wait on tables. She worked for a boat broker, ferrying boats back and forth between here and Mexico and Hawaii, sometimes the South Pacific. His name was Frank something.

She met him in Acapulco, but he worked at that marina out by the airport. Bridgepoint?"

"I know it," I said. I couldn't think of anything else to ask her, so I stood up. "Thanks very much for your help."

"My pleasure." She stood too and we shook hands. "Do you mind if I keep your card?" she said. "I might need a photographer someday."

16

It was almost two when I left the tennis club. I drove to the studio, tried to catch up on the paperwork I'd been neglecting, then went home at four-thirty, battling the rush-hour traffic across the Granville Bridge. Simpson Marine & Salvage's electric-blue van was still parked by the boardwalk, blocking a number of parking spaces. Inside the truck an air compressor thumped monotonously and I had to step over a pair of fat, black air hoses that snaked from the van, dropped off the edge of the embankment, and ran along the docks before disappearing into the water beside the house. Air bubbles boiled on the surface of the water and an eerie green glow shone from below. There were divers down there with powerful lamps, inspecting the hull, I presumed.

On the dock, the little purple pump thrummed away, still sounding a little strained as it jetted water into the harbour. Inside, Hilly perched on the rim of the bilge hatch, from which issued ominous thumping and banging and scrunching sounds. Beatrix sat on her lap, staring intently into the rectangular hole, head cocked and tiny teddy-bear ears perked.

"Do you think they really know what they're doing?" Hilly asked.

"I sure hope so," I replied. I went into the kitchen, got an apple from the refrigerator, then rejoined Hilly. "How was your day?" I asked, peering into the bilge.

"All right," she replied with a complete lack of enthusiasm. "Oh, yeah, Bobbi called. She wanted me to remind you that you have to work tomorrow morning."

"I remember," I said. We were scheduled to take publicity photos for the Shakespeare-in-the-Park production of *Hamlet*. Stanley Park at dawn, for god's sake. Morning sun slanting through the mist rising off Beaver Lake. Bobbi's idea, not mine. I'd arranged for Hilly to stay overnight with Daniel.

"And," Hilly added after a lengthy pause, "Aunt Mary-Alice called. Do we really have to go there for dinner tomorrow? Her husband is such an asshole."

"Mind your tongue," I said. "That's Uncle Asshole."

"Can I bring Beatrix?"

"I don't think that would be a good idea," I said. "Mary-Alice and David don't like animals."

"You mean they don't have any pets at all?"

"Not everyone has a pet. I don't."

"What about Bodger?"

"Well, he's not exactly a pet. Besides, he doesn't live here. I think Mary-Alice has a plant, but it may be plastic."

There was a loud bang from the bilge and the house suddenly tilted a few degrees to starboard – or was it port? – then slowly levelled.

"Yipes," Hilly said. "Abandon ship. Children and animals first."

"Shut up, Hilly," I said. "Hey!" I shouted down the hatch. "What the hell's going on down there?"

Bernard Simpson's gnomish head appeared below the hatch. He was wearing a blue surgical mask and safety goggles and his fringe of white hair was flecked with bits of wet Styrofoam insulation.

"Eh?" he asked, standing up in the hatchway and pulling the mask down.

Beatrix stretched out her neck and sniffed at him. A bit of Styrofoam stuck to the tip of her nose.

"What's happening?" I asked. "The house is tilting."

"Oh, that," he said, reaching out slowly and gently brushing the fleck of Styrofoam from the ferret's nose with his fingertip. "It's all right. Y'ain't goin' to sink."

I was relieved he was so confident. Unfortunately, I didn't have as much faith in him as he seemed to have in himself.

"What are you doing down there?"

He slowly shook his head, as though it was the stupidest question he'd ever heard, and it may have been, but I wanted an answer. "Haven't finished inspecting the hull yet," he said, "but it looks like you might've got stove in by a deadhead. Rare in these waters. You know what a deadhead is?"

"Of course. A Grateful Dead fan."

"Eh?"

"Never mind. Yes, I know what a deadhead is." He looked as though he wanted proof, so I added, "A water-saturated log that floats just under the surface. Usually they float more or less vertically."

"Right. It prob'ly drifted under yer house at high tide." He held his left hand horizontal, palm down, and slowly moved his right hand, held almost perpendicular, under his left. "Then, when the tide went out, yer house settled onto the end of the deadhead and the hull cracked." He lowered his left hand until the fingers of the right touched his palm.

"Where's the deadhead now?" I asked.

He shrugged. "Drifted away. No marks on the bottom of the hull, so it prob'ly happened a while ago."

"Wouldn't I have felt it?"

"Not if you weren't here."

"How much damage did it do?"

"Hard to tell till we finish the inspection. Gotta scrape the hull and take out some insulation. Then find the leaks."

"How do you do that?" Hilly asked.

"With our magic leak detector," he said, round face crinkling with a smile. "Condensed milk. Put it in a squeeze bottle and squirt it against the bottom of the hull. It gets drawn into the leak with the water. Air bubbles work pretty good too, but the milk shows up better in the lights."

"Neat," Hilly said.

"So, once you find the leak," I asked, "then what?"

"If it ain't too bad, we seal it with what we call a 'hot patch.' Hydraulic cement. Dries under water."

"And if it is bad?"

"We install flotation bags under the house to keep it afloat and replace the damaged section of the hull. If we hafta do that we might hafta disconnect the water and sewage lines. Won't know for sure till we finish the inspection and see how much damage there is. But by the amount of water yer takin', it don't look that bad."

"I'm sure you know what you're doing," I said hopefully.

Bernard Simpson replaced his mask and goggles and disappeared back down into the bilge. I went into the kitchen. The telephone rang. I picked it up.

"Mr. McCall, this is Davy at the False Creek Community Centre. Do you have a minute?" I said I did and he went on: "Sir, your daughter got into a fist fight with another camper today."

"A fist fight?"

"Yes, sir."

"What was it about? Was the other child hurt?"

"We're not sure what it was about, sir. Hilly wouldn't say. But some of the other children say Conrad was teasing her about something."

"Conrad? Hilly got into a fist fight with a boy?"

"Yes, sir. He wasn't hurt, but his parents are pretty upset. You didn't tell us she knew martial arts, Mr. McCall. We like to know these things."

"I understand. I didn't know myself. I'll have a talk with her, of course."

"Yes, sir. And would you mind coming by with her on Monday morning? The director would like to speak with you."

"I'll be there," I said. "Thanks for calling." I hung up.

Hilly was standing in the doorway. "He made fun of my hearing aids, Dad. He kept talking real loud, yelling like I couldn't hear him."

"So you punched him out?" That's my girl, I thought. I had very low tolerance for the kind of cretin who would make fun of another person's handicap, especially when that other person was my only daughter.

"He asked for it," she said. "And he was bigger than me."

"Still," I said, "there are other ways to settle these things. You should have gone to the staff."

"I guess."

"Where did you learn martial arts?"

"Mom made me take lessons. Self-defence stuff."

"Self-defence, eh?"

"Uh, yeah."

After dinner I took Hilly for a soda. As we were walking home past the dive shop, we ran into Francine carrying a huge gunny sack. She was wearing shorts and a singlet and the muscles of her arms and shoulders and legs stood out in ridges under the weight of her load.

"Can I help you with that?" I asked, before I realized what I was saying.

She looked at me, smiling. "It's okay, I can handle it." She tossed the gunny sack into the back of her Jeep Renegade like it was filled with laundry. It sounded like it was filled with scrap iron. Maybe she wore chain-mail undies. I was grateful she'd refused my offer. "I saw Bernie Simpson's truck parked near your place," she said.

"He's saving my house," I said. "I think."

"He's a little unusual," she said. "But he's one of the best salvage guys around." She looked at Hilly. "Hi. I'm Francine." She stuck out her hand.

"I'm Hilly," Hilly said, shaking Francine's hand.

"Pretty name. Short for . . . ?"

"Hillary. Are you a diver?"

"Yes, I am. How'd you know?"

Hilly pointed to the "Diver Below" symbol on the spare-wheel cover, a red square with white diagonal stripe.

"Would you like to come over?" I asked. "You could see what Simpson's been up to. I'll make some tea. That is, if he hasn't disconnected the water. If he has, you may have to settle for a soft drink. Or beer. I think I have some . . ." I realized I was babbling and clamped my mouth shut.

"I'd love to," Francine said, "but I'll have to take a rain check." She climbed into the Jeep. "I'm taking a group to the Gulf Islands in the morning. Hilly, have you ever done any diving?"

"No, but I've done some snorkelling."

"If you can talk your dad into springing for some lessons, I'll see if I can get you a discount."

"That'd be neat," Hilly said. "Dad?"

"I don't see why not," I said.

"See you in a couple of days," Francine said as she started the Jeep.

"Wow," Hilly said as Francine's Jeep rattled off down the cobbled street. "Did you see her muscles?"

"Yes," I said. "I surely did."

17

The telephone rang at four in the morning, dragging me out of a dream in which Bernard Simpson had discovered that the reason my house was sinking was that the bilge was filled with huge barbells.

"You can go back to bed," Bobbi said. "The shoot's off."

"Why?" I asked.

"Lucky you live on a houseboat."

"What?" I became aware of the dull roar of rain on the roof. I peered out my bedroom window. I couldn't see a thing. Normally the lights of the Granville Bridge and the bright glow of the downtown core of the city beyond it were clearly visible. "Gee, that's too bad," I said.

"Yeah, sure." She hung up and I went back to my bed.

It was still raining at eight o'clock and according to the radio it was going to keep it up all day. Bernard Simpson and his crew arrived at eight-thirty. Hilly and I hung around, getting in their way until Mary-Alice came by to take Hilly shopping. Before they left, Hilly insisted on introducing Beatrix. Mary-Alice was less than enchanted by the creature, so Beatrix stayed home while Hilly and Mary-Alice went out to make their contribution to the Pacific Rim economy.

At eleven o'clock, for want of anything better to do, I got out the Porsche, took Granville Street south toward the airport. I exited Granville at 70th and crossed the Oak Street Bridge over the North Arm of the Fraser River to Lulu Island and the City of Richmond.

I'm not sure what the architect had in mind when he designed the Bridgepoint complex. It sprawled over a couple of acres of riverfront, the predominant colours grey and red. The public market, vacant as the day it was built, resembled an unhappy marriage between a discount food mart and a New Age church. There was even a clock tower, starkly angular and completely superfluous, looking as though it had been added as an afterthought. We need a clock tower, the developer had said, and, lo, there was a clock tower. A separate building, looking as though it had been lifted bodily from the set of *Miami Vice*, lots of smoked glass and blue neon, housed a restaurant/bar and the offices of Bridgepoint Yacht Sales.

I locked up the Porsche and went into the sales office. Behind the counter, a florid-faced middle-aged woman in slacks and a sweatshirt that read "PMS: Putting up with Men's Shit" was pecking something out on an old IBM Selectric typewriter. I asked her if Frank was around.

"Frank?" she said. For a second I was afraid she was going to say "Frank who?" but she said, "Yeah, he's around. Probably in the bar. You can go through that way."

I went through the door she'd indicated. It led to a narrow hallway, at the end of which was a door labelled BAR. It opened into a dimly lit lounge that smelled of pine-scented cleaner, frying bacon, fresh coffee, and stale cigarette smoke. A dozen or so customers, mostly boat people, judging from their attire, drank coffee and stared wistfully out the windows at the rain. Two men in business suits sat at the bar. Do boat brokers wear suits? I wondered. One of them was drinking coffee and reading the newspaper. The other was talking to the bartender.

A thin young woman in a pseudo–French maid's uniform sat at the end of the bar, smoking a cigarette and reading a fat Stephen King paperback. She had a mass of streaked and teased hair and small breasts mashed together in the middle of her chest by some kind of sado-masochistic lift-and-shape brassiere in a futile attempt to form cleavage. She had very good legs, though, which her short skirt showed off nicely indeed. When I asked her if Frank was around, she nodded toward the man talking to the bartender.

Frank was about my age, but his arteries were probably ten years older. He was thirty pounds overweight and his clothes smelled of cigarettes. His suit needed pressing and I thought his hair might have been store-bought.

"Best goddamned blow job I ever had in my life," he was saying to the bartender. "My ex-wife was okay, but this broad was fan-fucking-tastic. I kept hearing this weird whistling sound, then realized it was air being sucked in through my asshole."

The bartender laughed hollowly. I didn't think it was very funny either.

"Excuse me," I said. "Frank?"

He swivelled toward me. "That depends," he said. "You buying or selling?" The bartender moved down the bar to where the waitress sat.

"Neither," I said.

"You're not buying and you're not selling," he said, lighting a cigarette with a disposable lighter. "What're you doing?"

"I'm looking for a friend," I said.

"Sorry, pally," he said, blowing smoke. "Boats I got, friendship I can't help you with."

"Her name is Carla Bergman," I said.

He looked at me for a long time, then said, "You a cop?"

"No, just a friend." I handed him a card.

He read it, looked at me, and said, "You take pictures for skin mags or something?"

"No."

"What makes you think I know her?"

"She told me she used to work for a boat broker at this marina."

"I'm not the only one sells boats around here."

"Frank Something, she said. That you?"

"Yeah, I guess that's me. Frank Poole." He tucked my card into his shirt pocket. "Okay, so she used to work for me," he said. "That was a long time ago. I haven't seen her in a couple of years." He took a hard drag on his cigarette, shortening it by half an inch. "I'll say this, pal, she was a truly world-class piece of ass," he said, smoke dribbling from his mouth. "If looks could kill, she'd be a mass murderer. But I can't tell you the grief she caused me."

"What sort of grief?" I asked, trying hard to keep my voice neutral.

"Coupla years ago she showed up outta the blue lookin' for a place to crash. I said, sure, for old time's sake, and let her stay on one of the boats. But three days later she was gone, along with fucking near everything on that boat that wasn't nailed down, and some that was."

I was beginning to see a definite pattern. A blind man could have seen it.

"Billy," he called to the bartender. "Bring me a rye-and-ginger, would you?" He lit another cigarette from the butt of the first, which he then ground out in the ashtray. The bartender gave him his drink and he downed half of it in one shot.

"How long did she work for you?" I asked.

"About two years, on and off, whenever I had a boat to deliver or pick up."

"Why did she quit?"

"She didn't. I fired her."

"What for?"

"I had my reasons. Look, what's this all about, anyway? Let's see some real ID. Anyone can have a fucking business card printed up."

I took out my wallet and showed him my driver's licence.

"All right, so you're who you say you are, that doesn't prove anything. You could still be a private cop or an insurance investigator."

"I could be," I said, "but I'm not. I told you, I'm a friend. I'm just trying to find her."

"Tell you what, pally." I didn't have to be psychic to know what was coming. "Things have been kinda slow lately and I'm getting fucked by my ex-wife more now than when we were married. If you were to come up

143

with, say, a hundred bucks, I might be more inclined to answer your questions. I'll bet there are a few things I could tell you about Carla."

He'd put me in an interesting position. Was it worth a hundred dollars to find out what he could tell me about Carla? What if, despite his claim, he didn't have anything worthwhile to tell me? I could hardly ask for my money back. Besides, my cash-flow situation was lousy. I'd come this far, though, there didn't seem to be any point in turning back now.

"I don't have that much cash on me," I said. "Will you take a cheque?"

"I don't think so," he said sarcastically. "How about this? You got a credit card. Pay off my bar tab."

"And how much is that?" I asked.

"Hey, Billy. What do I owe you?"

Billy opened the cash register and took out a small spiral-bound notebook. He flipped it open. "A hundred and sixty plus change."

I took out my MasterCard. "Put a hundred of it on this," I said, hoping there was sufficient credit available.

Billy took the card.

"And I want a receipt," Poole said to Billy.

After I signed the credit-card slip, Billy wrote out a receipt and handed it to Poole. "Ask away," Poole said, tucking the receipt into his shirt pocket.

"When did you meet her?"

"I dunno. A while back. Six or seven years. She liked hanging around boats and the people who owned 'em."

"Was that in Mexico?"

"Christ, she tell you I've got a ten-inch dick too?"

"No," I said.

"Yeah, I met her in Mexico. Acapulco. I was down there to pick up a boat and she was hanging out at the marina. My guy got drunk and broke his fucking leg and I needed help bringing the boat back. She needed transportation out of there, so we made a deal. Man, that was some trip. She knew all the tricks. Goddamned near had cardiac arrest a half a dozen times."

To say that I did not like Frank Poole is putting it too mildly. I do not like walnuts or situation comedies or junk mail. Frank Poole was a detestable boor and was pushing all my buttons. Or maybe it was just that he was telling me things about Carla I didn't want to know.

"After we got back here," he said, "she hung around for a while, crewin' and screwin'." He laughed at his attempt at poetry.

"Why did you fire her?"

"She'd become, y'know, unreliable. Never knew when she was going to be available for either."

"Do you know where she lived?"

"No one particular place," he said. "For a time she was shacked up with this guy who had an old Bradley custom sloop out of one of the marinas in Coal Harbour."

Coal Harbour was on the eastern flank of Stanley Park. It was home to a couple of public marinas, as well as the Vancouver Rowing Club, the Westin Bayshore Resort and Marina, and the winter quarters of the Royal Vancouver Yacht Club.

"Do you remember his name?"

"No. He was an over-the-hill hippie type. Must've had money, though, otherwise Carla wouldn't've been interested."

"Do you remember the name of the boat?" I asked.

"The *Dragon*, I think it was. Yeah, something like that. Pretty thing. Sixty-footer. But getting a little long in the tooth."

The telephone behind the bar warbled. Billy the barman listened for a second, hung up and said to Frank Poole, "Irma says you got a call in the office."

Poole stood up. "Gotta go." He was taller than I expected him to be, well over six feet. He started to leave, turned back. "You think of any more questions, you know where to find me. Just don't forget your plastic."

"Sure," I said.

On my way out, the waitress with the nice legs looked up from her book, smiled and said, "Have a nice day." It was a warm, friendly smile and she sounded as though it genuinely mattered to her that I have a nice day.

18

The rain had stopped by the time I drove back across the Oak Street Bridge, and there was blue sky to the west. I spent the remainder of the afternoon at the studio, wrestling with the design for a brochure advertising our services. The only way we were ever going to be able to afford to borrow the sixty- to seventy-thousand dollars needed for a decent digital set-up was to significantly increase our revenues. (If you want weekends off, work for someone else.) At four o'clock I concluded that I wasn't going to be able to avoid spending the money to have a professional graphics person design the brochure. I packed it in and headed home. I'd walked halfway to the Hornby Street ferry dock before I remembered the Porsche.

When I got home there were two electric-blue Simpson Marine & Salvage vans parked by the embankment, taking up four parking spaces between them. The little purple pump sounded as though it wasn't long for this world and the list had worsened. Two divers were doing mysterious things in the water under my house, god knows what, and the dock was cluttered with metal pipes and rubber hoses, wire-rope cables and shackles, and what looked like gigantic reinforced plastic garden bags. I assumed they were the flotation bags to which Bernard Simpson had referred. Their presence wasn't reassuring.

The message light on my answering machine was blinking furiously, indicating that there were four messages. The first was from Mary-Alice, reminding me about dinner. The second was from Ginny Gregory, wondering if I'd had any word from Carla. The third was from Mr. Oliphant, Sea Village's self-appointed guardian of taste and decorum, complaining about Simpson's trucks and the mess on the docks around my house. The last message was from Bobbi, informing me that the Stanley Park shoot was on for tomorrow morning, weather permitting.

I opened a can of Kokanee beer, took it and the cordless phone up to the roof deck, flaked out in a deck chair, and did something I hadn't done in a long time. I thought about Linda, my ex-wife. I thought about her for all of ten seconds, then I must have dozed off, because the next thing I remember was being awakened by the warble of the telephone.

It was Mary-Alice wondering where the hell I was, it was almost six-thirty. I apologized and told her I'd be there in half an hour, then went into the bathroom to grab a quick shower. When I turned the water taps, nothing happened.

On my way out I noticed the yellow Post-it note stuck to the mirror in the front hall. It read: "Had to disconnect the water. B.S."

Mary-Alice and her husband David Paul lived in the community of West Bay, on the north shore of English

Bay, about six kilometres west of the Lions Gate Bridge. Their house clung precariously to the rocks above Marine Drive and seemed to be constructed mostly of glass, so as to take best advantage of the view. As I parked the Porsche between a pair of steel cantilevers next to Mary-Alice's little BMW 325i – Mary-Alice may have had poor taste in husbands, but I approved of her car – I wondered if there was a limit to the number of guests Mary-Alice and David could entertain at any one time; the cantilevers didn't look that thick.

David answered the door. He was tall and slim and very distinguished, with thick grey hair and a neatly trimmed salt-and-pepper beard. "Hello, Tom," he said, offering a pale, long-fingered hand. "Glad you could make it. Come in." He had a deep, wet voice that always made me want to clear my throat. "Mary-Alice is in the living room with Hilly," he said. "If you'll excuse me, I'll put the salmon on."

Hilly and Mary-Alice were sitting side by side on the huge curved sofa that wouldn't have looked out of place in a hotel lobby. In fact, I was certain there was one just like it in the lobby of the Hotel Vancouver. They were surrounded by shopping bags and fancy flat boxes and an almost palpable aura of satisfaction.

In our society it's not generally acceptable to have incestuous thoughts about one's sister, so I don't, but if there ever were a sister to have incestuous thoughts about, it was Mary-Alice. They'd saved all the good genes for Mary-Alice, as my father was wont to say; I was just a trial run. The only thing average about Mary-Alice was her height. The rest of her was definitely superior, from her fine golden hair to her rounded calves and trim ankles. Of course, Mary-Alice worked at it. Hard.

"Hello, Tom," she said, standing and kissing me lightly on the cheek. "You look like shit." Mary-Alice only *looked* as though she wouldn't say shit if she had a mouthful.

"Daddy," Hilly said, "look at the neat stuff Mary-Alice bought me." She stood up and held a pair of jeans in front of her hips. They looked like they'd been run through a paper shredder. "Aren't they great?"

"You bet," I said. "Let me know the next time you go to the Salvation Army, though. I've got a couple of bags of old clothes I've been meaning to give them."

"Oh, Daddy." She tossed the jeans aside and picked up a scrap of black fabric.

"Why don't you model them for your father," Mary-Alice said.

"Be right back," Hilly said, grabbing her jeans and dashing upstairs before I could stop her.

"I hope you didn't spend too much," I said to Mary-Alice.

She shrugged. "Of course I spent too much. What's the point otherwise?"

At the risk of being accused of sexism, likely justifiably, I don't understand the pleasure my sister and other women I've known derive from shopping. Most men I know hate shopping. I do. I don't mind browsing through photographic supply stores or bookstores, but that's different. And I know a guy who loves hardware stores, especially the power-tools section. When he travels he visits hardware stores like other people visit museums or historical sites. But shopping as recreation is a mystery to me. There are undoubtedly women who dislike shopping, but I don't know any, leastways none who admit it.

"Do you want a drink?" Mary-Alice asked.

"No, thanks."

Hilly came back downstairs dressed in her new jeans and a lacy black strapless brassiere-like garment.

"Hilly," I said. "Put a shirt on, for god's sake. You can't walk around in just a bra."

"Oh, Daddy. It's not a bra. It's a *bustier*." She pronounced it boost-yay.

"It sure looks like a bra."

"Well, it's not."

"I'm relieved," I said. "It makes me feel a lot better that you're parading around in something that only looks like a bra. Don't let me catch you wearing it outside of the house, though."

"Tom," Mary-Alice said. "Aren't you being a bit stuffy?"

"You bloody damn well betcha I'm being stuffy," I said. "If Linda ever found out I let her wear something like that in public, she'd think me to death all the way from Toronto."

"Mom lets me wear stuff like this," Hilly said.

"Fine," I said. "Save it for when you're at home."

Hilly turned and ran upstairs.

"Way to go, Tom."

"At least I didn't say anything about the make-up," I said. Hilly's eyes had been made up, none too subtly either, and there had been too much rouge on her cheeks. "Did you buy her that too?"

"Tom," Mary-Alice said. "Hilly told me she's started her period. I know it probably frightens you, but it's a big thing for a girl. She's turning into a young woman and there's nothing you can do about it. You might as well learn to live with it."

"Easy for you to say," I said. "The only thing you ever raised was a sweat."

"Just goes to show how much you know," Mary-Alice said. "I don't sweat."

David announced that the salmon was ready and we sat down to dinner. The meal was served by Doris, Mary-Alice's tiny Filipino maid. Her name wasn't really Doris, but Mary-Alice couldn't pronounce her real name. After dinner Mary-Alice and Hilly went back into the living room, leaving me alone at the table with David. I refused brandy and a cigar, pouring myself another cup of very good coffee from a beaten-silver thermos.

"Mary-Alice hates it when I smoke these things in the house," he said as he lit up.

"Why do it then?" I said.

"Women need something to complain about," he said. "Otherwise they are not happy."

I couldn't comprehend what Mary-Alice saw in the man. I'd once asked her and she'd told me stiffly that he was a kind and caring person who was very good to her. I could name half a dozen men who would be more than happy to be very good to Mary-Alice.

"How was California?" I asked.

"Bahah," he said in his wet voice.

"I'm sorry to hear that."

"No, I meant the convention was in Baja."

"So, how was Baja?"

"Overrated. The convention was worthwhile, though."

"That's nice," I said, hoping it wouldn't encourage him to tell me about it. I didn't want to know what went on at a convention of proctologists.

David drew on his cigar, tipped his head back, and made a fat, blue smoke ring. It drifted toward the ceiling until it was shredded by a vagrant air current. Now there was a reason to regret I'd quit smoking, I thought. I sipped my coffee, resisting the urge to look at my watch. Hilly and Mary-Alice chattered in the other room, rattling through the pages of fashion magazines.

"So," David said with elaborate casualness. "Mary-Alice is quite upset about this thing between your parents."

"Yes, I suppose she is."

"It's not an easy thing for her," David went on. "She's very close to her mother."

"Maybe too close," I said. "But I think she's worrying for nothing."

"You don't believe your father is having an affair?"

"No, I don't."

He nodded. "Hilly's growing up fast," he said.

"Yes, she is."

"I hope you don't think I'm presumptuous, but would you like me to arrange for a friend to examine her?"

"What? Oh. No, I . . ."

"It couldn't hurt," he said.

"No, of course not," I said. "But she's seen an army of specialists and the diagnosis is the same each time. The nerves are damaged and there's nothing they can do."

"I just thought I'd offer."

"Thanks for your concern," I said, wincing at the stiffness in my voice.

We lapsed into silence once again. As much as I tried, I could not like him. There was no logical reason for it. He was not a bad person. As Mary-Alice had told me, he was a kind and socially aware man who contributed to charities and participated in fund-raising events for people living with AIDS, abused children, the homeless, and the environment. Perhaps it was chemical or something about his deep wet voice that got to me, like the tines of a fork scraping across a dinner plate.

"David," I said. "I'm sorry, I didn't mean to sound ungrateful. Believe me, we haven't given up hope that someday someone will be able to restore Hilly's hearing. If you think your friend has something new to offer I'd be more than willing to let him look at her."

David shook his head. "Please, don't apologize, Tom," he said. "I'm the one who should apologize. It was arrogant of me to think you and Linda hadn't done everything possible for Hilly."

"Forget it," I said.

"I know little about the speciality," he said, drawing out the British variation of the word. "But if you have no objection, I will speak to my friend and see if there is anything new she can offer."

"I'd appreciate that," I said. We sat in silence for a while longer. Finally, when I was finished my coffee, I looked at my watch. It was almost ten-thirty. I stood up. "I think we should be going," I said. "I have an early morning shoot and I've arranged for Hilly to stay with a neighbour."

We didn't get home until after one o'clock in the morning. A drive that normally takes less than half an hour took over two hours. I'd forgotten about the Symphony of Fire, the annual international fireworks competition held Saturday and Wednesday nights during the last two weeks of June. Staged from a pair of barges anchored off English Bay Beach in the West End, the fireworks had drawn tens of thousands of people into the area along Beach Avenue between Stanley Park and Burrard Street, and the West End was closed to non-residential vehicular traffic until eleven o'clock.

The traffic started piling up as soon as we hit the approach to the Lions Gate Bridge. Gambling that Stanley Park Drive would be better, I exited the Park Causeway as soon as we were across the bridge, but it was worse, stop-and-go all the way to Burrard. Even after we'd crossed the Burrard Bridge to the Kitsilano side of False Creek, the fun wasn't over; we had to fight our way onto Granville Island. Thousands of people take boats out into English Bay to watch the fireworks. The boats start trickling out of the False Creek basin as early as five in the afternoon to get a good anchorage, and when the fireworks end at about eleven, all those hundreds of boats, from kayaks and canoes to ninety-foot yachts and tour boats, make their way back under the Burrard Bridge into the narrow inlet. My house and the others in Sea Village rock all night in the wash from the power boats, too few of the drivers evidently capable of grasping the meaning of the "No Wake" speed limit of five knots.

It was too late for Hilly to go to Daniel's as planned, so she brushed her teeth with bottled water and slept in her own bed. As I lay in my bed, waiting for sleep to come and listening to the wash of the waves against the hull and the creak of the moorings, I wondered what had become of Carla. It had been five days since she'd asked for my help to get away from Vince Ryan. But where was she? Had Vince Ryan caught up with her? And why did I care? I didn't want to care, but I did, even though it was becoming clear she wasn't the person I had thought she was. What had she stolen from Ryan? I had the feeling that, whatever it was, it was something a lot more important to him than my stereo, computer, and camera had been to me.

19

The next morning Bobbi picked me up at four-thirty for the shoot in Stanley Park. I considered dragging Hilly along to the shoot, but waking her at four A.M. would have been tantamount to child abuse. So I left a message on Daniel's answering machine that I'd left her home alone. The shoot went well – the Shakespeare-in-the-Park people were all set up by the time Bobbi and I got there – and I was home by seven forty-five. Hilly was still fast asleep. I went back to bed for an hour, then woke her and we both went next door to use Daniel's shower. Then I took her for a late breakfast in Stanley Park. After breakfast we rented bikes and spent the day in the park, pedalling around the seawall, en route visiting the aquarium, riding the miniature railway, eating greasy fish and chips from the snack bar by the kids' water park, playing pitch 'n' putt, things I'd rarely done even though I'd lived in Vancouver for years.

The bike-rental place was just across Georgia from Devonian Harbour Park and Coal Harbour. After we returned the bikes at the end of the day, we walked along the park path that runs parallel to the water. There were hundreds of boats moored in the public marinas, boats of all sizes, from fifteen-foot outboards and little twenty-five-foot day sailers to yachts three times the size of my house, and the majority of them seemed to be sailboats, creating a dense and noisy forest of masts and spars and stays.

The office of the Harbour Ferries Marina was in the forward cabin of an old tour boat called the *Hollyburn*, permanently moored at the end of the dock. I asked the woman at the desk if there was a boat called the *Dragon* registered at the marina.

"Half a dozen at least," she said.

"This one was described to me as a sixty-foot Bradley custom sloop."

"That sounds like the *Pendragon*." She gave me the slip number and directions.

Poole had been right: the *Pendragon* was a lovely thing, sleek and tidy and well kept, although the bright-work could've used some polishing and the varnish was beginning to flake off the teak trim. According to a leathery, sun-baked woman who was reading on the afterdeck of a stubby and nondescript little cabin cruiser in the next slip, *Pendragon* was owned by a man named Christopher Hastings who, like the *Pendragon*, seemed to match the description Poole had given me.

"But his Zodiac is gone," she said.

"Meaning?"

"He's not aboard."

"Does he live aboard?"

"You're not supposed to," she said warily.

I nodded. Like most of the marinas around Vancouver, Harbour Ferries wasn't zoned for live-aboard moorage, but you could get away with it as long as you were careful about waste disposal and had a permanent address elsewhere.

"If I see him," the woman said, "can I give him a message?"

"No," I said. "I was just admiring his boat."

All in all, it was a good day, and both Hilly and I were exhausted by the time we got back to the house, which was more or less on an even keel again, thanks to the flotation bags under the hull. Hilly went upstairs to check on Beatrix while I tried the water: it was still off. When I went upstairs to see if Hilly wanted something to eat, I found her asleep on her bed, Beatrix curled up against her chest.

For the next couple of days I was too busy to worry much about Carla or to check out the owner of the *Pendragon*. Monday morning, after awakening to the rattle and clank of Bernard Simpson and his crew setting up below my bedroom window, I shaved and showered at Daniel's, then took Hilly to the community centre, where I spent a frustrating half-hour with the director. He was a wispy fifty-something man with pale, powdery skin and manicured nails, and try as I might I could not seem to make him understand that, while I did not condone violence, Hilly had been raised to take responsibility for herself, and the next time some barbarous lout decided to make fun of someone's handicap, he might not get off so easily.

I spent the rest of the morning in my office, still struggling with the promotional brochure until I finally gave it up and called the designer I used from time to time. The afternoon was taken up with a couple of portrait sittings (an aspect of the business for which I have little aptitude and less patience, but which pays moderately well for the time involved) and preparations for a movie-location shoot later that evening.

Around four, Bobbi came into my office to tell me that everything was ready for the movie-location shoot. She looked so down in the dumps I took her downstairs to Zapata's for a Corona with lime and tried to cheer her up with silly stories about my sinking house, the trial by ordeal that was modern parenting, and the pathetic state of my social life. She smiled briefly when I told her how Francine Janes's muscular development frightened me, but otherwise I enjoyed little success. Otherwise I enjoyed no success at all.

"Okay," I said, "so what's eating you?"

"Nothing's eating me," she said.

"C'mon, Bobbi. We've known each other a long time and I've never seen you like this. You're usually so cheerful I want to strangle you. But if you don't want to talk about it, I can't make you. Tell me to butt out and I'll drop it."

"Butt out."

"What was that stuff in the office the other day?"

"What stuff?" she asked.

"When you went storming out."

"Nothing important," she said.

"You damned near tore the door off the hinges."

"Butt out."

"Nope," I said, shaking my head. "I'll stay out of your personal life, but what goes on in the studio is my business."

"It was personal."

"Then keep it out of the office."

"Fine," she said stiffly. "You finished?" She didn't mean my beer.

"Yes." I hated being a boss.

"I've got some work to do," she said, standing. "Are you going back up?"

"No, I think I'll go home."

"I'll pick you up at seven?"

"Fine," I said.

"Tom?"

"Yeah?"

"Thanks. You're a good friend." She leaned down and kissed me. She'd never kissed me. All right, so it was just a peck on the cheek, but it made the blood rush to my face. "Sorry," she said. "I didn't mean to embarrass you."

"You haven't," I said.

Hilly had asked if she could bring a friend to the movie set and I said sure, as long as they stayed out of trouble. I was a little surprised when the friend turned out to be a girl. I'd half expected a pimply-faced boy with an earring, a half-shaved head, and paratrooper boots. Courtney was slim and fine-featured, with flawless skin, straight blond hair worn long and loose, and a mischievous laugh. Although she was the same age as Hilly she wore make-up and a skin-tight Spandex tank top that accentuated her tiny budding breasts. She was proud of them and they undoubtedly earned her a lot of attention from the boys, but I couldn't help feeling there was something slightly pathetic about it. She was also an outrageous flirt. I found myself wishing Hilly's friend had been a boy. Adolescent boys I understand. Sort of.

"I don't like her," I said to Bobbi after the shoot. We were packing the equipment into the back of the Land Rover. Hilly and Courtney had gone to the mobile commissary to see if they could get George Clooney's autograph.

"Why not?" Bobbi asked.

"She makes me uncomfortable," I said. "She's like a pre-adolescent Madonna. Did you dress like that when you were a little girl?"

"Sure I did," Bobbi said. "And everyone thought I was a boy. But Courtney's not a little girl. Neither is Hilly." She laughed. "Pubescent girls make many men uncomfortable," she said. "You feel guilty because you're sexually attracted to them."

"I am not sexually attracted to her," I said emphatically, knowing as I said it that there was some truth in what she was saying.

"Don't worry about it," she said. "It's a perfectly normal reaction. A healthy male wouldn't do anything about it, though."

"Jesus," I said.

Bobbi shrugged. "What can I tell you, boss? Kids grow up fast these days."

"Don't call me boss," I told her.

She shrugged again.

On Tuesday we had three portrait sittings before lunch. After sharing a quick lunch of barbecued-pork buns with Bodger, I sat with the graphic designer for a couple of hours working on ideas for the brochure. The balance of the afternoon I spent with Mrs. Szymkowiak, going over the books for the semi-annual meeting with my accountant. It was never an experience to which I looked forward with any great enthusiasm, but it was especially discouraging given the sorry state of my bottom line. I wondered why I ever left my job at the *Sun*.

After supper Hilly asked if she could go to the arcade. I said okay, but reluctantly and only after extracting a promise from her to be back at Daniel's by eight o'clock. She grumbled a little at the early curfew, but I did not want her to be out after dark or alone in the house. Perhaps I was being overly cautious, but I wasn't going to take any chances. After walking her to the arcade, I took a ferry across False Creek, and walked along the Sunset Beach bike and foot path to the edge of Stanley Park, then across the narrow neck of the peninsula to Coal Harbour and the Harbour Ferries Marina. A total distance of slightly more than three kilometres. I was mighty proud of myself.

20

Christopher Hastings was fiftyish, tall and slightly shaggy, a comfortably worn man with a large head, a wild shock of greying brown hair, pale blue-grey eyes, and a battered and uneven nose. We sat on the afterdeck of the *Pendragon*, drinking herbal tea brewed by a strikingly handsome woman with long straight pale hair who looked eighteen in the slanting light of the lowering sun but who was probably closer to thirty. He called her Reeny, although she'd introduced herself as Irene Lindsey. I was sure I'd seen her on television, commercials or perhaps a locally produced syndicated series, but I didn't fawn, at least not too much, and she admitted she'd been in a couple of episodes of *The X-Files*.

I didn't know what to make of Chris Hastings. He claimed to be a television writer and affected a laid-back, ageing hippie demeanour, but there was a cold, almost feral watchfulness lurking behind his steel-coloured eyes. There was a tiny cellular telephone in the breast pocket of his baggy Indian cotton shirt. Perhaps he augmented his income as a people-smuggler or drug-dealer.

At first he volunteered nothing, responding to my questions but otherwise telling me very little. After fifteen minutes the only thing I'd learned that was even remotely interesting was that about a month after Carla had run out on me, Hastings had bought her a one-way airplane ticket to Montreal, for which, of course, she'd never reimbursed him. That was the last time he'd seen her.

"Do you know a boat broker named Frank Poole?" I asked.

"Only by reputation," Hastings said.

"Which is?"

"Not good." I waited for him to elaborate. He finally said, "I wouldn't buy a boat from him, but otherwise I know very little about him."

"He said you and Carla were shacked up – his words – for a couple of years before she started working at the tennis club."

"She crewed for me on occasion for a couple of years," Hastings said. "*Pendragon* has a wooden hull," he added, "and I winter her on the Fraser River; fresh-water kills the teredo worms. Carla helped me move her a couple of times. She also stayed aboard when she was between crewing jobs. But we weren't 'shacked up.' It was around that time Reeny and I got together."

"And I like my men exclusive," Reeny said.

"Carla had a serious case of wanderlust," Hastings said. "She was your basic boat bum when I met her, hanging around the marinas and yacht clubs, offering her services –"

"So to speak," Reeny interjected.

"– in exchange for passage to South America, Fiji, or Australia. She never lacked for takers, usually single older men –" he smiled wryly at Reeny "– but she was usually back within a few weeks, a couple of months at most, looking for something else."

"Tough life," I said.

"Not much of a retirement plan, though," Hastings said. He paused for a few seconds, then added, "Although she always seemed to have money. Sometimes quite a lot."

"How much would she make helping Frank Poole pick up and deliver boats?"

"Not that much. Nor do I think he was a particularly reliable employer. She called me once from Mexico to ask me to wire her some money. I think it was a couple of months later that she started working at the tennis club. I thought she was finally settling down, but more likely she was just making a slight career adjustment."

"Staking out new territory," Reeny said.

"It does seem a little more in character," I said. "Did you know that she had a brother in jail for killing a man in a bar fight?"

"Stepbrother," Hastings said. "Pierre Deguire. Petey. And he didn't kill the man in a bar fight."

"That's what she told a friend," I said.

Hastings shook his head. "It may have happened in a bar," he said, "but Deguire was a small-time coke dealer in the Laurentians, the resort country north of Montreal. The victim was a competitor."

"Did Carla tell you this?" I asked.

He shook his head. "I ran a background check on her. A few phone calls to some friends in law enforcement."

"Why would you do that?"

He didn't answer right away, watched me from behind those steely eyes. Reeny Lindsey finally nudged him gently with her elbow.

Hastings shrugged and said, "I inherited this lifestyle, Mr. McCall. Perhaps if I'd earned it I wouldn't have to write some of the stuff I write. My grandfather had the good fortune to own a modest ball-bearing factory at the outbreak of World War Two. My father never did an honest day's work in his life. Fortunately for me, his lifestyle caught up with him before he was able to spend everything. Unfortunately for me, I was even easier prey for people like Carla. However, by the time Carla came along, I'd learned – the hard way – to recognize the sharks. A little late, though; there isn't much of my grandfather's money left."

"So you've learned to be suspicious."

"That's right."

"What else did your law enforcement friends tell you?"

"I don't suppose it'll come as any surprise to you that she has a record."

It didn't, but I was disappointed nonetheless.

"Nothing very serious," he went on. "When she was nineteen she was arrested a couple of times for soliciting, pled guilty, and paid the fine. After that, nothing. It was the eighties," he added. "Fear of AIDS drove quite a few of them out of the business, I imagine."

"No arrests for theft?" I asked.

He shook his head. "Why?"

"She's stolen from just about everyone I've talked to," I said. "I'm guessing she stole from her boyfriend, which is why he's so eager to find her."

Hastings shrugged. "Adaptability is a good survival trait."

"Vince Ryan isn't the kind of person I'd want to cross," I said. "I think he's used to getting his way and willing to do just about anything to get it."

"What was that name again?"

"Vincent Ryan," I said.

"What do you know about him?"

"Nothing, really. He introduced himself as a developer of some kind. He and Carla became lovers after his wife died in a hit-and-run accident while he and Carla were in Europe."

Hastings was silent for a few seconds, eyes half closed, then stood up.

"What?" I said as he disappeared below. Reeny shrugged and looked as puzzled as I felt. Hastings returned a few minutes later with a slim file of newspaper and magazine clippings. He handed me a clipping.

It was a grainy black-and-white newspaper photograph of Vince Ryan glaring into the camera lens, mouth open as if snarling "No comment." Or "Fuck off." He made no effort to conceal his face, unlike the pale, dark-haired woman on his arm whose face was partly obscured by a paperback-sized handbag. The caption read, " 'No comment' says Toronto businessman Vincent Ryan after being questioned by police in connection with the brutal rape and murder of his wife Elizabeth Giordini Ryan in their Forest Hill home."

A cold fist of fear tightened around my chest.

"Is that the man you spoke to?" he asked.

"Yes," I said. "And I'm almost certain the woman in the photograph is Carla."

"Ryan's wife died," Hastings said, as he thumbed through the clippings. "But it wasn't hit and run. It was murder. She was raped and murdered in her home. And it was evidently pretty brutal. Her throat was slashed so deeply her head was almost severed. Although Ryan was in Europe at the time," Hastings went on, half reading, "he was questioned by the police. He and his wife had been separated for almost a year and, according to her sister, she was going to file for divorce. And there was a sizeable life-insurance policy. The sister screamed murder most foul, but the police were never able to connect Ryan to the murder."

"Connect him how? You mean, he might have hired someone to kill his wife."

"It happens all the time," Hastings said.

"How do you come to have this?" I asked.

"Research," he said. "For a script I wrote. One of those true-crime shows about people who hire professional assassins to kill their spouses."

He handed me the rest of the clippings. I quickly read though them. They added little to what Hastings had already told me.

Although Margaret Giordini was certain Ryan had had her sister killed, she wasn't a very credible source. She had a history of emotional instability and her sister's death pushed her very close to the edge, perhaps beyond it. On top of that, she and Ryan had been lovers before he'd married her younger sister and she was very bitter about it. But she and her sister had been close and she told the police that her sister had told her on more than one occasion that she was afraid of Ryan, that he'd threatened to kill her if she tried to divorce him.

"According to the police," Hastings said as I returned the folder, "there was motive aplenty. A divorce might not have ruined him financially, but it would have hurt. On the other hand, the insurance would have helped him over a fairly serious cash-flow problem. But Ryan's alibi was airtight and there was no evidence of any kind to implicate him in a conspiracy. These kinds of murders are almost impossible to solve unless the police get lucky – someone with a score to settle comes forward, or the hitman himself gets caught for something else and talks, either to make a deal or just to boast."

I got up and went to the rail, looked out over the harbour. Dusk had fallen quickly and the lights of the city were reflected in the glassy water.

"Did he do it?" I asked without turning.

"At a guess," Hastings said, "I'd say yes. Her death was too convenient to be coincidental. But that doesn't mean it wasn't. However, the possibility puts Carla's situation in a whole new light, doesn't it?"

"I don't understand why she lied to me about how his wife died, though," I said. "If she wanted my help she'd have had a better case if she'd told me the truth. You don't think . . ." I left the thought unspoken.

"I know what you're thinking," Hastings said. "Carla may be a thief and a grifter, but I don't think she's a killer."

"I hope you're right," I said.

The three of us stood surrounded by the deepening night and the subdued grumble of the city. Hastings, rangy and rumpled; Irene Lindsey, quiet and lovely; and yours truly, certain now that I'd got myself in way over my head. On one of the nearby boats a woman laughed. In the distance, a SeaBus whined across the harbour on the regular run between Vancouver and Lonsdale Quay in North Vancouver. The lights of the ski-runs on top of Grouse Mountain gleamed like a ragged string of pearls floating in the sky to the north over the dark mass of Stanley Park.

"Thanks for the tea," I said.

"Nice to have met you," Irene Lindsey said.

"If I hear from her," Hastings asked as I stepped onto the dock, "I'll tell her to call you."

"Thanks."

"But to be honest," he said, "I hope I don't hear from her."

When I got back to Sea Village a little after nine, Hilly was in Daniel's living room, watching a video on his giant television. Daniel called me into the kitchen, where he told me he'd had to go looking for her when she hadn't returned by eight-thirty.

"I didn't tell you to get her into trouble," he added. "I just think you ought to know there have been reports about a man hanging around and treating the kids to free games."

"Oh, wonderful," I said.

"Don't overreact," he said. "Not every older man who likes kids is a pedophile. Hilly's a smart girl. I don't think you have anything to worry about."

I returned to the living room, watched a little more of the movie with Hilly, then kissed her goodnight and went back to my place. Pouring myself a couple of fingers of single malt whisky, neat, I took it up to the roof and settled into a deck chair without turning on any lights. My life seemed to have become exceedingly complicated in the short time since Hilly had arrived. I like things simple. When they get complicated, I get edgy. I was also rattled by what I'd learned from Chris Hastings about Vince Ryan. Rattled and more than a little scared. Of course, there was a good chance Ryan may not have had anything to do with his wife's death.

Nevertheless, I was worried. And why had Carla told me that Ryan's wife had been killed by a hit and run? Maybe it was time to send Hilly to stay with her grandparents in Victoria. She wouldn't want to go, nor did I want to send her, but I had to get her out of potential harm's way. Perhaps, I thought, I should go with her.

I could hear the telephone ringing, but I let the machine take it, being too lethargic to answer it. A few minutes later, though, I levered myself out of the chair and went downstairs (or below, if you prefer). I pressed the PLAY button.

"Thomas, this is your mother speaking. Are you there? Oh, I hate these things. If you're there, please answer." She paused, waiting for me to pick up. "All right," she said at last. "Call me as soon as possible, please. It's urgent."

I reset the machine, picked up the handset, and pressed the memory button that dialled my parents' number in Victoria.

"It's me," I said when she answered.

"So you were there after all."

"I was up on the roof. What's so urgent?"

"I have something to tell you," she said.

"Yes?"

"Your father and I have decided to get a divorce."

"What? A divorce? What do you mean, a divorce? When did you decide this? Why?"

"I know it must come as a shock to you, Thomas, but these things happen, you know."

"Not to my parents," I said. My voice felt strange in my throat, as if it belonged to someone else. Nor did it sound like my own voice. Nevertheless, it was oddly familiar.

"We're human beings too," my mother said. "You, of all people, should understand."

"What should I understand?" The voice I heard was my own, but it was as if I were ten years old again.

"You know what I mean."

"No, I don't," I said. I did, of course. I knew what she meant. And I understood. "Look," I said, "I know things have been difficult lately, but a divorce is a little drastic, isn't it?" She didn't really believe he was seeing another woman, did she? I couldn't bring myself to ask.

"It's the only way," she said. "I'm through making sacrifices. I have myself to think about. My needs. I've been thinking about going back to work."

"Work? What kind of work?"

"Why, acting, of course. What kind of work did you think I meant?"

"Acting?"

"Yes, acting."

"You don't have to get a divorce to do that," I said.

"What else can I do? Your father made it quite clear he didn't want me going back to work."

"Have you at least talked to him about it?"

"What good would it do? He's never taken me seriously. He thinks it's all a big joke."

"Maybe you should see a counsellor."

"I won't have strangers prying into my private life. I've made up my mind, Thomas, and there's nothing you can do to change it."

"Have you told Mary-Alice?"

"Not yet."

"Before you tell her, are you absolutely certain this is what you want?"

"Want?" she said. "I don't *want* a divorce," she said. "I don't think anyone *wants* a divorce."

Now it was my turn to say, "You know what I mean. Don't tell her unless you are sure there's no hope."

"I'm sure," she said.

Ten minutes after my mother hung up Mary-Alice called. It went much as I expected it would.

"There must be something we can do," she said.

"If there is," I said, "I don't know what it is. If I did, I might've saved my own marriage."

"Is it because of Daddy's affair?"

"She didn't mention it and I didn't ask. She says she wants to go back to work."

"Work? What kind of work? Surely you don't mean acting. My god, that's ridiculous. She's sixty years old." I agreed that it was a little ridiculous, but not because of her age. "Maybe it will just blow over," Mary-Alice said hopefully.

"And maybe it won't," I said. "They haven't been very happy lately."

"Happy? Who's happy?"

"I was," I said. "For a while. Aren't you?"

She didn't answer. "Think of something," she said.

21

I slept fitfully and woke up in a foul mood, made fouler by having to go next door to Daniel's to shower and shave. I grumbled and growled my way through the day, moody and irritable, impatient with Bernard Simpson and how long the repairs were taking, with Bobbi's continuing absent-mindedness, with Ron's constant surliness. I even snapped at Mrs. Szymkowiak when she reminded me that I hadn't signed the pay-cheques she'd left on my desk. When I went into my office to sign them, Bodger hissed at me as I tried to remove him from my chair.

"Don't push your luck, stir-fry," I told him, and tipped him onto the floor.

A little after two o'clock Bobbi hung her baseball cap on a yardstick and waved it in front of my office door.

"What is it?" I said, taking my heels off my desk. "Can't you see I'm busy?"

"There's someone here to see you."

"Who is it?"

"He says his name is Vince Ryan."

"Tell him to go away," I said.

"I told him you were busy," she said, "but he said it was important." Lowering her voice, she added, "And he's got a guy with him who looks like he could pick up a small car."

"All right," I said without enthusiasm. "Show them in."

"Hey, McCall," Vince Ryan said cheerily, a broad smile on his homely face. He settled onto the old worn leather sofa opposite my desk. Sam stood in the doorway, leaning against the jamb, arms folded across his broad chest.

"What do you want?" I asked sourly. As if I didn't know.

"Having a good day, are we?"

"It's getting worse by the minute."

"I was in the neighbourhood," Ryan said. "So I thought I'd just drop by to see how things were going."

"What, exactly?"

"Pardon me?"

"How what's going?"

"I didn't come here to talk philosophy, McCall. Did you find out where Carla is?"

"No, I didn't."

"You talk to anybody at all?"

"Correct me if I'm wrong," I said, "but didn't I tell you I wasn't going to help you find her?"

"I guess I didn't believe you."

"Believe me," I said.

"Why don't we go get ourselves a drink and talk about it."

"There's nothing to talk about," I said. "Besides, I've got work to do."

"Work later. You need to relax."

"You're probably right," I said. "But if you don't mind, I'll choose who I relax with."

Ryan looked up at Sam. "Sam, go get yourself an herbal tea or something. I want a private word with our friend here."

Sam heaved himself away from the door jamb and went into the outer office. Ryan reached out and closed the door. It banged shut with a rattle of glass and cheap plastic blind.

If you believe a tenth of the stuff on television or in the newspapers, it's difficult to avoid the conclusion that the majority of North American males are beer-guzzling wife beaters, rapists, child molesters, serial killers, or ambulance-chasing lawyers; that women, when not obsessing about cleanliness or worrying about leakage from their sanitary products, regularly poison their husbands and children, seduce teenage boys or elderly men, and turn their sons into homophobic sociopaths and their daughters into pathological victims; that every black kid in the inner cities carries a handgun and wants to be a crack dealer when he grows up, if he grows up; and that every politician is a self-serving egomaniac who can't keep his fingers out of the till or his dick in his pants. (Okay, so some things are true.) If beings from Alpha Centauri are monitoring our television, who could blame them for deciding to blow us into the fifth dimension before we can mess up any more of this spiral arm of the galaxy. Assuming, of course, that they don't have problems of their own.

While I did not swallow much of anything I saw on television or read in the papers, it had nevertheless skewed my perspective and I was having a difficult time making up my mind about Vince Ryan. Had he or had he not hired someone to kill his wife? Nothing in my life had prepared me to make that kind of judgement. On the one hand, I did not want to believe people were capable of cold-blooded murder; on the other hand, the evidence that some indeed were, was irrefutable.

When Ryan closed the door of my office my mouth went dry and my heart began to pound in my chest.

"I'm running out of time," he said. His voice seemed unnaturally loud in the small office. "If I don't find her soon there's going to be some serious hell to pay."

"What does that mean?" I asked, gratified, and a little surprised, that my voice didn't quaver.

"It means," Ryan said, "that if you're smart you'll tell me where she is. This is a stupid and dangerous game she's playing. I don't think she has a clue how stupid and dangerous it is. People could get hurt. I don't want to see anyone get hurt. Do you?"

"No. But I don't know where she is. Even if I did," I said, "I'm not sure I would tell you."

Ryan shook his head slowly. "I thought you were smarter than that, McCall. It just goes to show how wrong you can be about people. Look, why make more trouble for yourself? You seem to have enough to worry about."

"Pardon me?"

"I went by your place this morning," Ryan said. "Is your house really sinking? Remind me never to live in a houseboat."

"What do you know about my house sinking?" I asked.

"Me? Nothing. Nothing at all. All I'm saying is that there's lots worse kinds of problems than your

houseboat sinking, trust me. Save yourself the aggrava-
tion, just tell me where Carla is."

"Are you threatening me?"

"Threatening you," Ryan said, smiling widely. "Hell,
no. I wouldn't hurt a fly. Did it sound like a threat?"

"Yes, it did."

"Well, it wasn't. I'm just telling you the way things
are. Look," he added, standing, "I gotta go to L.A. for
a few days. Think about what I said. I'll give you a
number you can reach me at." He wrote the number on
a business card and dropped it onto my desk. "Think
about it," he said again. "Think about it real hard." He
opened the door and left.

I got home around four o'clock, still a little unnerved
by my conversation with Ryan. There was no sign of
Bernard Simpson or his crew, but they obviously hadn't
finished; their equipment littered the docks and the
house was still exhibiting a slight list. The water was
back on, at least.

Hilly would be home around five-thirty. Day camp
let out at five and she usually hung around the arcade
for a while before coming home. The message light on
the answering machine was blinking rapidly, indicating
three messages.

"Mister McCall, this is Davy at the community
centre. Your daughter did not come to day camp today
and as per our policy I am calling to confirm that you
are aware of it. Thank you."

I didn't wait to hear the other messages. I hit the
STOP button and immediately began to panic. The first

thing that popped into my mind was that Ryan had kidnapped her to exchange for information about Carla, information I didn't have. Christ, was that what he'd meant by "lots worse kinds of trouble"? Then I remembered what Daniel had said about a man hanging around the arcade treating the kids to free video games.

"Get hold of yourself," I said aloud.

The message light on the answering machine was still blinking. I pressed the PLAY button. Maybe one of the other messages was from Hilly.

"Thomas, this is your mother speaking . . ."

I hit the FAST FORWARD button until the machine beeped. All I heard when I released the button was a hollow click.

I rewound the tape a little and pressed PLAY.

". . . speaking. If your father is there, would you please tell him the repairman says it will cost two hundred dollars to replace the dishwasher motor."

She rambled on pointlessly for half a minute more while I jittered in frustration and kept my finger away from the FAST FORWARD button. Finally she hung up and the machine beeped.

The third message was nothing but a second or so of silence followed by a hollow click.

I swore and hit the button that speed-dialled Daniel's number. He'd told me he was going to be spending most of the day on a job site, but if Hilly was watching television, perhaps she'd pick up. His line rang four times, then clicked as the call was forwarded to his cel-lular. He answered it on the second ring. There was construction noise in the background.

"No," he said. "I haven't seen her, but she knows where to find the key. If she isn't there, though, don't let your imagination get the better of you."

Easy for him to say, I thought as I hung up.

She wasn't at Daniel's. I rang Maggie Urquhart's bell, but no one answered. I went to the arcade and asked the kids there if any of them had seen the girl with the ferret. None had. Discouraged – I really had hoped to find her there – I went to the ferry dock and checked with the drivers and attendants. A number of them remembered her, but none of them recalled seeing her this morning, sorry.

On my way back to the house I stopped at the dive shop. Perhaps Hilly had taken Francine up on her offer of diving lessons. But the man behind the counter told me that Francine wouldn't be back until late that evening. And, no, no little kids had come in asking for her.

Back home I dithered about for a moment, wondering what to do next, then I called the police. Within fifteen minutes two constables were at my door, a woman in her late thirties or early forties and a man in his twenties. They looked around, exchanging looks, but did not comment on the equipment on the dock or the condition of the house.

"Am I overreacting?" I asked after the policewoman had taken the report and Hilly's description. The tag on the breast pocket of her uniform blouse read M. FIRTH.

"No," Constable Firth said. "Technically, there's still a forty-eight-hour waiting period for reporting missing persons, but we don't apply it to children."

"I'm not sure I find that reassuring," I said.

"Now you're overreacting," she said. "Look, we get lots of calls like this. Most of them are false alarms. Kids being kids. But we take them seriously, believe me. The best thing you can do is keep calm and call everyone you can think of she might be with."

"She hasn't had time to make many friends," I said, realizing I didn't even know Courtney's last name or where she lived.

"Kids make friends easily," she said. "She's probably with one of them right now. We'll check with the community centre and see if there are any other kids who didn't show up today."

I mentally kicked myself. I hadn't thought of that.

Constable Firth wrote a number on the back of a business card and handed it to me. "That's the case number. When your daughter comes back, or if you hear from her or think of anything else, call the station and give the desk sergeant that number. He'll pass the message on to me."

I wanted to tell her that it was possible that Hilly had been abducted by Vince Ryan, but I couldn't bring myself to say the words. I didn't really believe it – I didn't want to believe it – and I was afraid that if I said it I would believe it, that saying it would make it true.

"And when she gets home . . ." Firth said.

"Yes?"

"Be firm with her, let her know how badly she scared you, ground her for a couple of days, but don't go overboard. By the looks of things around here you've had other things on your mind lately. Maybe she's just trying to get your attention."

"I hope you're right."

"I got three kids of my own," she said. "Between them and this job I've got a pretty good feel for these things." We shook hands and they left.

Hilly got home at quarter to six, acting as though nothing was wrong. But she was a lousy actor. Guilt was written all over her.

"How was your day?" I asked casually, although I was almost faint with relief.

"Okay." She put Beatrix on the kitchen counter. The ferret jumped into the sink and began licking the drops from the faucet. "What's for dinner?"

"I haven't thought about it," I said, picking up the telephone. I started dialling the number on the card the police had left.

"Who are you calling?" Hilly asked.

"The police."

"The police? Why?"

"To tell them you're home."

"Oh."

"Oh, indeed."

I gave the desk sergeant my name and the case number and told him that everything was okay.

"The officers who took the report will be there within half an hour."

"Is that really necessary?" I asked.

"Yes, they have to see the child to close the report."

"All right, we'll be here."

I hung up.

"You called the police," Hilly said.

"I was worried," I said. "Actually, I was scared half to death. Where were you?"

"With Courtney."

"Okay, you were with Courtney. Now *where* were you?"

"Just hanging around."

"Could you be more specific? I checked the arcade and a few other places."

"Just hanging around," she said again. "Different places. We went downtown and took the SeaBus across to North Van."

"Why didn't you go to the day camp? Did that kid give you a hard time again?"

"No," she said. "It's just boring."

"Listen," I said. "I'm pretty upset. And angry. Some kind of punishment is definitely in order. Until further notice the arcade is off limits." I stood up and turned the cold-water tap until the faucet ran slowly. Beatrix drank thirstily. "Haven't you given her anything to drink today?"

Hilly looked stricken. "I forgot."

The police constables arrived ten minutes later. I called Hilly down from her room. We sat around the kitchen table and the policewoman introduced herself to Hilly as Mabel Firth and asked her where she'd been during the day, with whom, and was there any particular reason why she'd not gone to the day camp? Hilly told her what she'd told me.

"Don't you think you should have told your father you were going to spend the day with your friend?" Officer Firth asked.

"I suppose. I didn't think it'd really matter, though. He was busy."

I winced inwardly.

"Had he arranged for other people to look after you when he's at work?"

"Sure. Daniel or Mrs. Urquhart."

"Did you tell them you were going to spend the day with –" she consulted her clipboard "– Courtney?"

"Uh, no."

"Your father was very worried about you. And those other people you mentioned, they're probably worried too. It's a very scary thing for grown-ups when kids are missing."

"I know. I'm sorry, Daddy."

I hugged her and said, "Next time tell me, all right."

Constable Firth stood up. "Okay, I guess we're done here."

I shook hands with them both. "Thanks again."

"No problem," the policewoman said. "You," she added, spearing Hilly with a look. "I know sometimes it looks like grown-ups don't have time or aren't interested, but give us a chance. We might surprise you."

Hilly said she would and went upstairs. I walked the officers to the door. Constable Firth told her partner she wanted a word with me. He nodded and said he'd wait in the car.

"I like Hilly," Constable Firth said. "She seems pretty level-headed. My youngest girl is only a year older than Hilly and I know how difficult it can be to hold down jobs and raise kids these days. My husband works for the city too, but his hours are a little more regular than mine. Still, it can be tough, especially when a child is handicapped. How long has Hilly been hearing impaired?"

"Since she was four," I said.

"My oldest has had epilepsy since he was nine," she said. "The meds keep it under control now, but when he was Hilly's age he didn't have an easy time of it and there were a few behavioural problems, nothing very serious, thank god. How is Hilly coping?"

"I think she's coping pretty well," I said. "It's something she's lived with all her life. There was a kid at day camp who harassed her, but that doesn't happen very often. She can be a little selectively hard-of-hearing from time to time, as can we all, and occasionally she's turned her hearing aids off, like kids will sometimes stick their fingers in their ears, but she's never used her handicap to get her own way."

"My husband calls it the 'guilt stick,'" Mabel Firth said. "You can't let them get away with it, of course. The thing is, though," she added, "they're the ones living with the handicap, not us. They have a right to feel sorry for themselves from time to time."

"Hilly is the least self-pitying person I know," I said. "She learned early that no matter how bad things might be for her, there were lots of kids worse off than she was."

Mabel Firth smiled. "That's a lesson all of us need to be reminded of now and again."

22

I wasn't in the mood to cook, so I decided to take Hilly out to dinner. As we reached the intersection of the finger dock and the main dock, we almost collided with my father, Maggie Urquhart, and Harvey. They were coming from the direction of the gate. My father was holding Harvey's leash. He seemed pleased to see me. Harvey, not my father.

"Hi, Stinkpot," my father said to Hilly.

"Hi, Grumps," she said.

"What are you doing in Vancouver, Dad?" I said.

"Eh? Oh, I had some business to take care of," he said. "I rang your bell but you weren't around. I bumped into Maggie here and she kindly allowed me to accompany her on her errands." He looked at his watch. "Goodness, I didn't realize it was so late. I've been bending this little lady's ear for hours."

"I'm going to do your father's chart," Maggie said.

"Oh," I said. Since when was my father interested in astrology? Or was it the astrologer?

Dad looked embarrassed. "Ahem, well, y'know. What's the harm?"

What harm indeed? I thought. "Hilly and I are going for dinner," I said. "Would you like to join us?"

"Ah, we've eaten," my father said. He looked at Maggie, then said, "Tom, Maggie's been telling me she's a little concerned about the lack of security around here."

"Lack of security? What do you mean? The gate's always locked. And you've got an alarm system, don't you?" Not to mention Harvey.

Maggie nodded, but added, "There was a man on the docks the other day, on this side of the gate. He was taking pictures."

"I wouldn't worry about it," I said. "Tourists are always trying to get onto the docks. Someone must have left the gate open. It happens."

"I'm sure this man wasn't a tourist," she said. "I'm very sensitive to people. He didn't *feel* like a tourist." I wondered what a tourist felt like. "There was something sinister about him." She shook her head. "Not sinister, exactly. I'm probably just reacting to his disfigurement. But he wasn't a tourist, I'm sure of that, even though he was dressed like one."

"What disfigurement?" I asked.

"His hand," she said. "It was like a claw. He was missing the middle fingers of his right hand."

It wasn't until Hilly and I were walking back home from dinner that I remembered the two-fingered tourist with the video camera we'd seen on the boardwalk last week.

In the morning, to make sure they got there, I delivered Hilly and Beatrix to the community centre, with instructions to go straight to Maggie's afterward. As I was walking to the ferry dock, I saw Francine loading diving gear into her Jeep. I waved and she waved back. She looked so nice in her cut-offs and T-shirt that I went over and said hi. Once you got used to it, her muscular development was really quite interesting.

"Hi," she replied with a smile.

"Um," I said, getting right to the point. "If you're going to be around later, maybe we could get together for a coffee or something and talk about Hilly's diving lessons. That is, if you're not too busy."

"No problem," she said. "Why don't you come by the shop around five."

I said, "Great. See you later, then."

She reached for a big gunny sack on the cobbles, but I got to it first and hoisted it into the back of the Jeep.

"Thanks," she said.

"No problem," I said, pressing my hand against my back just above my kidneys and exaggerating the strain in my voice, but not much. "I think I've hurt myself."

"You have not," she said. "Have you?"

"It's a small price to pay to preserve the honour of my gender."

She laughed, but I hobbled almost all the way to the ferry dock. I was walking more or less normally by the time I got to the studio.

"Thank god you're here," Mrs. Szymkowiak said. "I think they're killing each other."

"Who?"

"Roberta and Ronald." Mrs. Szymkowiak always called people by their full given names.

There was a muted crash from the back of the studio. Mrs. Szymkowiak moaned and wrung her hands. "Do something," she said.

"Damn," I said, but she expected more and pushed me toward the back of the studio.

The lab door was locked. It wasn't supposed to be, not ever. It wasn't supposed to even have a lock. There was another crash, followed by a heavy thud. The dividing wall shuddered. It wasn't a supporting wall, so it wasn't especially sturdy, but it wasn't exactly flimsy, either.

I banged on the door with my fist. "What's going on in there?" I called. "Ron. Bobbi. Unlock this door."

The door opened and Bobbi stamped out, face red and ugly with anger.

"You stay the fuck out of here," Ron Church shouted at her back. "I catch you goin' through my stuff again you'll be real sorry, I guarantee that."

She whirled. He backed away. "You bag of festering pus," she hissed. "If you know what's good for you, you'll —"

"That's enough, both of you."

Bobbi slowly brought herself under control. It didn't look easy. "Sorry," she said when she was able to speak.

"Fucking cunt is crazy," Ron Church said.

"Shut up," I said. There was an angry red welt on his forehead and blood on his lower lip. "Bobbi, I want to see you in my office. Ron, I'll talk to you later."

In my office I made Bobbi sit down, even though she was too agitated to sit still.

"Are you going to tell me what's going on?" I asked.

"Nothing's going on."

I shook my head. "You're not getting away with it this time," I said. "I want an explanation."

"There's nothing to explain," she said.

"Damn it, Bobbi. This is ridiculous. The guy's got a lump on his head and a bloody lip and you tell me there's nothing going on. Did you hit him?"

She massaged the knuckles of her right hand. "Yes."

"What the hell am I supposed to do, Bobbi? I know there's something bothering you. Did Ron come on to you or something? Is he harassing you?"

"You mean sexually?"

"Whatever. Sexually, physically, psychologically. Is he?"

"No."

"I'm not sure I believe you." She didn't answer, just stared at a spot somewhere in the middle of my desk and rubbed the knuckles of her right hand. They looked swollen. "I can't fire you," I said. "Not only could I not run this place without you, but you're my friend. I guess I'll have to fire Ron."

"Could you hold off on that for a little while?" Bobbi said. "I'll see if I can work things out."

"Why should I do that? You don't like him. You don't like his work. I don't like the idea of firing him, but why should you care?"

"Because it's not entirely his fault," she said. "I'm to blame too."

"For what? I wish you'd tell me what the hell is going on." I waved my hand. "Never mind. All right. You've got him a reprieve. I just hope I won't regret this."

"Me too," she said.

"You should go get that hand looked at," I said as I walked her out of the office.

Ron was picking supplies up off the floor and replacing them on the shelves. He stopped what he was doing and stared at me sullenly.

"I thought very seriously about firing your miserable ass right out of here," I said.

"Hey, man, you wanna fire me, fire me."

"You're not making this easy, Ron. You want to tell me what it was all about?"

"Hey, I got no idea, man. Maybe she's on the rag or something." He rubbed the welt on his forehead.

"Listen," I said. "She's my friend. On top of that, she does damned good work. You're not my friend and lately your work hasn't been particularly impressive. You're a good tech, Ron. You know more about this stuff that I'll ever know." That probably wasn't true, but it seemed like a good management tactic. "But if you'd rather move on I won't cry over it."

"So you are firing me."

"No, I'm not. It's up to you. Sort out this thing between you and Bobbi. If you don't think you can, just give me a couple of weeks' notice." I turned to go, then turned back. "The movie-location stuff. Have you sent it to be scanned yet?"

"No."

"Why not?"

"I been busy," he said.

"With what? Never mind. Do it."

"Sure, man," he said. "You want to give your customers that digital shit, fine, but the quality is crap compared to real photography."

"Maybe so," I said, "but that's what they all want these days. You'd better get used to it."

"Not me, man. I don't want anything to do with that shit."

I headed back toward my office wondering why I bothered. Maybe I should call Kevin Ferguson at the

Sun, see if they needed a photographer. As I passed her desk, Mrs. Szymkowiak held the telephone out to me. I took it. It was Wally Hoag, my insurance agent.

"Tom," he said. "I hate to be the one to have to tell you this, but Pacific Casualty has gone into receivership and its assets, those left, have been frozen."

"I have a confession to make," I said.

"About what?" Francine asked.

We were sitting at the bar in Bridges Pub. I could feel the solid warm pressure of her shoulder against mine. She smelled of salt and sunshine despite the smoky atmosphere of the pub.

"I lied."

"You did? You should be ashamed."

"Well, it wasn't a lie, exactly."

"What was it then, exactly?"

"An excuse, I suppose."

"For what?"

"To see you."

"Ah," she said. "I'm flattered that you felt you needed one. Does that mean you don't want to talk about Hilly's diving lessons?"

"Not necessarily, but I'm not sure I can afford them now."

"I got you a twenty percent discount," she said. "All she'll need is a mask and fins. A good set will only cost you about a hundred bucks."

"I suppose I can handle that." I told her about Wally Hoag's call. "Apparently the company's officers have been siphoning funds to Swiss bank accounts for years. There isn't much left for the courts to seize. So I'm stuck with the costs of the repairs to the house. Wally says I should consider myself lucky, some people lost their life savings." I drank, then said, "I can always sell the Porsche."

"That would be a shame."

"I think so too." Fortunately, the Porsche was insured through the business and my business insurance was handled by another carrier.

"Don't worry about the equipment," she said. "I'm sure I can find some stuff that'll fit her."

We chatted for a while. She told me about wreck diving in the Mediterranean and I told her about photographing the Rocky Mountains from a helicopter. The silences were comfortable too.

"Can I ask you a personal question?" she said.

"As long as I have the option of not answering."

"Are you attracted to me?"

"Oh, yes, very. Why do you have to ask?"

"Because I can't tell."

"Is it important to you?"

She shrugged. "I guess it must be. I think I should tell you something, though."

"Oh-oh. Here it comes. You're married?"

"No, I'm not married."

"You've taken a vow of celibacy."

"What? No."

I looked at her reflection in the mirror behind the bar. I could see she was getting upset. I am not completely insensitive.

"Sorry," I said. "I guess I'm nervous. So what is it?"

"It's no big thing," she said, "but you ought to know I don't usually stay in one place too long."

"Jesus," I said. "You had me worried. I thought you were going to tell me you used to be a man or something."

"No, nothing like that." She nudged me gently with her shoulder. "You're a nice guy, McCall. I just thought you should know."

"I like it when women call me by my last name. It's kind of sexy."

She shook her head slowly.

"How long are you planning to hang around?" I asked.

"As long as it's interesting."

"I'll do my best."

"You're doing fine."

"Am I to construe then that you are, um, attracted to me too?"

"You could construe that, yes. Is there a problem?"

"Frankly," I said, "you scare the hell out of me."

"Well, we're even, then. You scare the hell out of me."

"I do? How?"

"I'm not sure, actually. You just do."

"Let's get out of here," I said.

"Your place or mine?"

"I was just going to suggest we go for a walk."

"Right," she said. "Let's not rush into anything."

We held hands as we walked along the promenade east of Granville Island past the commercial marina. I kissed her under the Burrard Bridge (oh, shut up, you know what I mean). She didn't feel the least bit hard and muscular in my arms. She felt very good in fact. I began to regret not rushing into things.

"Damn," she said later as she was getting into her Jeep in front of the dive shop. She was looking across the street toward the lane that ran behind the Granville Island Brewing. "There he is again."

"Who?" I asked, turning around. I saw no one for the forest of sightseers and young couples pushing baby strollers.

"I don't know. The last couple of days I've been seeing this guy. At least, I think it's the same guy. He came into the shop a few days ago, didn't buy anything, just hung around, chatting with Chuck and Estelle. But he kept looking at me."

"I can understand that," I said.

"Not like that."

"What did he look like?"

"He was about fifty, fifty-five. Fit. Sort of ordinary looking except for his hand."

"What about his hand?" I said, a cold tingle of apprehension stroking my spine.

"He was missing a couple of fingers. The two middle fingers on his right hand."

23

I didn't have to be hit over the head. Barring a convention of the digitally challenged in town, it had to be the same man I'd seen on the boardwalk and Maggie Urquhart had seen on the docks. Of course, there was no reason to believe he wasn't simply a tourist, despite Maggie's "feelings," or a local, but I was certain it had something to do with Carla and Ryan. Perhaps Ryan had hired someone to keep eye on me, hoping I'd lead him to Carla. Or maybe the man was a cop, working on Ryan's wife's murder. Whoever he was, it was an eerie sensation, the feeling that I was being watched, and I didn't like it at all. I had to force myself to not hunch my shoulders as I walked home.

"Where have you been?" Hilly said sternly when I went into the kitchen. It was seven o'clock. "I made dinner."

I couldn't help but laugh at her manner.

"What's so funny?" she demanded.

"Nothing," I said. "I'm sorry I'm late. I was with Francine and we got to talking. I lost track of the time." She speared me with a dark look. "Sorry," I said again.

She opened the refrigerator and took out the big Wedgwood platter my grandmother had left me. It was at least a hundred and twenty years old. Lifting the edge of a metre or two of aluminum foil, she said, "I guess everything's still okay." She set out the food on the kitchen table.

She'd made crab-salad sandwiches on pita bread and a spinach-and-watercress salad and both were indeed wonderful. She'd even chilled a bottle of Chablis I'd forgotten I had. Where had she learned about chilling white wine? I wondered. Maybe I should have a talk with her mother. For dessert there was coffee, good but a little stronger than I liked, and the carrot cake we'd doggie-bagged from dinner the night before.

"You keep this up," I said, "and I might not let you go home at the end of the summer."

"I wouldn't mind," she said.

Mmm, I thought.

After I helped her clean up, she went upstairs to watch television while I put John Lee Hooker on the CD player and settled down to try to catch up on my reading. It was hopeless, of course. I was months behind, and the stack of to-be-read journals and magazines and books was growing taller by the day.

About half an hour after Hilly came down for her goodnight kiss I had just tossed a three-month-old issue of *Photo Life* onto the recycle stack when someone knocked at the front door. I got up to answer it, expecting one of my neighbours – a non-resident would have had to buzz from the security gate – but when I opened the door there was a young woman standing under the yellow porch light. She wore round sunglasses, had boyishly short peroxide-blond hair, and lipstick the colour of orange Popsicle. She was dressed in a creased and cracked black leather motorcycle jacket over a thin white T-shirt, distressed jeans that Hilly would have loved, and scuffed brown cowboy boots. She had a battered brown leather bag slung over her shoulder.

"Yes?" I said, wondering who she was and how she'd got by the gate. But the gate was designed to discourage casual strollers, tourists and the like; it wasn't much of a deterrent to a determined and moderately agile trespasser.

"Hi, Tommy," she said, taking off the glasses. "Don't you recognize me?" As soon as she removed the glasses, of course, I did. "Aren't you going to ask me in?" Without waiting for an answer, she pushed past me into the house. "What's with all the junk outside on the dock?" she asked as I closed the door.

"It's a long story," I said. "I like your outfit," I added. I did, too. It suited her, reminding me of the Carla I used to know.

She did a graceful pirouette and curtsied, finger under her chin. "It's a disguise," she said.

"A disguise?"

"You can't be too careful," she said.

"Aren't you being a little melodramatic?"

"It's better than getting my ass shot off."

"Yes," I said. "That would be a shame. It's such an important asset in your line of work." She stuck out her tongue. "So, who's trying to shoot your *toches* off? Anyone I know?"

"Get with the program, Tommy. Vince Ryan, of course."

"You think Ryan is trying to kill you?" I said. Then I remembered that he may have had his wife killed.

"Yes," she said. "Well," she amended, "maybe."

She took off the motorcycle jacket and slung it over the back of a chair in the entrance hall. The T-shirt had no sleeves and there were dark purple bruises on her upper arms, as though someone had gripped her, hard. She went into the living room, dropped her bag onto the floor, and collapsed onto the sofa. "I'm totally wasted," she said. She leaned over and dug into a pocket of her bag, taking out a pack of cigarettes. Lighting one, she blew a thick plume of smoke toward the ceiling.

"When did you start smoking?"

"It's part of my disguise."

"Giving yourself lung cancer is carrying it a little far, don't you think?"

"God, Tommy, you've gotten awfully damned self-righteous in your old age. Give it a rest. So I smoke. What the fuck's it to you?"

I thought about telling her that it was my house she was stinking up, but under the circumstances it would have sounded petty. I fetched her a dish to use as an ashtray, put it on the coffee table in front of her.

"First you tell me that Ryan wants you back," I said. "Now you tell me that he might be trying to kill you. Which is it?"

"I dunno. Both. Neither. Christ, Tommy, I'm tired. I haven't slept more than a couple of hours at a time for almost two weeks. I'm so tired I can hardly see straight. I'd swear your house is tilted." She pulled hard on the cigarette, drawing the smoke into her lungs. She hadn't started smoking yesterday. "I thought it would be easy, you know, like all the other times, just pull my famous disappearing act and that would be that. But things have gotten out of hand and I'm scared, Tommy, really scared."

"I suppose you have a right to be," I said. "I mean, how many of your other ex-boyfriends are suspected of hiring hit men to kill their wives?"

Her eyes locked onto mine, like a blue laser targeting system. "Who told you that?" she demanded. Perhaps it was some subtle change in the lighting or the increased blood flow as a result of accelerated heartbeat, but her eyes seemed to darken, going from indigo to an even-deeper blue.

"An old friend of yours," I said. "Chris Hastings."

"You talked to Chris?"

"And Ginny Gregory and Nancy Petersen and Frank Poole."

"You do get around, don't you? What did good ol' Frank have to say?"

"Nothing that was worth the hundred bucks it cost me," I said.

"That's Frank, a real prince of a guy. You want something from him, pay him or fuck him, he doesn't much care which."

"I should consider myself fortunate then," I said. "Why didn't you tell me the police suspected Ryan of having his wife killed? Why the crap about a hit and run?"

"I didn't want to get into it," she said, crushing out her cigarette in a pewter coaster instead of the dish I'd fetched. "It would have just complicated things."

I thought of Hilly asleep upstairs. "Goddamnit, Carla, if Ryan's dangerous –"

"Oh, relax, Tommy. You don't have anything to worry about. Look, I really don't want to talk about it."

"Come off it, Carla," I said. "You tell me your boyfriend might be trying to kill you, but you don't want to talk about it." I picked up her bag and tossed it at her. She caught it and glared at me, eyes hot and dark. "Why don't you just take your bullshit somewhere else?"

"Christ, you sure have gotten hard-assed lately," she said. "All right." She put the bag down and picked up the cigarette pack from the coffee table. "You don't mind, do you?" she said.

"Yeah, I mind, but go ahead." She lit up. "All right, what makes you think Ryan is trying to kill you?"

"Maybe he is, maybe he isn't. But a couple of guys tried to haul me into a car the other day. That's how I got these." She twisted her shoulders, exhibiting her bruises. "On the other hand," she added, "it could have been attempted robbery or rape. I haven't been frequenting the better neighbourhoods lately. I didn't wait around to find out what they wanted."

"Let me rephrase the question," I said. "What reason would he have to kill you?"

"Reason. Christ, he doesn't need a fucking reason. I left him, that's enough reason for him. He's a crazy son of a bitch, you never know what the fuck he's going to do. We were in Germany negotiating the sale of some construction equipment he'd picked up somewhere when one of the buyers said something that pissed him off. I don't know what it was, but Vince suddenly told the guy that he'd rather let the equipment rust away to nothing than sell it to such assholes, packed up, and walked out. He stood to clear half a million bucks for an afternoon's work and he just walked out, like it meant nothing to him. Another time I thought he was going to have a fucking stroke because some sales clerk short-changed him a dollar. And Sam," she added.

"Vince's fired and rehired him so many times, the poor bastard doesn't know whether he's poached, baked, or stir-fried."

"So he's a little unpredictable," I said.

"A little. Christ, it got so I was afraid to open my mouth, I never knew how he was going to react. Look, maybe he had his wife killed, maybe not, I don't know. I wouldn't put it past him, though. And if he hired someone to kill her, he can hire someone to kill me."

I silently watched her smoke her cigarette. As she removed the cigarette from between her sticky orange lips, she opened her mouth, almost releasing the ball of smoke, but with a quick intake of air, it was drawn deep into her lungs. I thought about what to say next, then said it.

"Ryan came to see me."

She sat up straight. "Christ," she said.

"A couple of times," I added. "The day after we met in the hotel and again yesterday." I thought I detected a slight tremor as she raised the cigarette to her mouth and took a hard drag. "He offered me money to help him get you back."

"And are you?"

"No."

"Why did you talk to Ginny and Chris and Frank then?"

I shook my head. "I'm beginning to wonder myself."

She crushed her cigarette out in the coaster. "Poor Tommy," she said, under control once again. She reached across the coffee table and patted me gently on the cheek. "I'm surprised your house isn't full of stray dogs and cats."

Her touch simultaneously heated me and chilled me. I jerked to my feet like a puppet whose strings had been yanked too abruptly.

"How about offering a lady a drink?" she said.

"I would if there were a lady present."

"Very funny."

"You still like tequila?" I asked.

"That's like asking me if I still like fucking," she said with a wicked smile.

"I'll take that for a yes," I said.

I got a lemon from the fridge and occupied myself with slicing it into wedges. I don't need this, I told myself. My life was complicated enough. Strangely, though, and perhaps stupidly, I wasn't afraid, although I should have been. If Ryan had had his wife killed and if he truly was trying to kill Carla, I should have been scared stiff. I was stiff, all right, but it wasn't with fear. What I was, was almost beside myself with desire for Carla.

I put the dish of lemon wedges, a shaker of salt, half a bottle of tequila, and a couple of heavy shot glasses on a tray and carried it to the coffee table. I put it down and sat opposite her. Carla twisted the top off the bottle and filled the shot glasses. Without a word, we performed the ritual of salt, tequila, lemon.

"How is Ginny?" she asked as she filled the glasses.

"She's fine," I said. "She wanted me to ask you to call her. If I saw you."

"Yeah, well, maybe I will."

"You've taken care of your business then?" I said.

She shook her head. "No, not quite. Soon." She rubbed a lemon wedge on the web of flesh between her thumb and forefinger and sprinkled salt. She licked the salt from her hand, downed a shot of tequila, and chewed the lemon wedge. "Have you got a girlfriend?" she asked.

"No," I said, reaching for the salt shaker. I tossed the tequila back. It went off like a slow, soft explosion in my gut. I bit down on the lemon, the hinges of my jaw aching from the tartness. I tore the pulp from the rind, chewed, and swallowed. "I can't afford the insurance rates," I said.

"You think I took something from Ryan, don't you, that's why he's after me?" She poured more tequila.

"Your track record makes it hard to think otherwise," I said. "You're a thief and a liar and god knows what else." I remembered what Hastings had told me about her past. I discovered that it didn't matter.

"But you still love me, don't you?" she said, smiling but perhaps only half joking.

"No, I don't still love you."

"You'll help me, though, won't you?"

"That depends on what you want."

"All I need is a bed for the night," she said. "And a small favour."

"Haven't we been through this before? I do you favours, you rip me off. Not exactly a good deal for me."

"You were willing to help me the other day."

"That was before I knew your boyfriend was a murder suspect," I said.

"Yeah, well, what can I tell you?"

"Your pal Frank," I said. "He seems like the type to do people favours if the price is right."

"That's the problem," she said. "The price."

"Do you know a man with the two middle fingers of his right hand missing?" I asked.

"Uh? No," she replied, finding her cigarette pack and taking out another cigarette. "Why?"

"It isn't important." The thought came unbidden and made my blood run cold despite the flames fed by the tequila. "You didn't have anything to do with Ryan's wife's death, did you?"

She didn't have to answer. The look on her face was enough. A mixture of shock and horror and disbelief. And something else. Disappointment. It was ironic, I thought, that she should be disappointed in me.

I felt I should apologize, but didn't.

She poured more tequila into the glasses, carefully filling them to the brim, then capped the bottle and looked at me. Her indigo eyes were unreadable.

"You're right, Tommy," she said. "I am a thief and a liar and god knows what else. It sort of came with the territory. Maybe someday I'll tell you all about it, the long sad story of the life of Carla Bergman, whoever the hell she is. But not tonight. I'm absolutely beat.

"I'll tell you this, though. I've done things I'm not proud of, but cold-blooded murder isn't one of them. I met her once, when I first started working for Vince. Things had already started to go bad between them, but you could see that it was painful for her. She was nice, sweet and sort of innocent. She reminded me a little of –" She paused, shook her head, then went on. "If the son of a bitch had her killed, he's crazier than I think he is. But I didn't have anything to do with it, you have to believe me." A tear spilled from the corner of her eye and rolled down her cheek.

"How did you do that?" I asked.

"I must have got some cigarette smoke in my eye," she said, wiping her cheek with the knuckles of her left hand. With her right hand she reached out and touched the rim of one of the shot glasses with a fingertip, breaking the surface tension of the tequila. The liquor flowed over the rim of the glass onto the table.

"You can stay the night," I said, reaching for the salt.

24

"Noooo," cried a voice in my head.

"Yessss," crowed another.

My left brain, wherein supposedly dwelled whatever logic and reason I possessed, was arguing with the more self-indulgent right half of my brain. Or perhaps it was a mammalian forebrain versus reptilian hindbrain thing. Whatever, I was seriously conflicted. I felt like that cartoon character from my childhood, a pious little angel droning "good" advice into his right ear and an impish little red devil whispering "bad" advice into the other. Or maybe it was just glandular overload.

"If there is even the remotest possibility of getting fucked," my ex-wife had once told me, "men will forget whatever good sense they possess, which isn't a whole lot to begin with, and listen only to the roar of testosterone."

I tossed back the tequila.

"That's nice of you, Tommy," Carla said. "But then, you always were a nice guy, weren't you? Tommy McCall, the last of the nice guys."

"That's me," I said, dropping a chewed strip of lemon peel onto the dish. The tequila made my head buzz gently and my arms and legs feel loose. It wasn't an unpleasant feeling, but I knew it could lead me into bad trouble if I wasn't careful, which I tended not to be when I mixed alcohol and hormones. "I think I need assertiveness training," I added.

"What?"

"Never mind." I stood up, a little surprised I didn't stagger. "You can sleep on the sofa," I said.

"Are you sure you want me to stay?" Carla asked.

"Hell, yes, I'm sure," I said. "I don't want you to stay."

When she'd puzzled that out she said, "If you don't want me to stay, why offer?"

"Fucked if I know," I replied.

"Ah," she said, nodding.

"Indeed," I said. "I'll be right back."

I went upstairs, got some bedding from the linen closet, and went back downstairs. Carla was sprawled languidly on the sofa. She'd taken her boots and socks off and refilled the shot glasses.

"No more for me, thanks," I said, dropping the bedding onto the end of the sofa at her feet.

"Oh, c'mon, Tommy. One more for old time's sake."

"One more and you'll have to put me to bed," I said, immediately regretting my choice of words.

"Getting you into bed was never much of a problem," she replied with a smile that made me think of Beatrix. Lifting a long leg, she rubbed her bare foot against my thigh. I moved away and she pouted. "I guess I was wrong," she said. "I thought you were glad to see me, but that must be a salami in your pocket after all."

I grinned despite my discomfort. "I won't deny you still have an effect on me," I said. I lowered myself into the easy chair facing the sofa across the coffee table.

She pointed a painted toe at the tequila. "C'mon, drink up." She kicked the bedding onto the floor. "And don't sit way over there. It's not friendly."

"No, but it's safer," I said.

"What's to be afraid of?"

"You. Me."

"Me?"

"Don't be coy," I said.

She stood up, stepped over the coffee table, and dropped into my lap. Her mouth fastened on mine, lips soft and hot, and her tongue probed between my teeth. I heard a low moaning, but didn't know whether it was her or me. Putting my hands on her shoulders, I pushed gently, trying to detach her, but her arms went around my neck and she held on.

"Goddamnit, Carla," I said against her mouth. Her tongue darted between my teeth.

I bit down, not too hard, though, not wanting to hurt, but she only probed deeper. She tasted of citrus, tequila, and tobacco. I reached behind my head, grasped her wrists and unwound her arms. She whimpered petulantly against my mouth, sucking greedily at my lower lip, trying to hang on. She twisted her wrists and broke my grip. I placed my hands against her chest and pushed her away. Pain flared as she bit my lip.

"Shit, Carla," I said, wiping the blood from my mouth.

She stood up.

"Serves you right," she said. She unsnapped her jeans, slid out of them, and stood in front of me in pale pink bikini panties. It was obvious she wasn't a natural blonde.

I ignored the need to squirm and pull at the crotch of my jeans to ease my discomfort. What if Hilly came downstairs? The noise wouldn't waken her – she took her hearing aids out at night – but Beatrix, the Hearing-Ear Ferret, was on the job.

"Will you please go sit down," I said.

She picked up her jeans, returned to the sofa, and sat down. Her stomach was hard and flat and beneath the thin fabric of her T-shirt her breasts were high and firm, dark nipples erect and standing out sharply. I looked away, but the image seemed burned into my retinas. Despite the blood in my mouth, I could still taste her and my hands ached to touch her.

"There wouldn't be any strings," she said.

"Yes, there would," I said.

"Have it your way," she said. "There won't be another offer."

"Fine," I said.

She picked up a lemon wedge, rubbed it against her hand, and applied salt. Raising the glass in a toast, she sucked the salt off her hand, downed the tequila and threw the shot glass at my head. It glanced off my right cheekbone.

"Son of a bitch," I said, pressing my fingertips against the bruised spot just below my eye. "Why the hell did you do that?"

"Just to get your attention," she said.

"Christ, you could've put out my eye."

"Oh, stop whining, for god's sake."

I picked up the glass and put it on the tray, picked up the tray and took it to the bar. Turning to her, I said, "I should throw your ass out of here."

"But you won't, will you?" she said, a challenge in her voice and in her eyes.

"No," I said. "I said you could stay the night and you can. But that's it. You're out of here in the morning. And don't even think about trying to rip anything off. Do and the first thing I'll do is call the police."

"And the second thing?"

"I'll call Ryan." I tightened the cap of the tequila bottle and put it on the shelf, then picked up the tray. "You know where the light switches are," I said as I took the tray into the kitchen.

I dreamed about her. At least I think it was her, but it could have been Francine. Or my ex-wife for that matter. It was one of those sweaty, hormone-induced dreams that brought me to the edge of orgasm before waking me, achingly stiff and unable to get back to sleep. On my back, staring into the darkness, I listened to the sounds of the night, the gentle creaking of the house as it moved with the tide, the lap of water outside my window, the distant whine of traffic, land and water, a dog barking somewhere, an angry drunken shout, sirens, and what sounded like a far-off gunshot, probably a backfire. Sleep came eventually, but some time around three I was awakened by the sound of someone coming into my bedroom.

I felt her weight on the bed as she slipped under the covers. She was naked and heated, her flesh hot against me. I was instantly rigid and churning with desire.

Alarms went off in my head, but the clangour was lost in the thunder of raging hunger. Her hands, cooler than the rest of her, sought me, stroked me. My breath caught as the tight ring of latex encircled me.

"I really did love you, you know," I said.

"That was stupid," she said as she straddled me, placed me inside her.

"Don't I know it."

25

I don't remember falling asleep, but I didn't wake up until it was morning. I could still taste her on my lips, smell her in the sheets, so it hadn't been another dream after all. I got up, showered, shaved, dressed and went downstairs. The bedding was neatly folded on the sofa. Hilly was in the kitchen eating Cheerios. There was a yellow Post-it note on the refrigerator. It read, "Thanks," and was signed with a big scrawled C partly encircling a happy face eyes and grinning mouth.

At least she hadn't taken the stereo.

July 1, Canada Day, almost everyone has the day off and, because they've got nothing better to do, they all come to Granville Island. They clog the streets and lanes and boardwalks with their cars and bicycles and skateboards and baby carriages. They fill False Creek with their Zodiacs and Boston Whalers and converted logging tugs. They fight over parking spaces and moorings and restaurant seating. The residents of Sea Village pray for rain. If it weren't illegal, we'd probably sacrifice a few small animals. Who'd miss a couple of pigeons, a squirrel or two, Mr. Oliphant's Yorkshire terrier?

Hilly took off early to spend the day with Courtney and the gang from the community centre. I spent the morning puttering around, periodically drifting off into a muzzy trance, wondering if I'd finally seen the last of Carla. Part of me hoped I had. A little voice in the back of my mind, however, when it wasn't telling me I was a complete idiot, which I already knew, told me I probably hadn't.

Restless, I went to the studio and tried to do some work. We had a three-day shoot in Whistler the following week and there was a lot to do to get ready. I discovered, however, that Bobbi had done most of it already. By four I was back home. The message light on my answering machine was blinking. Blink-blink. Pause. Blink-blink. Pause. Two messages.

"McCall," Francine's husky voice said. "My group cancelled out on me so I'll be around this weekend after all. Give me a call if you want." She rattled off a number.

The second message was from Mary-Alice. There was a desperate urgency in her voice as she said, "Tom, call me, please. We just have to do something to stop Mummy and Daddy from getting a divorce." Mummy and Daddy. Mary-Alice was retrogressing.

Putting off calling Mary-Alice, I dialled Francine's number.

"Yo," a man's voice answered.

"Ah, is Francine Janes there, please?"

"She's out for a while. Can I give her a message?"

"Just tell her Tom McCall called."

"Okee-dokee."

I hung up and got a beer from the refrigerator. I took the cordless phone up to the roof deck. The last thing I wanted to do was talk to Mary-Alice about my parents' divorce. The next-to-last thing I wanted to do was talk to my parents about it. But I knew I wasn't going to be able to avoid either. I punched Mary-Alice's number into the phone.

I was flaked out on the sofa, listening to disc three of B.B. King's boxed set, '69 to '75, when Hilly and Courtney came banging and squealing into the house, faces and arms and knees red from a day of sun and water. Little Canadian flags fluttered over their heads from elastic headbands. Bouquets of helium-filled balloons floated behind them, bouncing against the ceiling. They pranced into the living room and performed coy little pirouettes in front of me. Both wore sleeveless jerseys and there were big garish tattoos splashed across their shoulders. Courtney sported a bright green and red parrot, Hilly a hooded cobra poised to strike.

"Nice tattoos," I said as I got up to turn the volume down.

Their faces fell and they looked at each other.

"How did you know they weren't real?" Hilly asked.

"They're not real?" I said.

"Of course they're not real."

"That's too bad," I said. "I was really looking forward to the reactions of your respective mothers to real tattoos."

"Oh, Daddy, you were not." They exchanged looks again. "Were you?"

"No," I said. "I wasn't."

"They wash off in a couple of days," Courtney said.

"You hope," I said.

"You're awfully quiet tonight," Francine said. Hilly was downstairs, watching a video, and Francine and I were sitting on my roof deck, eating a late supper and watching the sun go down over the dark silhouette of Granville Bridge. "Something on your mind?"

The little voice in my head gibbered, *Tell her about last night.* I stuffed a mental rag in its stupid mouth.

While I looked forward with considerable anticipation to seeing Francine, and enjoyed her company, I felt a certain apprehension about the suddenness of what was happening between us. I wondered if I wasn't getting myself into something I might regret. Nevertheless, I didn't want to do anything that would end it before it was even on the runway. Naturally, I didn't say any of this.

I said, "No, not really."

She wasn't fooled, of course. "Look, I'm not going to throw a conniption if you tell me you think you've made a mistake. I'm a big girl."

"Conniption?"

"A word my grandmother used to use."

I reached over and placed my hand on hers. I ran my fingertips up her arm to her bare shoulder, her cheek. Her skin was warm and silky. Despite her physical strength and her self-confident manner, I sensed a certain vulnerability to her. "I haven't made a mistake," I said.

She turned her head and kissed the palm of my hand. "Glad to hear it," she said.

"When I told you that you scared the heck out of me," I said, "I meant your, well, physical development. I don't suppose I'm the first man to tell you that it can be somewhat intimidating."

"No, you're not," she said quietly.

"What did you mean when you said we were even because I scared you too?"

"I guess I meant that I'm afraid you're the kind of man I could fall in love with."

"Would that be so bad?" I said, feeling the adrenaline begin to rush through my veins.

"I've been in love," she said, as if she was telling me she'd had food poisoning. "Someone always gets hurt."

"It doesn't have to be like that," I said.

"So far, for me, it's always been like that," she said. After a pause, she added, "Look, you told me you like things simple. All right, let's keep it simple. I like you, McCall. You make me feel good. I can relax around you, be myself. And I think you like me. So what's the point in making it more complicated than that? It's okay that you don't love me, don't feel like you're obligated or anything. Besides, I'll be moving on before long anyway."

"Maybe if you didn't leave," I said, "if you hung around a while, things might be different."

"Are you asking me to stay?"

"I would like you to stick around at least long enough to get to know you," I said.

"I'm not leaving tomorrow," she said. "But don't you see, if I stay too long you might fall in love with me.

Worse, I might fall in love with you and you might *not* fall in love with me."

"I've fallen in love three times in my life," I said. "The first time was with Elsie Heatherington, who sat in front of me in my seventh-grade homeroom. The second time was with my ex-wife and the last time was with Carla Bergman. I got burned all three times. Elsie didn't know I even existed in the same space-time continuum as her, my ex-wife dumped me for the fast-food-franchise king of southern Ontario, and Carla Bergman ran off with a lot of expensive hardware and a substantial chunk of my self-esteem. If I'm not careful," I added, "I could get burned again."

"What are you trying to say?"

"That I'm willing to take the chance," I said, adding, "Would that I had a choice."

"Maybe I'm not willing to take the chance," Francine said, adding, "And I do have a choice."

The next day, July 2, was more of the same. Locals and tourists still mobbed Granville Island. In a futile attempt to escape, I rented a C&C 25 and took Francine, Hilly, and Courtney sailing on English Bay. It was a good thing Francine knew something about sailing. And it was likely her physique, not my diplomatic skills, that dissuaded the skipper of the boat we almost rammed from doing anything rash. On the way back to the marina I tried to explain to Hilly and Courtney that it is not polite to laugh at your captain.

26

On Sunday afternoon Daniel and I were playing chess on his roof deck when a long dark-grey limo rolled silently up to the embankment. The tide was out and Daniel's deck was almost level with the boardwalk. Sam, nattily attired in a blue blazer and grey trousers, got out of the car and lumbered down the ramp toward the gate.

"Is that who I think it is?" Daniel said. I had been bringing him up to date on the latest developments.

"Yes," I said. I got up and leaned over the railing. I could see Sam standing patiently at the gate.

"Should I buzz him in?" Daniel asked.

"I suppose," I said.

He pressed the button on the remote control he'd rigged to release the gate from his deck. I could hear the distant rasp of the gate lock as it released. Sam opened the gate, stepped through, and carefully closed it behind him, although it would have shut automatically. He walked slowly along the main dock, examining each house with interest, smiling at some of the more idio-syncratic touches to which some of my neighbours are prone. He turned onto the finger dock and, when he passed below me, I called down to him.

He looked up and said, "I wouldn't want to come home blind stumbling drunk some night. Especially in the winter."

"You sober up fast when you hit the water," I said. "Especially in the winter. Where's your boss?"

"In the car. He wants to talk to you."

"Is that right?" I said. "Well, he knows where to find me."

"Would you mind coming to the car?"

I felt like telling him to tell Ryan to take a hike, but my curiosity got the better of me.

Ryan was alone in the back of the limo, although there was room enough for a basketball team.

"Howzit goin'?" he asked as I settled into a buttery leather seat facing him. Sam closed the door and waited outside.

I didn't bother to answer.

"You get one guess why I'm here," he said.

"I don't need any guesses," I said. "Yes, I've seen Carla. And, no, she doesn't want to see you. I don't know what's going on between you two, and I don't really care, but you're an adult, you can live with the rejection. Forget her and get on with your own life." I silently added to myself that I should try taking my own advice for a change.

"I can't afford to forget her," Ryan said. "When she left she took something. I need it back."

"I figured as much," I said. "But I don't want to know about it."

"There are some people who will be very unhappy if I don't get it back."

"Unhappy with her or you?" I said.

Ryan shrugged. "Both, but I can handle it."

"I know about your wife. Is that what you mean by 'handle it'?"

His face was suddenly very hard, eyes narrowing to unreadable black slits. I wondered if I hadn't just made a serious mistake. I put my hand on the door handle.

"I didn't kill my wife," he said. "I loved her. Okay, we were having some problems, but what married couple doesn't? C'mon, McCall, do I look like the type of person who'd hire some scuzball to kill his wife?"

"I've never met anyone who would hire someone to kill his wife," I said, "so I have no frame of reference. Carla thinks you're crazy enough."

"And what do you think?"

"I'll give you the benefit of the doubt."

"Innocent until proved guilty," he said.

"You could put it that way."

"I was never charged," he said with a shrug. "But that could have been because cops fucked up, right? They're just dumb simple servants after all. Look at that poor schnook O.J. Simpson. Even though he was acquitted, there will always be people who believe he got off because he could afford to spend millions on his defence. Reasonable doubt works both ways." He pressed a button and a panel slid aside to reveal a small bar. "You want a drink?" he asked.

"No, thanks," I said.

He poured three fingers of Jack Daniels into a cut-glass tumbler and downed it in a single gulp.

"Carla hasn't been herself for some time," he said.

"Carla is never herself," I said. "She's always someone else."

"Seriously," he said. "I think she's mentally ill. Paranoid. Delusional."

"Oh, come on. She's strung tight. Maybe too tight," I added, pressing my fingertips to the tender spot on my cheek. "But in her line of work a little paranoia's probably a good thing. Keeps her cautious. And if she's suffering from a delusion, it's a common one shared by a lot of petty criminals, that so-called straight society is for clowns and losers. What did she take from you that was so important, anyway?"

"I thought you weren't interested?"

"Call it curiosity," I said. "What was it? Not money. You strike me as a man who's used to losing money."

"That's a funny way to put it," he said, "but, yeah, I've gone from dead broke, to swimming in the stuff, back to dead broke so many times I've lost count. Some people jump out of windows. Me, I just dust myself off and jump back in. Making money's easy. Almost as easy as spending it." He poured himself another drink, sipped this one. "You're right, it wasn't money she took, but it was the key to making a lot of money. And I'll be straight with you. I made some commitments to some people and now, thanks to Carla, I probably won't be able to keep them. These aren't the sort of people you want pissed off at you.

"But that's only part of the reason I want to find her. Christ, McCall, you know her. You know the effect she can have. Sure, I can buy all the woman I want, but I know, inside, it's just the money. With Carla, it was different. It wasn't the money."

Now who was delusional? I asked myself. "With Carla it's always money," I said. "Or a reasonable facsimile thereof. I've learned a lot about her recently, most of it I don't like. She isn't the person I thought she was and it's a safe bet that she isn't who you think she is. Maybe you really do care about her, but I've said it before and I'll say it again: you're better off without her. Write it off to experience."

"I can't do that."

"Fine," I said. "But just leave me out of it."

I opened the car door and started to get out. His hand clamped onto my arm. It felt as if my arm was caught in a vice.

"She's out of her depth on this, McCall. So are you. She's tough, but she's not that tough, not by half. I don't want anything to happen to her. I don't want to see anything happen to you either."

"Then I'll just have to keep my distance," I said.

"It may be too late for that. Losing is all part of the game, McCall. I don't like it, but I'm used to it. These people I'm involved with, though, they don't understand that part of it. They didn't earn their money, they just happened to own leases on the right chunks of the right mountains at the right time. They're tough old boys, though, and used to taking direct action. There's no telling what they'll do if they get desperate enough. They've made commitments themselves to some even more serious people to whom losing is just plain unthinkable."

"Goodbye, Ryan," I said. "Don't come back. I'm out of it."

"I'm not sure it's that easy," he said as I got out of the car.

Sam nodded as he walked around to the driver's side and got into the car. I watched the limo silently edge its way out of the parking lot, then started down the ramp.

A car horn blipped and I turned to see Mary-Alice's little white BMW slip with a quick snort of exhaust into the space vacated by the limousine.

"We have to talk," she said as she got out of the car.

"We talked last night," I said. "Nothing has changed."

"Tom, how can you be so . . . so uncaring? They're our parents."

"Plenty of people's parents get divorced," I said.

"They've been married for almost forty years."

"I'm not happy about it, M.-A., but I'm not going to Victoria with you to try to talk them out of doing something they've both decided they want. I know it's hard for you to accept, but they are adults, after all."

Her face grew red and blotchy. "You arrogant son of a bitch," she said, jaw clenched, voice cracking with anger. "How can you just stand by and let them tear their lives apart? Goddamnit, I used to look up to you. My big brother, so smart and self-confident and self-sufficient. But now I see you for what you really are, a selfish, insensitive, uncaring bastard. You're just like our father. No wonder Linda divorced you."

"What the hell does that mean?"

"Linda told me you had a girlfriend, some woman at the paper."

"Well, she was wrong. Mary-Alice, you aren't making any sense. I don't like what's happening any more than you do, but it's none of our business. Disapprove all you want, but keep your nose out of it. You won't make it any easier for them by butting in. You'll only make it worse. Believe me, they won't appreciate your interference."

"I prefer to think of it as intervention."

"Call it what you will," I said. "It's still poking your nose where it doesn't belong. They have a right to sort out their own affairs."

Without another word, she got into her car and drove away.

"Check," Daniel said as he blindsided me with his knight, catching me in a queen-king fork. If I moved my king out of check, he'd take my queen, and without my queen the game was as good as lost; I was already down a bishop and both my knights.

I toppled my king onto his fat stupid face.

"Are you all right?" Daniel asked. "You don't usually make it this easy for me."

"If my house weren't sinking," I said, "I'd cast it loose and paddle to a deserted island in the South Pacific." Daniel was setting up the pieces again. "No more for me, thanks. You could at least let me win one once in a while."

"Why would I do that?"

"Just to be neighbourly." I got up. "I need a change," I said. "I'm going to call up Howie and tell him to find another babysitter for the house. Then I'm going to sell the business to Bobbi, if she wants it, pack up the Land Rover, and drive into the mountains, where I will grow my beard long and spend the rest of my life taking pictures of rocks. When I'm dead they'll have a retrospective of my work. They'll call it 'McCall's Rocks: Those That Weren't in His Road Were in His Head.'"

"What about Hilly?"

"What about her? I'll send her back to her mother."

"And if she doesn't want to go?"

"I'll send her back to her mother. What do you mean, if she doesn't want to go? Why would she want to stay? What has she been telling you?"

"She likes it here," Daniel said. "With you."

"That's nice, but I don't think Linda would let her stay."

"Think of the money you'd save."

"I dunno. Child support isn't so bad. Like other people's dogs."

"Pardon?"

"I like dogs," I said. "As long as they belong to someone else."

"Ah," he said. "Responsibility."

"Yeah, you don't have to walk other people's dogs."

"Or scoop their poop."

"You got it."

"So what's bothering you?"

"Jesus, what isn't? My house is sinking and the guy who's supposed to save it looks like a Hobbit and talks like Yosemite Sam and is taking forever to do it. The insurance company has gone belly-up and my insurance agent has gone into hiding. My parents are getting a divorce and Mary-Alice insists that I do something to prevent it. What else? Oh, yeah. Hilly is running around with a pre-teen vamp who likes showing off her tits; Carla has me tied into knots, unable to stand her one minute, pounding the mattress with her the next; I am this close to losing my most important client; Bobbi punched out my lab tech; and, to top it all off, I think I am falling in serious lust with Miss Muscle Beach."

"I'll help you pack," Daniel said.

27

Bobbi came by at eight Monday morning, the back of the Land Rover piled high with equipment. After delivering Beatrix to Maggie Urquhart and leaving a message for Bernard Simpson tacked to my front door, we set out for Whistler, stopping on our way through the city to pick up Courtney. Hilly had asked if Courtney could come with us and I'd said it was all right with me if it was all right with her parents. Unfortunately, it was. In fact, they seemed almost eager to be rid of her for a few days.

By nine-thirty we were on the Sea to Sky Highway, rollercoasting north along Howe Sound. A little less than an hour later we dropped back down to sea level for the last time outside the logging town of Squamish at the head of Howe Sound, a little more than halfway to Whistler.

"Pee break," I announced as I pulled into a self-serve gas station.

The girls went into the convenience store attached to the service station, bopping to the beats of their respective Walkmans. Bobbi stretched her legs while I topped up the tank.

"I think we're being followed," Bobbi said.

"What?"

"That white car," she said, pointing to a white Buick Century parked at the pumps of the gas station across the road. "It's been behind us since we passed Lions Bay."

"What makes you think it's following us?" I asked. The driver wasn't paying any attention to us, seemed to be studying a map as the attendant filled the tank.

"I don't know," she said. "But why didn't he pass? You're driving like you're afraid the wheels are going to fall off any minute."

"Maybe," I said, "he's just a timid driver."

"Why did he stop when we did?"

"I never realized you had such a suspicious mind," I said.

I'd noticed the same white car in the rearview mirror some time back, but it hadn't occurred to me that it might have been following us, despite the driver's reluctance to pass, even on the three-lane passing sections. I was at least half sure it was a coincidence, but I figured it wouldn't hurt to take a better look, see if he was missing any fingers. I opened the back of the Land Rover to get out one of the cameras and a telephoto lens.

"False alarm, I guess," Bobbi said as the Buick pulled out of the gas station and sped north toward Whistler.

I watched it disappear around a bend. I didn't bother to mention that there was a high probability that most of the cars on this road were going to Whistler and you could just as easily "precede" as "follow."

From Squamish we continued on Highway 99 for a few kilometres to Brackendale, where it branches off and snakes along the Cheakamus River gorge for the climb into the Coast Mountains. It's a spectacular drive in any season and there are numerous lookouts along the road. The Buick was parked in the second one we passed, nose against the guard rail, the driver sitting behind the wheel.

Bobbi looked at me. "Well?"

"He's taking in the view."

She looked sceptical.

A few minutes later I saw the distinctive front end of the Buick in the rearview mirror. It slowly caught up until it was about five or six car lengths behind us. Bobbi kept glancing at the passenger-side mirror and soon saw it too.

"Pull off," she said. "Let him pass. Let him know we know he's there."

Hilly and Courtney seemed to be asleep, both with their Walkman earphones still socketed and issuing tinny, far-off sounds. I slowed for a sharp turn. The Buick came within a couple of car lengths. There was an Avis sticker on the front bumper.

"If he's following us," I said, "it doesn't look to me like he cares whether we know it or not. Either that or he's not very good."

She opened a *Photo Life* magazine. "Maybe you're right about me having a suspicious mind," she said and began to read.

Was it the mysterious Two-Fingered Man, I wondered, trying to drive with one eye on the road and the other on the rearview mirror, and damned near piling into the back of a Maverick bus as a result. Or was it simply a cautious driver, like us, going to Whistler? I tried to forget about it before I killed us all.

We arrived in Whistler Creek a little before noon and watched as the white Buick continued toward the main village of Whistler a few kilometres farther along Highway 99. When in Whistler I usually stayed at the Mountain Haus bed-and-breakfast about midway between Whistler Creek and Whistler Village. But the proprietors, Joanna and Bill Selkirk, were visiting Joanna's parents in Kansas or Oklahoma or Nebraska, so I'd rented a condo in Whistler Creek for four days. After checking into the condo and lunching at Boston Pizza, Bobbi and I dropped the girls off in Whistler Village to fend for themselves for the afternoon and hurried to the two o'clock meeting with the client and the people from the agency to go over the shooting schedule.

I consider myself a good photographer, technically competent and moderately creative, but hindered somewhat by a tendency toward verbal rather than visual thinking. Bobbi is better. She is the artist. What I have to work at comes naturally to her. To see us on the street you wouldn't mistake either of us for bank employees or insurance company executives, but neither would you say to yourself, these people are obviously creative, look at the way they are dressed.

There was no mistaking that Nigel Llewellyn-Smith was creative, though. A red neon sign suspended over his head flashing the words "I Am Creative" would have been redundant. Everything about Nigel, from the silk cravat and tinted glasses to the fake British accent to go with the fake British name and equally fake homosexual affectations, screamed CREATIVE. The thing of it was, though, he was very, very good at what he did.

"Thomas," he said, offering me his hand as though he expected me to kiss it. "Dear boy."

"Nigel," I said, barely touching his fingertips.

He hugged Bobbi. "Are you two doing it yet?" he asked her.

"Every chance we get," Bobbi said.

The first time we'd worked with Nigel, he had decided that Bobbi and I were made for each other. He claimed he could not understand how she and I could work together effectively without sleeping together. I think he was kidding.

"You're a liar," Nigel said, "but I love you. So, are you both ready to work your chaste little asses off?"

"Just because we're not fucking each other," Bobbi said, "doesn't mean we're chaste."

"I'm chaste all the time," I said. "Just never caught."

"Haw," Bobbi said.

"Let's get this tedious business over with," Nigel said. "Then we can go out and get laid."

In the evening Bobbi took Hilly and Courtney to the movies and I headed for Tapley's Neighbourhood Pub to see if I could track down Wes Camacho. The waitress had hair the colour and texture of straw and was sunburned despite her tan. I asked her if she knew Wes.

"Yah," she said. "I know Ves." She sounded like Arnold Schwarzenegger.

"Have you seen him tonight?"

"He vass here a vile ago," she said. She left to get my beer.

Wesley Camacho ran a one-man helicopter operation and I'd bartered services with him from time to time. He was also tapped into most of what went on in

Whistler. Tapley's was his home-away-from-home. A few minutes later, he dropped his lanky frame into the chair across the table from me.

"Hey, Flash. Long time no see." He thrust out a powerful hand. "Bobbi with you?"

"At the movies," I said. "How are you?"

"Same," he replied. "Still flyin' and getting laid regular. You here for business or pleasure?"

"Business," I said. "A brochure promoting Whistler as a summer resort. Skiing on the glaciers, hiking, mountain biking, golf, sail-boarding, all that stuff."

We played catch-up for a minute or two, then he said, "You'll never guess who I saw a coupla weeks ago."

"Carla Bergman," I said.

"Yeah," he said, disappointed I'd ruined his surprise. "I took her and her boss –" he came down heavily on the word "– for a fly-about over Rainbow Mountain. I dunno what I did to offend her, man, but she was colder'n Dracula's dick. Called me Mr. Camacho."

"Ouch," I said. "And after all you two meant to each other."

"Hey, I didn't mean any harm," he said. "You know me, Flash. It's just part of my shtick. The ladies expect it and it gives them something to tell their friends about when they go back home to Mississauga."

"Don't worry about it," I said. He shrugged. It was his most common expression. "What was your impression of Ryan?" I asked.

"Can't say I liked him much. A bit snakish. Came on friendly enough, but I wouldn't turn my back on him in a business deal."

"He was supposed to be working on some big development project up here. Know anything about it?"

233

"There's always somethin' goin' on," he said. "The most interesting rumour makin' the rounds these days is that there's some serious money, mostly Hong Kong and Japanese, behind a plan to open Rainbow Mountain to development. Some local-boys-made-good types are frothing at the mouth and lining up to buy into a piece of the action. But," he added with a shrug, "if there's anythin' to it, it's way out of my league."

Despite his flamboyant flyboy demeanour, Wes was a shrewd businessman who'd invested well and wisely in half a dozen local enterprises, from real estate to limousine services to launderettes. He still flew, but only because he liked it and, he claimed, it was a great way to meet women.

"How about Ryan?" I asked. "Is it out of his league too?"

"Unless my take on him is way off, yeah, I'd say so. He talks big, but he's little fish. Why you asking? You're not thinking about getting into anything with him, are you?"

"No," I said. "Nothing like that."

"If you're looking to invest your money, Flash, I got a few things you might find interesting. Nothing too risky. You're a friend."

"Thanks," I said. "I think I'll stick to nice, safe mutual funds. That is, if I had any money to invest in the first place."

Wes shrugged, downed his beer, and stood up. "Got an early gig," he said. "Don't be a stranger," he added, sticking out his hand. "Give my love to Bobbi."

Hilly and Courtney were blurry-eyed and yawning with fatigue by the time we got back to the condo. They headed straight for bed. They were sharing one of the small upstairs bedrooms, Bobbi had the other, and I was consigned to a Hide-A-Bed in the living room.

Over a couple of cold Kokanees we'd picked up earlier in the day, Bobbi and I talked over the next day's shoot, biking, hiking, and glacier skiing on Blackcomb Mountain. By ten she was stifling yawns and rubbing her eyes.

"Go to bed," I said. "I don't want to have to carry you up the stairs."

She stood up. "Tom?"

"Mmm." I noticed that she hadn't called me "boss."

"I know I haven't been very good company lately and that you've been carrying me, and, well, I want you to know I really appreciate it, your patience and all that, I've had a lot on my mind and I promise I'll have it all sorted out soon, I just wanted to say thanks."

"Bobbi," I said, "if there's anything I can do, all you have to do is say so. I think you know that." She nodded. "I hate to see you like this, but if you don't want to talk to me about it, I understand. Would you like the names of, ah, some people you could talk to? I mean, if that's what you think you need."

She shook her head, long brown ponytail swishing. Her eyes were dark fathomless pools. "No, it's nothing like that," she said. "It's just some personal stuff I have to sort out for myself."

She went upstairs.

I brushed my teeth in the downstairs bathroom, folded out the Hide-A-Bed, undressed and climbed between the cool sheets. Through the open window I could hear voices raised over loud rock music. Whistler is a year-round party town. And here I was in bed at eleven o'clock. The exciting life of a single.

I thought about Francine, which was a mistake.

28

The next day's shoot went well. Hilly got a kick out of being on the glacier in shorts and a T-shirt, was only mildly disappointed that corn snow didn't make good snowballs. Courtney tried hard to be blasé about it, but squealed with delight at the antics of the hot-dogging skiers and snowboarders we'd hired for the shoot. After Bobbi lent them one of the spare cameras, an old ruggedized Canon, plus a couple of rolls of film, and gave them a quick lesson on loading and using it, we didn't see very much of them until it was time to leave.

As I turned into the big day-parking lot across from the main village complex, the white Avis Buick pulled in behind us. The sun was reflecting off its windshield so I couldn't make out the driver's face. I found a space between a battered pickup and a Mercedes with two pairs of skis and a sailboard on the roof, probably golf clubs in the truck. The Buick continued down the row and, failing to find a free space farther on, went around the end and came back up the next row. Very casual.

"Stay here," I said to Bobbi and the girls. Jumping out of the Land Rover, I moved to intercept the Buick, hoping to get a better look at the driver. He saw me coming and increased speed, jouncing through the pot-holes. I ran. He stomped it, spitting gravel. The car skidded around the end of the row and sped toward the exit.

"Well?" Bobbi said when I got back to the Land Rover.

"I know. You told me so." I found a pen and wrote the licence number on the pad of yellow Post-its I keep stuck to the dash. "I got the licence number," I said, "but I don't know what good it's going to do."

Bobbi peeled off the Post-it. "Can't hurt to try," she said, getting out of the car.

The Avis office was in the Blackcomb Lodge. The clerk was a slim, balding, well-tanned man of about thirty. His name tag read Clint. He had a cast on his left arm.

"Hey, Clint," Bobbi said as though he was her best friend in the world.

"G'dye," he replied. "What can I do for you folks?"

"Clint, this is my boss, Tom McCall." We shook hands. Bobbi introduced Hilly and Courtney, then said, "I was wondering if you could do us a favour."

"Name it," Clint said agreeably.

She handed him the Post-it. "If you typed this licence number into your computer," she said, "could you call up the name of the person who rented this car?"

"Ah, yes, I can do it," Clint said. "But I'm not sup-posed to unless I have a request from the police."

"It's important," Bobbi said.

"We're being followed," Hilly blurted out.

"Followed?"

"Well, maybe," I said. "We've been seeing the same car almost since we left Vancouver. A white Buick Century with an Avis sticker on the bumper."

Clint looked at Bobbi.

"I don't want to get you into trouble," she said, hitting him with a megawatt smile. "But it sure would mean a lot to me if you could help us out."

He didn't have a chance. With a bemused expression, he shrugged and tapped his keyboard. He watched the screen for a few seconds, then said, "The car's rented to a William Henderson, 1424 Hillcrest Circle, Thornhill, Ontario."

The name meant nothing to me, of course. I wrote it down anyway.

"You want his driver's-licence number?" Clint asked.

I nodded and he read it off the screen. I added it to the name and address on the Post-it.

"Thanks," I said.

"I owe you one," Bobbi said. She handed him a business card. "Call me."

"Too right," Clint said.

Tuesday was Prime Rib Night at Tapley's and it was not to be missed. For ten bucks you got an inch-thick slice of rare prime rib, mashed potatoes, Yorkshire pudding, gravy, broccoli with a cheesy sauce (okay, so nothing's perfect) and horseradish guaranteed to clear your sinuses. We placed our orders with the straw-haired waitress, I gave her my last name, and when our order was ready, they called my name over the PA system. We picked up our meals from the service window by the entrance.

"I can't eat that," Courtney said, staring aghast at her heaping plate. Hilly was already digging into her mashed potatoes and gravy.

"Eat what you can," I said.

"I'm a vegetarian," Courtney said.

"There was meat in the spaghetti sauce last night," Bobbi said.

"That's different. Spaghetti sauce doesn't look like meat. This isn't even cooked," she added, poking at the pinkish-grey beef.

"Don't eat it, then," I said. "Eat the vegetables."

"They look gross too," she said.

But she ate, even nibbled a few bites of beef. Hilly ran out of steam about halfway through hers, so I finished it for her. I was so stuffed by then I wasn't even tempted by Courtney's leftovers.

"You are Tom McCall?" the waitress said as she cleared the table. I admitted I was. "Ves told me that if I saw you to tell you he vould be here at eight, to vait."

It was ten to eight. "No problem," I said.

"You vant coffee?" she asked.

I said I did. Bobbi and the girls shook their heads. Wes arrived a few minutes later. He set a mug of coffee in front of me.

"Hiya, darlin'," he said to Bobbi.

"Hey, Wes," Bobbi said.

I introduced Hilly and Courtney. He shook hands with both of them.

"Got a minute, Flash?" He tilted his head toward the bar.

"Sure," I said. "Be right back," I said to Bobbi and followed Wes to the bar.

Wes leaned his elbows on the bar and said, "I asked around about your pal Ryan."

"He's not my pal."

"Good thing, 'cause there's a couple of those local boys I told you about that're mightily pissed with him. They got in deep with him on a three-way deal to buy a piece of the Rainbow Mountain action. Way deep. And it cost them big. Those boys are not exactly brain surgeons," he went on. "But they're both of 'em bright enough to know when they've been left holding the stinky end of the stick."

"It was a con?" I said. "Ryan took their money?"

"Ryan lost a bundle too," he said. "Although not half as much as Henry and Layton. Near as I can tell, the reason they lost their money was because Ryan wasn't able to come up with another couple of million to close the deal. And the people they were dealing with don't give refunds. Apparently Ryan was in the middle of trying to liquidate some assets when the deal went south and he went chasing off after it."

"That would be our friend Carla," I said. He cocked a shaggy eyebrow. "She stole something from him. I don't know what, but he called it the key to making a lot of money."

Wes shrugged. "Next time you see him, tell him that it would probably be a good idea to stay clear of this place for a couple of hundred years. Henry and Layton may not be smart, but they've got long memories, especially when it comes to money. They're rough old boys, too, apt to settle differences with the blunt end of an axe."

"Thanks," I said.

He said, "What're friends for?"

Wednesday was not a good day. The weather didn't co-operate. Bobbi was in a foul mood. Nigel was impossible. The motor drive on the Hasselblad crapped out. The golf club steward bitched endlessly about the disruption and that everyone on the crew, with the exception of Nigel and the models, was in violation of the dress code. And Hilly and Courtney took a golf cart for a joy ride and drove it into a water trap.

I was about to ground Hilly until she was twenty-one, leaving Courtney to the mercy of her parents, when Nigel stuck his two cents worth in, claiming it was the high point of the day and that I shouldn't be so stiff-necked. I told him to fuck the hell off.

"What's with you?" Bobbi said as we packed up the Land Rover at the end of the day.

"Nothing," I snapped.

"Dry it off, it'll work fine," she said.

"What?"

"The golf cart. A little water isn't going to hurt it. Besides, they've got insurance for this kind of thing."

"I don't care about the damned golf cart," I said.

"I'm sure you got into your share of trouble when you were a kid. Why be so hard on Hilly?"

"It's in my job description," I said. "Anyway, I wasn't that hard on her."

"None of my business," Bobbi said with a shrug.

I looked at her. Pert nose. Big eyes. Generous mouth. Long brown ponytail stuck through the opening in the back of the Blackcomb Mountain baseball cap. If only she had tits. "McCall," the mouthy little voice in my mind said, "you are a disgusting bastard. She's your friend."

"Sorry," I said to her. "Of course it's your business. You're almost family. Hell, you are family."

She stared at me for half a dozen heartbeats, then hiccupped, held her hand to her mouth, and almost ran into the clubhouse. Christ, now what?

Hilly and Courtney came out of the clubhouse a second or two later.

"What's wrong with Bobbi?" Hilly asked accusingly.

"I don't know," I said. She didn't look as though she believed me. "Listen, scout, I'm sorry I came down on you about the golf cart." Courtney was standing mutely behind Hilly. "You too, Courtney. I should have realized you guys were gonna get bored."

"It's okay, Daddy," Hilly said. "We shouldn't have taken it."

"We didn't drive it into the water on purpose," Courtney said.

"I know," I said.

"Did you get any pictures?" Hilly asked.

"Yes, of course," I said.

They grinned at each other.

Nigel drove up in a golf cart with a pink fringed canopy. "You two keep away from it," he said to Hilly and Courtney as he parked it beside the Land Rover. "I think it went well today," he said to me. "Don't you?"

I nodded, closing the back of the Land Rover. He didn't need me to tell him how the job had gone.

He was just trying to ease the tension between us. I knew him well enough to know he wasn't going to apologize for sticking his nose into my domestic life and he knew me well enough to know I wasn't going to apologize to him for telling him to butt out.

"I'll have the films ready for you tomorrow," I said, telling him something he already knew. "I'll send them over as soon as they're dry."

"We'll take care of scanning them," he said, which I already knew. He offered his hand. "Good job," he said.

"Thanks," I said.

"Let's have lunch sometime," he added as I let go of his hand.

"Let's not overdo it," I said.

There was no sign of the white Buick on the drive back to Vancouver. The girls dozed or listened to their Walkmans and Bobbi spoke perhaps half a dozen words the whole way. If she wasn't going to tell me what was bothering her, I sure as hell wasn't going to beg. But I could have used the distraction; my mind kept circling back to Carla and Ryan. I didn't particularly care what Carla had stolen from him, I just didn't want my family, my friends, or myself to get caught in the middle. I tried to tell myself that I was worrying for nothing, that Carla was out of my life for good now, but the man in the white Buick had been strong, albeit circumstantial, evidence to the contrary.

Bobbi and Hilly waited in the Land Rover as I delivered Courtney to her parents' door. Her parents weren't home and I didn't feel comfortable about leaving her on her own, but she assured me she'd be all right. She thanked me for letting her come along and I said that I'd enjoyed having her along, which, to my surprise, I meant. Perhaps *enjoyed* was overstating it, but it hadn't been as unpleasant as I'd expected. She was a good kid.

Bobbi dropped Hilly and me off at Sea Village and took the Land Rover to the studio to unload it. I said I'd see her in the morning. There was no sign that Bernard Simpson had done any more work on the house. It still listed slightly but didn't seem to be taking on water. Hilly went next door to Maggie Urquhart's to retrieve Beatrix while I checked the answering machine.

There was a message from Bernard Simpson, apologizing for the delay and assuring me that the repairs to the hull would be completed soon.

There was a rambling, disjointed message from my mother, to the effect that my father had moved out, abandoning her to the cruel whims of fate, what was she going to do, how was she going to live, and how was she going to break it to Mary-Alice, would I do it, please?

And there was a message from my father: "Your mother has probably already called and told you that I've moved out. Not my idea, believe me, but her constant whining was driving me crazy. I told her it wasn't my fault she was getting old and she screamed at me that sixty wasn't old. I think she needs help, but I'm afraid to suggest it. Maybe you could talk to her." He hung up without leaving a number.

The dissolution of my parents' marriage made me feel like a six-year-old again, huddling under the covers listening to them fight, not understanding any of it, just wanting it to stop. Out of duty, I tried calling my mother, but there was no answer. I hung up with a mixture of relief and guilt.

I was too much of a coward to call Mary-Alice.

29

The next morning I was running late and didn't get to the studio until almost nine. There wasn't a soul in sight save for Bodger, who was asleep in the sun on the windowsill of my office. The Land Rover wasn't parked out back, although the cameras and lighting equipment had been returned to the storage cabinets. It wasn't unusual for the studio to be deserted early in the morning. I didn't run a particularly tight ship, we had no walk-in trade to speak of, and the answering service handled phone calls. As long as people did their jobs, they were free to define their own hours. But I'd promised Nigel the films for today and if Ron didn't show up soon I was going to have to process them myself. It had been a while since I'd spent any time in the lab.

I made coffee and Bodger and I ate the sweet rolls I'd picked up at the Chinese bakery. At a quarter to ten I went into the lab. The film we'd shot in Whistler was in the refrigerator, neatly labelled. Damn, where was Ron?

"Hey!"

I turned to see Ron at the door to the lab.

"What are you doing in here?" he demanded, moving to stand between me and the revolving blackout door into the darkroom. "What are you looking for?"

"I'm not looking for anything," I said. "You weren't here and I need the Whistler films processed by noon."

"I'll do it," he said. "You'll only fuck it up."

He was probably right, but I was damned if I was going to admit it. "I know my way around a lab," I said, handing him the canisters.

"Yeah," he said, "but this is my — my job."

"Don't get your territorial imperatives in an uproar," I said. "I promised the client he'd have the films by lunchtime. Damn it, I don't have to explain myself to you. Where were you, anyway? It's almost ten."

"All of a sudden you got problems with what time I come to work. I work late a lotta nights, y'know."

It was true, he was often still in the lab when I went home at night, but for all I knew he was practising shadow puppets under the enlarger. "Forget it," I said. "Just have those done by noon."

"Yes sir," he said.

There was more than a hint of sarcasm in his voice, but it wasn't the time to get into his attitude. I needed those films. But I thought, not for the first time, that it was time to start looking for a new lab tech.

"Do you know where Bobbi is?" I asked.

"How the fuck would I know where she is?"

"Take it easy," I said. "I just thought she might have said something to you."

"Well, she didn't." He disappeared through the revolving blackout door into the darkroom.

I went back to my office and did some paperwork for an hour or so. By eleven Bobbi still hadn't arrived. I picked up the phone and dialled her home number, only to get a taped message to the effect that the number I had dialled was no longer in service. I tried again, but got the same message. I dialled once again, very carefully. Same thing. What the hell? I called the operator, explained my problem.

"That number is no longer in service, sir," she said.

"Could it just be out of order?" I asked.

"No, sir."

"Why is it out of service?"

"You'll have to contact our business office, sir."

I thanked her and hung up.

I flipped through my card file, looking for Bobbi's father's number. There were two numbers on the card. On the off-chance that he was home, I punched in the first number. There was no answer, not even a machine. I tried the other number on the card and got the Richmond police.

"This is he," the gruff voice said when I asked for Norman Brooks. "Who's this?"

"Thomas McCall," I said. "Bobbi – Roberta's employer."

"I know who you are. What do you want?"

Friendly guy. "Mr. Brooks, is Bobbi in some kind of trouble?"

"What makes you think she's in trouble?"

"She hasn't shown up for work yet," I said.

"So she's late for work."

"And her phone's been disconnected."

"Gimme your number."

I did and he abruptly hung up. This guy's inter-personal skills could use some work, I thought. He called back fifteen minutes later.

"When was the last time you spoke to her?" he asked.

"Late yesterday afternoon. We were on a job in Whistler; she dropped me off at my place then came back here to unload the equipment. She was driving my Land Rover."

"She hasn't paid her telephone bill in six months," he said. "And she's been evicted from her apartment."

"When did you last see her?"

"We haven't been close since – for some time."

"It sounds like she's having money problems."

"No kidding. Maybe you oughta pay her more."

"She makes as much as I do," I said. "Maybe more."

"You own the business," he said.

"A business that employs a total of four people, myself included. And I don't give myself bonuses. If she's got herself into financial difficulties, it's not because I'm not paying her enough."

I heard the elevator door open and close and heard Bobbi say good morning to Mrs. Szymkowiak.

"She just came in," I said.

"Have her call me sometime," Norman Brooks said, and hung up.

I put the phone down and went into the outer office. Bobbi looked as though she hadn't slept in a week, eyes red-rimmed and puffy, with bags under them so dark she looked like she'd been punched. She might have been wearing the same clothes she'd worn yesterday, but since she habitually wore jeans and a jean jacket over a T-shirt, I couldn't be sure.

Mrs. Szymkowiak looked at me, her eyes big with worry.

"Bobbi," I said, "what the hell is going on? I just spoke to your father and –"

"I hope you had a nice chat."

"He told me you haven't paid your phone bill in six months and you've been evicted from your apartment."

"Did he also tell you my car's been repossessed?" she said flatly as she dropped onto the old leather sofa in my office. "Shit," she said, laying her head back and closing her eyes.

She sat up as Ron strode into the office and dropped a thick stack of glassine film sheets on my desk. "There you go," he said and left. He didn't look at Bobbi, but if her eyes had been lasers, he'd have been burned to a crisp.

I looked over the transparencies then got up and went into the outer office. Mrs. Szymkowiak was leafing through bills and invoices, entering the data into her bookkeeping program. I asked her to courier the films to Nigel, then went back into my office and closed the office door. I sat on the edge of the desk.

"What have we got on the books for the next couple of weeks?"

"Nothing much," Bobbi said.

"So if I fired you, I could probably handle it."

She looked at me. "I suppose."

"All right," I said. "You're fired."

She stood up. "Fine. See you around." Her mouth quivered and her voice sounded as though her throat were filled with shards of glass. Her eyes were bright with suppressed tears.

"Sit down," I said gruffly, struggling to control my own emotions.

She sat. "Am I fired or not?"

"No, you're not fired," I said. "But let's pretend for a few minutes that you are, that I'm not your employer and you're not my employee. We're just friends, all right?"

She nodded.

"Where did you stay last night?"

"Here." She patted the sofa.

"And where are you going to stay tonight?"

"I was planning to stay here again," she said.

"You used to be some fun to work with, Bobbi. We used to have a good time. Are you ready to tell me what's going on or do I have to fire you for real?"

She took a deep unsteady breath and said, "I lent Tony some money." She took another breath, let it out, and went on. "He was trying to get ready for a show and had some extra expenses. He promised to pay me back after the show, but he didn't. He netted over fifteen thousand dollars, but instead of paying me back, the son of a bitch bought a fucking *van*."

"How much did you lend him?"

"Ten thousand dollars," she said. "I had three thousand saved and borrowed the rest. But he also forged my signature and ran both my credit cards to the limit, another six thousand."

"Swell guy," I said. "How much back rent do you owe?"

"Five months. Seventy-five hundred dollars."

"How did you get that far behind?"

"The landlord doesn't trust banks so we paid our rent in cash. I'd leave my half with Tony, but he never paid it."

Twenty thousand dollars was a heavy load to have hanging over her head. If I'd had the money I'd have written her a cheque right then and there. As it was, I had a couple of thousand in my personal chequing account, maybe a couple of thousand more in the business account. Ryan had said making money was easy. For him maybe; I've always found it a chore, all the work involved.

"I don't blame you for being preoccupied the last couple of weeks," I said. "All right, the first order of business is to get you a lawyer."

I walked my fingers through my card file. Glenda Gilbert would make short work of Tony Chan and we could use a new van; the Land Rover was beginning to show its age.

"Then we'll see about getting your personal belongings back." She started to speak but I held up my hand. "You're going to have to find a less expensive place to live," I said as I dialled the phone. "In the meantime, if you need a place to stay, you can move in with Hilly and me."

Glenda's service answered. I left a message for her to call me and hung up.

"Now," I said, "let's go see your landlord about getting your stuff back."

"There's something else," she said.

"What?" I asked.

"I'm not sure how to tell you."

"Just say it straight out," I said. "That's usually the easiest way."

"Ron has some pictures of me," she said. Her face was hard and her voice was strained, as if the words had been forced out of her.

"What do you mean, pictures?"

"I posed for him."

I knew Ron did a little photography on the side, but I didn't know what kind. It wasn't hard to guess, though, given his taste in magazines and calendar pin-ups.

"I don't suppose we're talking art here." She shook her head. "Damn," I said.

"I needed the money."

"You don't have to apologize," I said.

"Yes, I do," she said.

I'd always thought she'd make an interesting study, but I'd never had the nerve to mention it.

"I really didn't know what I was getting myself into," she said.

"You don't have to explain it to me."

"I'm not trying to justify anything," she said, an edge of anger in her voice. "If it was just straight nudes, it wouldn't matter all that much. I worked my way through school modelling for photographers and painters, usually nude. I've got no problem with that. But this was different."

I wanted to tell her to stop, that I really didn't need to hear this, but she seemed to need to get it off her chest, so I let her go on.

"Ron had been after me for a long time to pose for him, telling me that it was an easy way to make a couple of thousand dollars. I'd always turned him down, but when my money problems started to get serious I told him I might be interested, as long as it wasn't hard core. He showed me some samples, your basic third-rate dirty magazine stuff, mostly – what do you guys call them? – beaver shots. Sorry. Anyway, it wasn't even remotely artistic, but I'd seen worse, so I said all right, if he agreed to some ground rules. He said sure, no problem."

She laughed bitterly. "Yeah, right. No problem. What an idiot I was. Before we started shooting the bastard brought out a bottle of wine and suggested that I have a couple of glasses to loosen up. I don't know what he put in it, but fifteen minutes later I was higher than a bloody kite. The last thing I remember is another girl fondling me and telling me to relax and go with the flow. The next thing I remember is throwing up in the bathroom at home with Tony holding my head and asking me what the hell I'd had to drink.

"A couple of days later Ron showed me the contacts and I almost got sick all over again. I told him there was no way I was going to sign the release and he said I already had. He showed it to me. It was my signature, but I don't remember signing it. I must have done it while I was drugged. He told me the other girl would swear I'd signed it before he'd started shooting.

"I told him I wanted the prints and the negs and he told me that if I paid him the two grand he could get for them, he'd give them to me. Otherwise, he'd send them to the magazine."

"You could probably have him charged with extortion or something."

"I thought of that," she said. "But the photos would become evidence and if my father ever saw them I don't know who he'd kill first, me or Ron. Probably me. And if my mother ever saw them, she'd die."

"Why didn't you tell me about this sooner?"

"I was too embarrassed," she said. "I thought I could handle it on my own."

"Has he sent them to the magazine yet?"

"I don't think so."

"Even if he did, what are the chances of anyone you know seeing them, let alone your parents?"

"He told me that if I didn't pay him, he'd make sure my parents saw them."

"Right. Where does he keep this stuff?"

"In the lab," she said. "But the filing cabinets are locked and he's got the only keys. I didn't want to break into them."

"Why not?" I asked.

"Because they're your property," she said.

I got up. "C'mon," I said. Mrs. Szymkowiak was at her desk. "Is Ron in the lab?" I asked her.

"I think so," she said.

"Take the rest of the day off," I told her.

30

The outer room of the lab contained Ron's desk, a set of industrial-strength grey metal shelves for supplies, a pair of equipment cabinets, a refrigerator, and five file cabinets, all of it bought secondhand. Two of the cabinets consisted of a dozen or so wide shallow drawers for storing drawings and prints.

"Wait here," I said and went through the revolving blackout door into the darkroom.

The red safety lights were on. Ron was stirring a print in the developer tray with a pair of long-handled plastic tongs. I flipped on the overhead fluorescent lights.

"Hey, the fuck you do that for? You just ruined this print."

"Don't worry about it," I said. "You're fired. Get out. I'll mail you a severance cheque."

"Fine with me," he said, tossing the tongs into the developer tray.

"Give me your keys."

He took a key ring out of his pocket, removed one key, and tossed me the rest.

"All of them," I said.

"One of 'em's personal private property."

"You're right," I said. "But it's *my* private property, since it's in my place of business." I held out my hand.

"Fuck you, man."

He brushed past me and went through the revolving door. I had to wait for it to rotate back before I could follow him through. When I emerged into the outer room of the lab, Ron was trying to open one of the legal-size file cabinets and cursing because the key wouldn't turn in the lock.

Bobbi grinned at me. "He kept the wrong key."

He snarled at her, snapped the key off in the lock and slammed out of the lab.

The pry bar from the toolbox made quick work of the jammed lock of the file cabinet. Ron's collection filled all four drawers. Fortunately, he was a very orderly person and the material was organized alphabetically, each hanging file containing colour contact sheets and negatives in glassine sleeves. Some also contained a selection of eight-by-ten prints. The best of the lot, presumably. I looked through a few of the A's in the front of the drawer, just to satisfy my curiosity, then stepped back.

"You look for them," I said, to Bobbi's obvious relief.

She finger-walked through the files while I cleared Ron's desk of anything that looked personal and dumped it into a cardboard file box.

"Got them," Bobbi said after a couple of minutes.

She took a folder out of the cabinet, flipped through it, then quickly closed it. I didn't even think about trying to peek. Okay, so I thought about it.

"You should take a look at these," Bobbi said, taking a second file folder off the top of the adjacent file cabinet.

"Do I have to?"

"They're not mine," she said, handing it to me.

The folder contained colour contact sheets and a slim stack of eight-by-ten colour prints.

I have no particular objection to looking at photographs of scantily clad woman, but I do have some artistic standards. Nothing too high, mind you. However, the small sample I'd seen of the material in Ron's collection didn't even come close to meeting my standards, as low as they were. The images were utterly banal and totally devoid of artistic merit. Nor were they particularly erotic, except in a very adolescent way; too little was left to the imagination. It was too much like looking at the illustrations in a textbook for a home-study course in amateur gynecology.

The dozen or so photos in the file Bobbi had handed me were no different, but they hit closer to home.

"Shit," I said as I leafed through them. "Shit," I said again.

The file contained photographs of Carla, reclining on pink satin sheets, half-dressed in her lounge-act mini-dress and doing things with a microphone that would have made Tina Turner blush.

I felt a strange sense of transition, as though I'd just moved from one state of consciousness to another, not unlike awakening from a dream. When Carla had posed for me she'd been girlishly shy and self-conscious, yet according to the date on Ron's file, these pictures had been taken long before I'd taken mine, only shortly after

Carla and I had first met. I didn't want to believe that the woman in the photographs I held in my hands was the same woman I'd photographed, but I knew I was deluding myself. Either Carla was a far better actor than I'd given her credit for, or she was able to change personalities to match the background, as though she were a human chameleon. For the chameleon, the ability to adapt was a survival trait. For Carla too perhaps.

"Maybe Ron drugged her, too," Bobbi suggested.

"I doubt it," I said. I found a large kraft envelope and slipped the file into it. "Let's go see your landlord now."

"What about the rest of this stuff?" Bobbi asked.

"What do you suggest?" I asked.

"Run it through a goddamned shredder."

When we got back to Sea Village, Bernard Simpson's crew was hard at it. One of the blue vans was parked near the embankment, air compressor thumping. Air hoses dropped over the edge of the boardwalk and snaked along the dock to the divers working under the hull of my house. Parked next to the blue van was a small ready-mix truck, a miniature version of the huge Ocean Cement trucks, that emitted a harsh chemical smell. A fat hose ran from a pump mounted on the back of the truck, over the embankment, along the dock, and through the front door of my house.

Mr. Oliphant and his Yorkshire terrier stood at the intersection of the main dock and my finger dock. Both wore expressions that were more sour than usual. When Bobbi and I got closer to my house I knew why. The stink of sewage hung in the air like a foul invisible fog.

"*Mister* McCall."

Mr. Oliphant's first name was Lionel, but no one called him Lionel. "Lionel," I said. I didn't know the dog's name, so I ignored him as he sniffed at my pant leg.

"This is really quite intolerable," Mr. Oliphant said.

"What is?"

"Why, this terrible smell."

"What smell?" I asked. I turned to Bobbi. "Do you smell anything? Is Daniel cooking dog again?"

She shook her head, trying hard to keep a straight face. She made a lousy straight man.

"*Mister* McCall," Mr. Oliphant said again, not amused. "I hope you realize the great inconvenience you're causing the other residents."

"Yes, I'm very sorry," I said. "It is really very inconsiderate of me. I should have just let my house sink."

"I have half a mind to call Mr. Silverman."

I wanted to ask him what he'd do if he had a whole mind, but said, "If it will make you feel better, by all means, call him. Give him my regards. Now, if you will excuse me."

The little purple pump had been decommissioned and sat quietly out of the way. We followed the fat hose from the ready-mix truck into the house. It disappeared into the bilge hatch.

Bernard Simpson emerged from the bilge. He was wearing a filter mask that made him look like a chubby praying mantis. Something was going on down in the bilge, something that made loud gurgling and splooshing sounds and was accompanied by the same harsh chemical smell I'd noticed by the ready-mix truck, mingled with the rank odour of human waste.

"Hadda disconnect the sewage system," Bernard said, taking off his mask.

261

"What's that other smell?" I asked.

"Hydraulic cement," he said. "Sorry for the inconvenience," he added, "but we should be done by tomorrow evening, the day after tomorrow at the latest. You got some place else you can stay? Insurance should cover it."

I locked the envelope containing Ron's photos of Carla in the filing cabinet in the upstairs office, collected the cordless telephone, and we went next door to Daniel's. Hilly and Beatrix were already there.

"Of course you can stay here," Daniel said. "The place is yours. I'm going to Halfmoon Bay for the weekend. To get away from the smell."

31

Friday morning, after a couple of portrait sittings, Bobbi went apartment hunting. The locksmith arrived shortly before lunch and changed the locks on the stairwell door and in the elevator. After lunch, I tilted my chair back, put my feet up, closed my eyes, and began composing an ad for a new lab tech. Around one-thirty I was roused from a half doze by the annoying warble of the telephone. I was tempted to let it ring through to the service – Mrs. Szymkowiak didn't work Fridays – but I picked it up. After all, it might be a client wanting a portrait of his prize-winning poodle.

It wasn't. It was Chris Hastings.

"Carla's here," he said. "On my boat."

"Lucky you. I hope you're not insured by Pacific Casualty."

"What?"

"Never mind."

"She's hurt," Hastings said.

"How bad?" I asked.

"Not seriously," he said. "She was beaten up."

"I'm sorry to hear that," I said. "But what do you want me to do?"

"She asked me to call you. She wants to see you."

"I don't think I want to see her," I said.

"She says you're the only one she can trust."

"I hope that didn't hurt your feelings," I said.

"Not at all," he replied. "I'm rather relieved, to tell you the truth."

"All right, I'll be there in an hour or so."

"She told me to tell you to make sure you're not followed."

Bobbi had taken the Land Rover. It took me twenty minutes to get back to Granville Island and pick up the Porsche. Keeping an eye out for a white Buick and cops, I opened it up across the Burrard Bridge, turning right onto Pacific, then right again and looping under the bridge approach onto Beach. I cruised along Beach toward Stanley Park. At Jervis I executed a quick right, then right again at Harwood and back down Bute to Beach. I did it again at Broughton. No one seemed to be following me.

I parked near the bicycle-rental place, locked up, and walked through the pedestrian tunnel under Georgia. To be on the safe side, I strolled around for a few minutes, watching the roller girls in their Spandex shorts and halter tops, then walked over to the marina. The gate was open. I wandered through the marina for five minutes, pretending to admire the boats, before finally stepping aboard the *Pendragon*.

Chris Hastings was mopping bird droppings off the sail covers. Reeny Lindsey, hair tied back and looking very young, was polishing chrome. Sailboats are not low-maintenance toys.

"She's below," Hastings said.

I went into the wheelhouse and knocked on the sliding cover over the hatch leading down to the main cabin.

"Who is it?" Carla's voice demanded.

"It's me," I said.

The hatch opened and Carla pointed a small automatic pistol at my face.

"Christ," I said, stepping back, heart thudding.

"Quick," she said. "Come in."

"Put that thing away first."

She did something to the pistol and shoved it into the side pocket of her motorcycle jacket. I went down the steep narrow steps of the companionway into the cabin. Carla closed and dogged the hatch.

By landlubber standards, the interior of *Pendragon* was cramped, but for a sailboat it was moderately roomy. It would have been roomier still had it not been for the books. Hardcovers and trades and paperbacks. They were stacked everywhere, on the deck, the chart table, the dining table, the shelf behind the long upholstered bench that ran the length of the salon, even in the galley. Any leftover space was filled with magazines, yellowing newspapers, and thick stacks of computer printouts.

"At least you won't run out of reading material," I said. I picked up a heavy hardcover volume, a high-school geography text.

"I'm not much of a reader," she said. Atop the pile of books on the chart table was a small colour television, flickering silently, a rerun of *Cheers*.

"Where did you get the gun?" I asked.

"It's Chris's."

What did Hastings need with a gun? I wondered. They weren't easy to come by in this country.

"It's awfully stuffy in here," I said. "Why don't we go out on deck and talk."

"No," she said, shaking her head. Her hair was growing back quickly, already black at the roots.

"It's time you started levelling with me, Carla. It'll be a stretch, I know, but give it a try. Who knows, you might find it refreshing."

"Yeah, right," she said.

"I mean it," I said. "No more bullshit. If you lie to me, I'm going to walk."

"And what have you got, a handy-dandy little Radio Shack lie detector? Your own personal polygraph?"

"If you lie," I said, "I'll know it."

Her indigo eyes flashed. "Tommy, if I put my mind to it, I could make you believe the sky was falling."

"If that's the way you want it, I wish you luck." I started toward the hatch.

"All right, fine," she said. "The truth. I need you to run an errand for me."

"I'm not interested."

"I can make it worth your while."

"You don't have anything I want," I said.

"At least listen, for chrissake."

"All right," I said. "I can do that." I made room on the bench by the end of the dining table and sat down. The table had a raised edge around it. It wouldn't do much to keep the books and magazines from sliding off in rough weather. Carla sat on a high stool by the chart table, hooked the heel of her scuffed cowboy boot over the foot rest, but when she leaned back against the table, she winced suddenly and sat up straight.

"Are you all right?" I asked.

"Yes," she said. "Just a little banged up."

"Let's see," I said.

She raised the hem of her T-shirt. There were dark bruises on her stomach and ribs. She slipped her jacket off her left shoulder, showed me fresh dollar-sized bruises on her upper arm, darker than the fading yellow of other, older bruises.

"It might be a good idea to have those ribs looked at."

"It hurts a bit when I take a deep breath," she said, shrugging the jacket back over her shoulder, "but nothing's broken."

"What happened?"

"I was on my way to a meeting when a couple of uglies tried to hustle me into a car. They weren't pros, thank god. Just guys who thought they could get by on size and bad manners. But I know a few nasty tricks. I got one in the kneecap with my boot heel and jabbed the other one in the eye." She held up her hands, waggling her fingers. Her fingernails were half an inch long.

"Who were they?"

"Thugs working for Vince. Who else would they be? The same ones who tried it last week."

"One of them wasn't missing a couple of fingers from his right hand, was he?"

"I didn't have time to count their fingers," she said, "but, no, I don't think so."

"Ryan told me you took something from him. Maybe if you gave it back . . ."

"I can't do that."

"You're going to make me ask, aren't you?" I said. "All right, what was it?"

"A videotape," she answered. I waited for her to elaborate. She found a cigarette pack on the chart table,

267

but it was empty. She crumpled it and tossed it in the general direction of the galley. Just as well; I wasn't particularly keen on the idea of her smoking around all that paper. I waited some more, the silence broken only by muted footfalls on the deck above us. Finally, she said, "It was a tape of . . . a well-known divorce lawyer extorting sex from his clients."

"Of course," I said. "It would be something as banal as blackmail. The lawyer," I added. "He wouldn't happen to be named Brian MacIlroy, would he?"

Her eyes widened. "How . . . ? Ah," she said. "Ginny." I nodded. "I took the tape from him four years ago. He's got a whole collection of them. The silly son of a bitch likes videotaping himself getting it on in his office. And he likes watching them with company."

"He should be more careful about the company he watches them with," I said.

She gave me a twisted smile.

"I take it that not all of the women with whom he has sex are completely willing."

"The tape shows him having sex with half a dozen women," she said. "But he forces one to give him a hand job by telling her that if she doesn't, he can guarantee she won't get custody of her children. Another agrees to have sex with him only after he threatens to arrange for some compromising information to fall into the hands of her husband's lawyer."

"You weren't planning to send the tape to the bar association I'll bet."

"What do you think?"

"Well," I said, "I won't say he doesn't deserve it."

"I told him that unless he deposited three thousand a month into an account I set up, he could kiss his legal practice goodbye. Not to mention his political ambitions."

"He paid, of course."

"Of course he paid. He isn't that stupid. Besides, he can afford it. He probably wrote it off on his taxes or charged it to his clients. I could have taken him for a lot more, but I'm not that greedy."

"Hmm," was my only comment on that. "So you weren't broke when we first met," I said.

"Sure I was," she said. "Three grand a month isn't much and, well, I had expenses."

"I'll bet," I said. "Okay, you'd been blackmailing MacIlroy to the tune of thirty-six grand a year for — what? — three years, when you hooked up with Ryan. Why did you give him the tape?"

"When Vince came up short on the Rainbow Mountain deal — the insurance company is dragging its feet about paying off on his wife's policy — I told him I knew someone who might be interested in buying in. Brian's always on the lookout for good investment opportunities for himself and his clients."

"And with the tape hanging over his head," I said, "how could he refuse?"

"Yeah," she said. "He couldn't."

"So he went along," I said. "That is, until he came up with a way to force you to double-cross Ryan. You were on your way to deliver the tape to MacIlroy when Ryan's goons jumped you, weren't you?"

"Christ," she said. "I should never have showed Vince that fucking tape."

"Don't whine, Carla," I said. "You cooked your own golden goose. You sicced Ryan on MacIlroy. Thirty-six thousand a year he could live with, but Wes Camacho told me Ryan needed two million to keep his end of Rainbow Mountain alive and that may have been just too much for him to handle, especially since he's got political ambitions and a by-election not too far down the road. How am I doing so far?"

"Oh, just great."

"What was it, Carla? What does MacIlroy have on you?"

"What makes you think he's got anything on me?"

I had to laugh at the self-righteous indignation in her voice. "You wouldn't have double-crossed Ryan for mere money. If Rainbow Mountain paid off, Ryan stood to make millions. No, it has to be something else."

"What difference does it make?" she snapped. "I don't need a fucking confessor."

"I can't promise I'll help you, but if you don't level with me, I can guarantee I won't."

She glared at me, blue eyes darkening almost to black. From somewhere toward the stern of *Pendragon* a pump kicked in, producing a low-pitched thrum that I could feel through soles of my shoes.

"All right," she said. "If you have to know, I killed someone."

32

My stomach clenched and my heart rattled against the walls of my chest. Had her tearful denial of complicity in Ryan's wife's death been just another lie?

"It happened in Acapulco," she said. "Five years ago. A crooked Mexican cop named Miguel Alvarez. I didn't mean to kill him, but he was trying his best to kill me. Somehow Brian found out about it and told me that if I didn't get Vince off his back, he'd tell Alvarez's friends where to find me. Alvarez was bent as they come and his friends were some very unpleasant people. I have no desire to spend the rest of my life in a Mexican prison or chained to a crib in a Mexican whorehouse."

"How did you get mixed up with a corrupt Mexican cop?" I asked.

"He was a business associate of Frank's."

It didn't require much imagination to deduce the sort of business Poole and a corrupt Mexican cop were into.

"You were smuggling drugs in the boats you were transporting for Frank Poole."

Value systems are curious things. That Carla was a liar and a thief and a blackmailer, that she'd apparently killed one man and had possibly been involved in the death of Ryan's wife, that she'd twice been arrested for prostitution, none of that disturbed me half as much as learning that she'd been involved in drug trafficking.

Seeing something in my face, she said, "You're not going to get all self-righteous on me now are you, Tommy? It was just a little grass."

"That makes it all right?"

"People have been using naturally occurring drugs like marijuana, peyote, opium, or coca for as long as they've been using alcohol," she said. "Maybe even longer."

"Don't try to rationalize it," I said.

"And don't you be such a fucking hypocrite," she said. "Like you've never fudged on your income tax a little."

"There's a difference between that and smuggling dope," I said.

"Yeah? What is it?"

"A matter of degree."

"Right," she said sourly. "Like being a little bit pregnant."

This wasn't getting us anywhere. "Why was Alvarez trying to kill you?" I asked. "Surely you weren't so stupid as to try to rip him off."

"No," she replied. "Alvarez had been trying to get me into the sack for months. He was a pig, but one night, when I was down there to pick up a boat, we were at a party and I let him talk me into going back to his boat with him. I didn't make it easy for him, though, and by the end of the evening he was so loaded on booze and coke he could hardly walk. I helped him to his boat, put him to bed, then crashed in the galley.

"About four in the morning I heard someone banging around in the cabin. It was Alvarez. He was tearing the place apart and ranting in Spanish about something, I'm not sure what. I tried to calm him down, but he started hitting me and throwing me around the cabin. I tried to get away, but he grabbed me, threw me down, and fell on top of me, knocking the wind out of me. I must have blacked out for a second or two, because the next thing I knew he was standing over me. He had a speargun in his hands and was pressing the tip of the spear against my throat. I could feel the blood running down my neck." She put her hand to her throat.

"What happened next isn't too clear," she went on. "I think I screamed and kicked him. I remember scrambling toward the hatch, but he caught me and pulled me back. All the time he's crying and babbling in Spanish. He had a diver's knife and showed me how sharp it was by slashing his arm. I knew then he was going to kill me. I told him I'd do anything he wanted, but he didn't hear me. The speargun was lying on the deck. I picked it up. It had a handle like a pistol. I pointed it at him. He just laughed and came at me with the knife. I pulled the trigger and the spear went straight into his mouth.

"It was awful," she said. "He staggered around, making these horrible choking sounds and spraying blood everywhere and trying to pull the spear out. But I could see these spring-loaded barbs sticking out of the back of his neck. Then he fell, thrashed around for a few seconds, and lay still. I thought he was dead, but when I checked, he was still breathing. I didn't know what to do, so I went up on deck and waited."

"Waited for what?" I asked. A feeling of unreality crept over me like a bitter January fog.

Carla looked at me. "For him to die," she said. "What do you think?"

"Why didn't you call for an ambulance, take him to the hospital?" I asked.

"He was into more than just dope and he had a lot of very rough friends. If he died, I'd be arrested for sure, maybe even killed. And if he lived . . ." She shrugged. "I couldn't very well count on him being grateful for saving his life."

"What did you do?"

"I thought about taking the boat out a few miles and scuttling it or setting the auto-pilot on a course to Hawaii, but I just turned the air-conditioning up full blast, locked up, and got the hell out of there. I figured it would be a couple of days at least before anyone went looking for him, plenty of time for me to get out of the country. I called Chris and he wired me some money."

It was warm in the saloon of Hastings's boat, but I was as cold as if it were mid-winter.

"What about Frank Poole?" I asked.

"What about him?"

"Did MacIlroy's investigation uncover him too?"

She shook her head. "He kept a low profile," she said. "He hardly ever went down there."

"Does he know about Alvarez?"

"That I killed him? Hell, no. He'd've sold me out to Alvarez's pals a long time ago."

I took a deep, deep breath and blew it out quickly, emptying my lungs, but it did nothing to relieve the tension. I felt as though a dull spike had been hammered into the base of my skull, and the ache spread down my back and across my shoulders.

"Will you help me?" she said. "There's no one else I can trust."

"I don't know," I said.

"All you have to do is deliver the tape to MacIlroy and pick up a package."

"So Ryan's thugs can beat up on me instead. No thanks."

"They probably won't bother you," she said. "It's me they're looking for."

"I'm not sure 'probably' is good enough," I said. "What's in the package?"

"The money I mentioned," she said. "Compensation for my trouble."

"How much?"

"Fifty thousand," she said. "He didn't want to pay, but I told him if he didn't I was prepared to take my chances with Alvarez's friends. And then he'd either be out two million bucks or facing disbarment. It was a small price. C'mon, Tommy, I'll just make a call and set up another meeting. You be there, make the exchange, and bring the money here. Once I've got the money, Chris has arranged for a boat to take me out of here." She got up and went to a locker below the chart table, from which she removed a padded envelope. Handing it to me, she said, "Go ahead, take a look, if you want." She pointed to the little television. It had a tape slot next to the screen.

"Thanks," I said. "I'll pass. You've kept a copy, of course."

"I have to protect myself, don't I?"

"Absolutely," I said.

"I'll pay you," she said. "Five thousand dollars, how's that? Not bad for a couple of hours of your time."

I could use the money, I thought, but I said, "I don't want your money."

"What do you want?"

"I want you out of my life. For good."

"Aw, Tommy," she said, pouting. "I'm hurt. Fine," she added. "Do me this favour and you'll never see me again."

"I should know better," I said. "All right, make your call."

She found the handset of a cordless telephone and punched in a number. "It's me," she said a few seconds later. After a pause, she said, "Yeah, well, circumstances beyond my control and all that. But I'm sending someone with the tape. His name's Tommy McCall. You just say where and when." She listened, then said, "He'll be there," and hung up.

She wrote something on the corner of a magazine cover, tore it off, and handed it to me. It was a down-town address, one of the office towers near Canada Place. "Be at Brian's office at five today," she said.

Carla stood close to me at the hatch, kissed me on the cheek. She smelled of soap and shampoo and musk. Even on the run, Carla managed to keep herself cat-clean.

"Thanks, Tommy," she said. "You're a sport."

"I'm an idiot," I said.

33

I had a couple of hours to kill before my appointment with MacIlroy. I thought about going back to the studio, but went home instead. After locking up the Porsche, I dropped by the dive shop to see if Francine was around, but she was in the pool conducting a class. I hadn't spoken to her since returning from Whistler, but had left a couple of messages, which she hadn't returned, and I wondered if something was wrong. My pulse quickened just thinking about her and that was not a good sign. Normally, that happens to me only when I fall in love, and I didn't want to fall in love with Francine. Of course, I've been known to fall in love involuntarily, so I shouldn't have been surprised.

The Land Rover was parked illegally in a space reserved for staff of the art college. As usual in the summer, the free parking lot was full to bursting and some tourist with Seattle plates had parked in my reserved slot. There was no sign of Bernard Simpson and his crew. The flotation bags were still in place under the hull, but most of the other equipment had been removed. I patted the purple pump, congratulated it for a job well done, and let myself into my house. I could still detect the residual chemical odour of the hydraulic cement, but I could no longer smell sewage. The bilge hatch was closed and everything looked level. I went into the kitchen. Bobbi was sitting at the kitchen table with the newspaper spread out in front of her, opened to the classified section.

"How'd it go?" I asked her.

"Not good," she said. "How would you feel about a permanent boarder?"

"Ah . . ."

"Don't panic," she said. "I'm just kidding."

"Thank god," I said.

She made a face, then said, "Speaking of panic, Nigel called. He's got a quick and dirty job he needs on his desk first thing Monday morning. Product beauty shots. Looks like we're going to have to work tomorrow."

"Swell," I said.

"Oh, yeah, and Mr. Baggins said they'd be taking out the flotation things tomorrow."

"Who?"

"Mr. Baggins, the contractor?"

"His name is Bernie Simpson," I said.

"I thought you said his name was Fred Baggins or something."

"Bobbi, haven't you ever read *Lord of the Rings?*"

"The story about the kids stranded on the island?" She shook her head. "I saw the movie, though."

After I explained who Frodo Baggins was, I went upstairs and took a shower, then headed downtown for my appointment, telling Bobbi on my way out that I was taking the Land Rover before it was towed away.

The Friday afternoon traffic was horrendous, but by five I was cooling my heels in the spacious but austere reception area of the offices of MacIlroy & Raymond, Attorneys at Law, watching the trim rump of the flaxen-haired thirty-something receptionist as she fed and watered the dozen or so potted African violets scattered about the room. When she came near me to tend the plants on the coffee table I caught a whiff of her perfume, so heavy and sweet it made me want to lick her. I controlled myself; she probably wouldn't have understood. At five-fifteen, without any apparent communication from her boss, she rose from her post behind the reception desk, announced that Mr. MacIlroy would see me now, and opened the door to the inner office.

Brian MacIlroy was tall and sleek, carefully coiffed and impeccably tailored. The only jarring note was thick dark-rimmed eyeglasses, through which his pale hazel eyes appeared coldly reptilian. He stood behind a huge, dark wood desk that was bare except for a modern black-and-chrome telephone, an antique wood-and-brass desk set, and a thin buff business envelope.

"Come in, Mr. McCall," he said as the door hissed closed behind me.

MacIlroy's office resembled my lawyer's office like my home resembled the Queen of England's – that is, not at all. It was a matter of scale. Glenda had a nice antique partner's desk, a little too big for her office and usually piled high with files, but MacIlroy's desk was the size of a snooker table. And there was plenty of room left over for the two matching four-seat leather sofas that faced each other across a massive black marble coffee table.

"I assume you have brought the, ah, package." His voice was as smooth and unctuous as his smile was thin and icy.

"Yes," I replied, showing him the padded envelope. I looked around the office, wondering where the video camera was hidden. Next to a bar that would have put a four-star resort hotel to shame, there was a tall, mirror-fronted cabinet. It was positioned directly opposite one of the big leather sofas. Perfect.

"I am a busy man, Mr. McCall," MacIlroy said.

I said, "You've got Carla's money?"

"Of course," he said, indicating the slim buff envelope.

I placed my package on the desk and slid it toward him. It stopped about two thirds of the way across, well within his reach, but he didn't touch it.

"Don't you want to check it?" I asked.

"It's not necessary," he said. "It's really just a symbolic gesture. I have no doubt Carla has kept a copy as a guarantee of good faith."

I picked up the envelope.

"You look disappointed," he said.

"I expected a bigger bundle."

"It's a cashier's cheque," he said.

"Oh," I said.

I slipped the envelope into the inside pocket of my jacket. I felt I ought to say something snappy, but settled for, "Well, I won't take any more of your time."

He surprised me then by coming around the big desk and walking me to the door. He opened the door. "Good day, Mr. McCall," he said.

"Ah, thanks," I said, and we shook hands. If he expected to get anywhere in politics he was going to have to do something about his handshake.

The door closed silently behind me. I looked at the sweet-smelling receptionist and sneezed suddenly.

"God bless you," she said and offered me a box of pink tissues.

I didn't waste any time on evasive tactics this time and drove straight north on Commissioner toward Stanley Park and the marina. As I turned onto Cardero, the telephone burbled, startling me so thoroughly I almost side-swiped a truck. I'd had a cellular telephone installed a few months ago, after a breakdown had stranded Bobbi and me close to the middle of nowhere. I paid the minimum monthly fee and used it for emergencies only. So far none had arisen and I'd forgotten all about it. And almost forgotten how to answer it.

I fumbled at the hands-free switch. "Yes, hello," I said. "Hello."

"Don't shout," Bobbi said. "Boss, you'd better get home toot sweet."

Panic closed an icy fist around my heart. I pulled off to the side of the road and stopped, ignoring the bleat of horns, shouts and upraised digits. "What is it? Is it Hilly?"

"No, Hilly's fine. It's your parents. They – your father – your mother says she caught him with another woman."

"Give me that," I heard my mother snap. "Thomas, is that you?"

"Yes, of course it's me. What's going on?"

"It's your father," she said. "He's – I've never been so humiliated in all my life."

"Oh, for god's sake, Eleanor," I heard my father say. "Will you for once in your life shut the hell up and listen."

Bobbi came back on the line. "Boss," she said imploringly.

"I've got something to take care of," I said. "I'll be back as soon as I can."

"I don't think this can wait," she said. "Oh, god."

"What?"

"Your sister's here."

34

I t was after midnight before my parents and my sister left. I checked on Hilly – she and Beatrix were fast asleep – then went into the kitchen. Bobbi was removing dishes from the dishwasher and putting them away. I'd tried calling Carla, to reassure her that all was well and that I'd be there as soon as I could, but Chris Hastings's number was unlisted.

"I'm sorry you had to put up with all that," I said. "Thanks for taking Hilly out."

"I like your family," Bobbi said. "But your mother is silly and self-indulgent and your sister isn't much better."

"Neither of them has had much opportunity to be anything else," I said.

"And your father," she added. "My dad is bad, but your father is so stiff-necked he must have to sit down to pee."

"They're quite a pair," I agreed.

"Do you think either of them has ever really listened to what the other was saying?"

"Probably not. But at least Maggie got them to agree to see a counsellor."

"Do you think he was having an affair with her?"

"No," I said. "I think she really was doing his astrological chart." I looked at my watch. "Look, I know it's late, but I've got an errand to run. Will you be all right?"

"Of course," Bobbi said. "Go do your errand."

I drove to Coal Harbour, parked in the near-empty lot at the northeast corner of Devonian Harbour Park near Denman, and walked to the Harbour Ferries Marina. It was half past midnight and the still waters of Coal Harbour were ablaze with reflected light. The bulbs strung from the masts of the sailboats in the marina swayed with the slow roll of the boats. Dance music drifted across the water from the brightly lit clubhouse of the Vancouver Rowing Club, perched on stilts above the harbour.

Pendragon showed no lights, but there was plenty of light spilling from the other boats and the low lamps along the docks. I went aboard and into the pilothouse. The hatch was partly open, light shining through the gap. I knocked and waited for an answer. When none was forthcoming, I knocked again, harder, and said, "Hello. Is anyone there?"

There was still no answer. I opened the hatch and went below.

The only light came from a single bulkhead-mounted lamp in the galley, but I could see that the main salon was a mess. The books and magazines and newspapers that had covered every flat surface were now mostly spilled onto the deck. The little TV was half buried, face up, screen cracked, tape-slot door torn off. The galley and chart lockers hung open, contents strewn across the carpet of paper. There was no sign of

Carla, nor of Hastings or Reeny Lindsey. Something glowed greenish amid the paper. I bent and picked up Hastings's little cellular telephone. The keypad was still illuminated but the flip-down microphone hung by a short length of flat ribbon cable and the liquid crystal display screen was cracked and blackened.

It seemed reasonable at this point to start worrying, and even maybe get a little scared. So I did. Both.

"Carla," I called out, unconsciously lowering my voice. Louder, I called, "Hastings." There was no answer from either.

I went forward, picking my way through the sea of paper, magazine and book spines cracking underfoot, to the passageway that led to the staterooms. I found a switch on the bulkhead near the passageway and flipped it. An overhead fluorescent flickered to life. The additional light revealed nothing but more mess. Someone had made a very thorough search of the boat.

The passageway was barely wider than my shoulders and maybe ten feet long. There were two narrow louvred doors on the left, storage lockers on the right, and another louvred door at the forward end. The deck of the passageway was littered with clothing, probably the contents of the lockers. I carefully opened the first door. The room beyond was dark, but my nose told me it was the head. I turned on the light. There was a stainless-steel toilet, seat up, a stainless-steel washbasin built into the bulkhead, and a shower stall the size of a telephone booth. I slid the shower curtain aside. No dead bodies. No live ones either. I turned off the light and closed the door.

The next door opened onto a small stateroom containing a built-in berth, rumpled and unmade, a small dresser-cum-writing-desk, a wooden captain's chair, and a narrow wardrobe. I turned on the lamp over the desk. Except for the unmade bed, the stateroom did not look as though it had been used much lately. There was a thin film of smudged dust on the top of the desk. The drawers under the bunk were open and empty.

I returned to the passageway and went to the door at the forward end. The skin of the back of my neck felt as though it were being pricked by a million tiny hot needles and my hand was slick with perspiration as I gripped the handle. With a pounding heart and dry mouth, afraid of what I would find, I turned the handle.

They were on the wide double berth, back-to-back, wrists and ankles bound together with silver-grey duct tape, arms outstretched and secured with loops of tape to the head of the berth, ankles likewise secured to the foot. Chris Hastings lay facing me, a length of duct tape wound around his head, covering his mouth. His eyes were closed. Reeny Lindsey's long blond hair spilled across his shoulder, limp and stringy.

I stood rooted in the doorway of the stateroom, trying to get my mind around the scene before me, but it was as if I had suddenly become incapable of processing sensory input, of translating the data collected by my eyes into an image my brain could understand. Something was wrong, I knew that much, but it took me a few moments to realize what. Then I became aware of the sour reek of urine.

I moved to the edge of the bed and tried to remove the tape from Hastings's mouth. At my touch his eyes half opened and he thrashed weakly, breathing noisily and messily through his nose. Without regard for his comfort, I found the free end of the tape and quickly unwound it from his head, taking a hank of hair with it. When I tore the tape from his face he opened his mouth wide and breathed with great heaving gasps.

Leaning over him, I unwrapped the tape from Reeny's head. She whimpered fretfully when the tape pulled her hair, like a child awakened from a disturbing dream, but otherwise did not respond.

"Is she all right?" Hastings asked, voice hoarse.

"I don't know," I said as I started to unwind the tape from their wrists. "I think so." Their hands were white with reduced circulation and cold to my touch. Their fingers were intertwined.

When I'd removed the tape from their wrists, Hastings sat up and tried to free their ankles, but his fingers would not co-operate. I did it for him. Once free, he lifted Reeny in his arms, stroked her hair with clumsy fingers, and spoke her name. She moaned fitfully, but did not rouse. Her lips were dry and cracked and the skin of her face where the tape had been was an angry red. The crotch of her faded jeans was dark with urine.

"What happened?" I asked. "Where's Carla?"

"They took her," he said.

"Who?"

"Two men." He rubbed Reeny's pale hands, trying to restore circulation. She made small mewing noises of complaint.

"You should call an ambulance for her," I said. "And the police."

"No police," he said.

I helped him lay her down on the bed and elevate her feet. Her breathing was regular and her colour was good, except for her hands.

"What happened here?" I asked again, following him to the main cabin.

"Christ," he said, when he saw the mess. He picked up the cellular telephone from the table where I'd placed it, punched the buttons, then tossed it aside.

"Hastings, for chrissake. What happened?"

"Two men came aboard," he said as he kicked through the paper on the deck. "It was about ten o'clock, I guess. Reeny and I were in the wheelhouse. Carla was in her cabin. One of the men took Reeny and me to the stateroom and taped us together. Ah," he said, finding the cordless phone.

"Chris?" Irene Lindsey called. "Chris? Where are you?"

He hurried to the master stateroom. I followed. Reeny was sitting up, looking dazed, eyes heavy-lidded and a little crossed. Hastings went to her.

"Are you all right?" he asked.

"I have an awful headache," she said, words a little slurred. "And I wet myself."

"C'mon, let's get you cleaned up," Hastings said. He helped her to her feet. She was wobbly, but managed to stand on her own. When he started to strip her clothes off, I left the room and waited impatiently in the salon. I began picking up books and magazines, stacking them on the table.

35

The clock in the radio display read 2:44 as I pulled the Land Rover into my parking space and turned off the engine. I sat in the quietness, staring at the iridescent glow of the city lights on the other side of False Creek. Chris Hastings hadn't been able to tell me much more about Carla's abduction. The men who'd boarded *Pendragon* hadn't spoken much, save to order Hastings and Reeny below. They hadn't shown guns, and when, with more bravado than good sense, Hastings had demanded to know what they wanted, one of them had simply grabbed him and thrown him through the hatch as if he were made of straw. Not that it was likely to do me much good, but Hastings and Reeny were able to give me a good description of them: big, rough-looking white men, one of whom had had a surgical patch over one eye. Both were in their late forties or early fifties, outdoor types, judging from their deep tans; very hard and strong. The man without the eye patch, who'd taped them to the berth, had had hands like hardwood, Reeny had added. And unpleasant body odour.

When I'd asked if they could have been loggers, Hastings had looked at me curiously for a second or two before answering. "More likely sailors or dock workers," he'd said. "They used words like 'below' and 'berth.'"

I locked up the Land Rover and walked toward the ramp. It seemed a safe bet that they'd been looking for MacIlroy's videotape. Their timing had been off, though, so they'd taken Carla instead. Why? Or had she gone with them willingly? They, or she, had gone to the trouble of packing her belongings. Hastings's little pistol was also missing.

As I walked down the ramp a sudden chill sent shivers up my spine. Something moved in my peripheral vision and I jerked around, heart in my throat, but it was my own shadow, cast by the lamp over the gate. With nervous fingers I punched the code into the gate lock and twisted the knob. Nothing happened. I took a deep breath and tried again. This time I got it right. Closing the gate behind me, I walked quickly along the dock toward my house, taking my keys out of my pocket. I fumbled and dropped them. They skittered along the rough surface of the dock, stopping just inches from the edge. I stooped quickly to pick them up and almost knocked them into the water. Straightening, clutching the keys in my fist, I almost ran the rest of the way to my house.

"Get a grip," I said aloud as I tried to insert the wrong key into the lock. I found the right key and inserted it.

A hand clasped the back my neck and shoved my face against the door. Something hard pressed painfully into the small of my back.

"Don't do anything stupid," a soft, cold voice said, the pressure on my neck increasing briefly.

Great advice. Just too bloody late. It felt like I was being held by a huge pincer or the claw of some great bird.

"Open the door," the voice said. The pressure on my neck eased slightly, but the claw maintained its grip. "Slowly."

I turned the key. The deadbolt thunked softly. "It's double locked," I said hoarsely. "I have to find the other key."

The claw released my neck, shifting its grip to my shoulder. "Careful," the voice warned.

My hands were shaking so badly now, I almost dropped the keys again. Biting my lip to control the trembling, I finally got the key into the lock. I twisted the key and eased the door open.

"No noise," the voice said quietly as the pressure in the small of my back pushed me into the foyer. "Let's not wake anyone up. Okay?"

"No problem," I said. The door closed behind me.

Bobbi had left the vestibule light on. I looked to my right. In the decorative mirror on the wall next to the entrance to the living room I saw standing behind me a man of average height and ordinary appearance. He glanced into the mirror and smiled, a broad and friendly smile, but his eyes were quick and cold. The first time I'd seen him he had been on the boardwalk, aiming a video camera at me. Now he held a blue-steel revolver in his good left hand. All things considered, I preferred the camera.

"Who are you?" I asked, turning around to face him. He backed up a couple of steps. "What do you want?"

"I just need a few minutes of your time," he answered quietly. His voice was different now, soft and well modulated, slightly reminiscent of a CBC television newscaster, as bland and nondescript as his appearance. "I'm a private investigator," he added, opening his jacket and snapping the revolver into a holster slung upside-down under his right arm. "Sorry about the melodramatic introduction, but I didn't want you making a fuss out on the dock. My name is —"

"William Henderson," I said, interrupting him.

His face tightened, then relaxed. "Not bad," he said. "You got the Avis office to run the licence-plate number of the rental car I used in Whistler. I'm impressed. As a rule they'll only do that for the police." He shrugged. "Those are the kinds of variables you can never anticipate; they make this business interesting. Just in case you're interested, Henderson isn't my real name. My real name's Jack Thompson."

"If you're a private investigator," I said, "you have identification. Let's see it."

"Sure," he said. He took out his wallet and showed me an official-looking card, complete with thumbnail-sized photo and Ontario provincial seal, that identified him as John Arthur Thompson, licensed investigator. With very little effort I could have made one up in the lab that looked just as authentic. He handed me a business card. It read, "J.A. Thompson, Investigations," with a Toronto address.

"Who are you working for?"

He put his wallet away. "I've been retained by Margaret Giordini, Vincent Ryan's former sister-in-law, to prove that Ryan is guilty of conspiracy in the death of Mrs. Elizabeth Giordini Ryan."

"So what do you want with me?"

"How about we get comfortable?" He extended his clawlike right hand toward the living room. "Maybe we'll have a drink. I don't know about you, but I could use one."

"Just tell me what you want," I said. "It's been a long day and I'm in no mood to be sociable."

"I want you to tell me where I can find Carla Bergman," he said.

"And why would I do that?"

"Because eventually Vince Ryan is going to catch up with her. When he does, he's most likely going to kill her."

36

"Ryan set up the hit on his wife through Petey Deguire," Thompson said, holding a glass of Scotch in his clawlike hand. "Deguire is Carla's stepbrother. He was a small-time coke dealer in the resort area north of Montreal until about six years ago. Another dealer tried to move in on his turf and he whanged the fat end of a pool cue off the side of the guy's head. Actually, Carla and Petey were a little more than just stepbrother and -sister; when Carla was sixteen her mother threw them both out of the house when she came home from work and caught them screwing their little brains out." He sipped his Scotch.

I wasn't drinking. My eyes burned with fatigue and my legs twitched from lack of sleep. A drink would have put me right out. "You're telling me that Carla conspired with Ryan to kill his wife by putting him in touch with her stepbrother?"

"Maybe she did, maybe she didn't," Thompson said. "I don't care. My client is only interested in Ryan. He's the one who ordered the hit. But Petey won't cooperate unless I can guarantee him that Carla won't be prosecuted and the only way I can do that is to convince her to testify that Ryan ordered the hit."

"What if she doesn't know anything?"

"And what are the chances of that? This isn't Miss Goody Two-Shoes we're talking about here, y'know. What do you know about her past?"

"Not much," I replied. Too much, I thought to myself.

"When her mother threw her and Petey out," Thompson said, "they went to Montreal, where Petey's old man ran an agency that booked strippers and nude dancers into clubs and hotels in Quebec and eastern Ontario. Deguire Sr. also dealt a little, which is how Petey got into the business. Carla worked the exotic-dance circuit for a couple of years, then one day she cleaned out Deguire's office safe and split for Toronto, where she changed her name – her real name is Charlotte Bergeron – and went into business for herself. By the time she was twenty she'd been busted a couple of times for soliciting. For a while she and a two-bit con man and coke addict named Quentin Holmes ran a series of multi-level marketing scams, but she got tired of him snorting everything they made and ratted him out to the cops.

"After that she worked at a string of nowhere jobs – waiting tables, tending bar, stripping, door-to-door sales, whatever. She even went back to school and studied business administration. But the straight and narrow was not for our Carla. Somewhere along the line she'd learned how to sail and for a couple of years worked the marina circuit all up and down the West Coast, during which time – you're gonna love this, I know I do – she allegedly committed at least one act of piracy on the high seas."

Did he not know about her drug-smuggling activities or Alvarez's death? Or was he simply keeping that information to himself? I wasn't going to ask.

"She told me she didn't have anything to do with Ryan's wife's death and I believe her," I said.

"Have I also mentioned that she's an exceptionally gifted liar?" Thompson said. "Look, I don't care one way or another. Sooner or later the cops will get lucky and pick up the psycho Ryan hired to off his wife. When they do, the guy will roll over on Ryan faster than you can say electroshock therapy, but my client isn't willing to wait that long. If I can get Carla to agree to testify, Petey will testify, and we can nail the son of a bitch. All you have to do is take me to her."

"I don't know where she is."

"You're not doing her any favours, y'know. If she doesn't help bang the lid down on Ryan, she'll go down with him. I want to at least give her the choice."

"It may be too late," I said. I told him what I'd found when I'd got back to Hastings's boat. "From the descriptions Hastings and his girlfriend gave me, they sound like the same two men who'd tried to abduct her earlier in the day. She assumed they worked for Ryan."

"You say that like you don't think they do."

"Ryan is in business with some old money in Whistler. Before it became a ski resort, it was logging country. There still is considerable logging activity in the area. According to Hastings, though, the men who abducted Carla used some nautical terms the average logger might not be familiar with."

"So Ryan hired sailors."

"Maybe," I agreed. "On the other hand, maybe you and Ryan aren't the only people interested in finding Carla."

I was awakened at quarter to eight by the smell of coffee. "You look like death," Bobbi said when I joined her and Hilly in the kitchen.

"Thanks," I said, pouring coffee. It was nice having someone around to make the coffee.

Hilly was eating toaster waffles floating in syrup. "You're up early," I said.

"I'm going to see the Lynn Canyon suspension bridge with Courtney and her mom and dad," she said. She stuffed half a waffle into her mouth and stood up. "An ah ate," she added, dribbling syrup. "Ould ou ook atter Eetrish?"

"Yes," Bobbi said. "Finish your milk."

She did, wiped her mouth with a serviette and left.

"Who were you talking to last night?" Bobbi asked as she poured us more coffee.

"Our friend in the white Buick," I said. She sat facing me across the table. I gave her a brief rundown, leaving out any mention of Carla's cashier's cheque, now securely locked in the little safe Howie had had installed under the floor of the pantry.

"I don't wish Carla any harm, of course," Bobbi said, "but you should be grateful you're out of it now."

But was I? I wondered, trying to drink coffee and yawn at the same time – not easy.

"I can handle things this morning," Bobbi said. "Why don't you go back to bed?"

So I did, and slept until awakened at ten-thirty by Bernard Simpson and his crew as they began to remove the flotation bags from under the house. The job was done; now all I had to do was figure out how to pay for it. By eleven-fifteen I was waiting on the ferry dock by the Public Market, eyes hot and grainy behind dark glasses and feeling as though I were standing at an odd angle. I must have looked pretty bad too; an elderly tourist couple with his-and-her video cameras – his was standard black, hers was a bright yellow – didn't seem to want to stand too close to me.

Francine pulled up to the dock in a battered orange Zodiac. She was wearing ragged cut-offs and a faded string bikini top, and was sitting on the backrest of the driver's seat. The big outboard burbled and stank.

"Hiya, guy," she said. "Can I offer you a ride?" She smiled brightly as the old man aimed his video camera at her.

"Uh, sure," I said. I stepped aboard, lost my balance and sat down heavily in the passenger seat.

The old lady slapped her husband on the arm and he lowered his camera.

"Where to?" Francine asked, squinting at me from under the brim of a threadbare and water-stained cap. The tops of her broad, muscular shoulders were sunburned and peeling.

"The Hornby Street ferry dock will be fine," I said.

"You okay?" she asked, pushing the throttle forward and moving slowly away from the dock, keeping well below the five-knot speed limit. "You look like you've had a rough night."

"You could say that," I said.

She was silent for half a minute, which took us most of the way across False Creek.

"Chuck said you came by the shop," she said without looking at me, watching the boat traffic in the narrow inlet. "I'm sorry I haven't been around much lately."

"That's okay," I said. "I've been pretty busy."

She manoeuvred the Zodiac up to the Hornby Street ferry dock. "I'm taking a dive group up Indian Arm inlet tomorrow," she said, "but I'm free on Sunday. How would you and Hilly like to go on a picnic or something?"

"That sounds terrific," I said. "Would you like to come for dinner tonight? We can work out the details then."

"Sure," she said. "I'd like that."

"Say around six?"

"All right," she said as I clambered onto the dock. "See you later."

37

By the time I got to the studio, Bobbi had finished the product shoot and was taking the films out of the processor. When they were dry we sent them to Nigel. Bobbi said that there were a couple of places she wanted to check out, but so far the hunt for an apartment she could afford was not going well. I kept my thoughts to myself, but ever since she'd raised the subject, I'd been wondering what it would be like to have Bobbi as a full-time roommate. She was quiet and clean and it wouldn't hurt for me to try to cut back on my expenses. But I also wondered what having a female roommate would do to my social life. Haw. What social life?

I spent the afternoon puttering around the studio and the lab, cleaning up, trying not to think about Carla and what might have happened to her. At four I went home. There was no one there except Beatrix, and she was asleep in her cage.

For want of anything better to do, I got the Porsche out and drove to Coal Harbour. Reeny Lindsey was sitting in the pilothouse, out of the sun, drinking tea and looking drawn, her skin dry, dark shadows under her eyes. Chris was somewhere around, she said dully.

When I asked her how things were going she said that Chris was talking about selling the *Pendragon* and moving to Arizona or New Mexico. I told her that I knew how he felt and she said that running away wasn't the answer.

"What's he running away from?" I asked.

"Himself," she said, tears leaking from the corners of her beautiful deep-set eyes. "Me."

"You? Why you?"

"He's ashamed of himself for not being able to protect me. I told him he was being silly and asked him if he thought he was supposed to be able to protect me from the Big One when it hits. He said, 'Yes.'" She shook her head.

I'd come to see if there was anything else she or Hastings could tell me about the men who'd come aboard last night, but I couldn't bring myself to ask. I just sat with her, listening to the creak and rattle of the boats as the tide came in.

Hastings ducked into the pilothouse. His hair was tangled and his face was bristly with grey stubble. He looked as though he'd aged ten years in a few hours.

"Wanna buy a boat?" he said to me, his breath sour.

"No, thanks," I said. "I have enough trouble keeping my house afloat."

He cocked an eyebrow, but then shrugged and said, "Want a beer?"

"Sure. Thanks."

He went below and returned with a couple of cans of Kokanee. Reeny stood up abruptly and went below.

"Wha'd I say?" Hastings said.

"Nothing," I said. "Maybe that's the problem." He flinched as though I'd hit him. "Look," I said. "What happened last night wasn't your fault. You couldn't have done anything to prevent it."

"I know," he said, pulling the tab on his beer. "But knowing it doesn't seem to make any difference."

"Maybe if you'd talk to her about it."

"I just can't seem to bring myself to do that."

He tipped his head back and downed most of the can, Adam's apple bobbing as he swallowed. I put my unopened can on the deck. Suddenly I didn't want it.

"If you don't talk to her," I said, "you'll lose her."

"Yeah, well, if that happens, it happens." He drank the rest of his beer.

"You'd be a bloody fool to let it," I said.

"Hey, get off my case, McCall."

I stood up. "See you around," I said.

It was six o'clock when I got back to Granville Island. Someone had parked in my private space again. It happens a lot — there must be a high rate of illiteracy amongst tourists — but it's usually more trouble than it's worth to have them towed. I cruised through the free parking lot and got lucky, finding a spot by the old freight crane. I thought I'd take Hilly and Bobbi and Francine out for dinner. Someplace nice, like Alaska. Running away from your problems works if you leave them behind and don't come back.

Bobbi was in the kitchen, chopping celery into tiny bits.

"Hi, honey, I'm home."

"Well, it's about time," she said. "You could have at least called and warned me that you'd invited someone to dinner." She scraped the chopped celery into a bowl containing equally finely chopped onions and green pepper.

"Oops. Sorry, forgot."

"Hilly and Francine are upstairs," she said. "She's nice," she added. "God knows what she sees in you."

There was a package of long-grain rice and a clear plastic tub of chicken livers on the counter, next to an unlabelled jar of evil-looking dark-brown paste and a collection of little plastic bags of herbs and spices: thyme, oregano, garlic powder, onion powder, cayenne, and cracked black pepper.

"I went shopping," she said.

"So I see. What are you making?"

"Cajun dirty rice."

"Yum. Where's the ground pork?"

"I leave that out," she said. "Too much fat."

Francine and Hilly came downstairs. Beatrix flowed down the steps behind them, a living Slinky, the bell on her collar tinkling. Francine came into the kitchen. Her short sun-bleached hair was slicked back and lacquered into place. The style accentuated the strong angles of her face. She was wearing jeans and an oversized raw cotton shirt with the top two buttons open, de-emphasizing the breadth of her shoulders. I was about to tell her how nice she looked, when the phone rang.

"McCall?" a man's voice said when I answered.

"Yes."

"I got a friend of yours here. She wants to say hello."

"Tommy –"

"That's enough. You still there, McCall?"

"I'm here." I recognized the voice. It was Frank Poole. "What do you want?"

"Don't be a jerk. You know what I want."

"The money?"

"Yeah, the money. What the fuck d'you think? Just bring it and everything'll be hunky-dorey. Fuck around, you'll just piss me off and I'll have to take it out on your girlfriend here. You don't want me to have to do that, do you? She won't like it, I can guarantee that."

"I'll bring it," I said. "Where?"

"Bridgepoint Marina, slip twenty-three, a blue and white Bayliner called *Moon Spinner*." I wrote the address on the pad by the phone. "And don't waste time," he added, and hung up.

I took out my wallet and unfolded the slip of paper on which I'd written the combination to the safe in the floor of the pantry.

"What's going on?" Bobbi asked as I went into the pantry and lifted the little hatch that covered the safe. "What money?"

I took the envelope containing the cashier's cheque out of the safe, folded it, put it in my shirt pocket and buttoned the flap.

"I don't have time to explain," I said to Bobbi as I closed the safe. "I've got to go out. Would you mind looking after Hilly?"

"No, of course not. Does this have something to do with Carla? Wouldn't it be simpler just to throw yourself under the wheels of a truck?"

"Probably," I said. "I'm sorry," I said to Francine. "I hope I won't be too long."

"I'll go with you," she said.

I was tempted to let her, but I said, "Thanks, but this is something I should do on my own. Will you be here when I get back?"

"Sure. If that's what you want."

I kissed her quickly, grabbed a jacket from the hall closet, and opened the front door. Vince Ryan was standing on the dock, finger poised to ring the bell.

"Ding-dong," he said.

38

Standing behind Ryan was a huge, fierce-faced man with curly black hair and terminal five o'clock shadow. He was so dark-skinned he was almost black, but his features were Semitic. He had tiny coal-black eyes and a single thick black eyebrow that merged with the wiry black hair on either side of his broad head. He wore a snowy shirt and a dark shiny suit that looked two sizes too small for him. The jacket buttons were done up. So was the top button of the shirt, although he wasn't wearing a tie. Despite his western garb I wouldn't have been surprised if he'd been carrying one of those wide-bladed swords out of *Arabian Nights*.

"What happened to Sam?" I asked.

"I fired him," Ryan said. "He was a pussy. This is Abdul. That's not his real name, but I call him Abdul the Assassin. He does what I tell him, no questions."

"He doesn't look very bright," I said, watching Abdul's eyes for a reaction. I saw none.

"He doesn't need to be."

"I suppose not." I stepped out onto the dock and closed the door behind me. "I'd love to stay and chat," I said. "But I have a business appointment."

"This late in the day?"

"You know how it is," I said.

"How about Abdul and I just tag along?" he said. "It'll be an education. Abdul will drive us, how's that? We can have a drink and chat on the way."

I wondered about my chances of getting past Abdul. Not very good, probably, but I tried anyway. Abdul grabbed me by the upper arm and squeezed so hard my hand went numb. I struggled, but I might as well have been Fay Wray to Abdul's King Kong.

"No more fucking around," Ryan said. "Where is she?"

"You're too late," I said.

"What do you mean?"

"I know about the videotape."

"Fuck the videotape. I don't care about that. I love her. I want her back."

Who was he kidding? "She doesn't want you back," I said.

"We'll see. Take us to her?"

"And if I refuse."

"Abdul will start tearing off pieces of you. Starting with an ear, maybe. I'll bet that smarts. Abdul, tear off his ear." Abdul looked confused. Ryan said, "Ear. Y'know, ear?" He pulled his own ear.

Abdul grabbed my left ear and started to pull. It hurt. A lot. As though someone had laid a red-hot poker against the side of my head. The pain brought tears to my eyes. I had no doubt if Ryan said do it, Abdul would do it.

"All right," I said through the bright sparkling haze of pain. "But you follow me."

Ryan laughed. "You in your jazzy little Porsche and us in a big lumbering limo. Do we look that dumb? Don't answer that. No, we'll all go together."

"That," Francine said as she emerged from the house, "will be enough of that."

Ryan stared at Francine for a moment, then began to laugh. "I'll take care of this," he said to Abdul. He took a step toward her. "This should be fun."

Francine dropped into a defensive stance, legs wide, back straight, hands cocked. She looked calm and confident.

"Very pretty," Ryan said, and mimicked her. Not very well, I thought, but then I'm no judge of these things.

Ryan tried to grab her rather than hit her, but Francine stepped out of the way and he staggered off balance. She swept his legs out from under him and he fell hard onto the dock.

Abdul had let go of my ear, transferring his relentless grip to my other arm, and in his excitement was jouncing me up and down, none too gently. I clenched my jaw to prevent my teeth from clacking.

Ryan got warily to his feet and adopted a boxing stance. He danced toward Francine, jabbing at her face with a fast left. She backed away, but there was very little room to manoeuvre on the docks. Ryan grinned and pressed his attack. He threw a hard right, she parried it, trapped his arm, and threw him over her hip.

He got up more slowly this time. "Fuck it," he said, rubbing his left elbow and backing away from Francine. "Abdul, you take care of her, I'll watch him."

Abdul let go of me and advanced on Francine. She held her ground, but her look of confidence wavered.

Abdul was at least three times her weight and over a foot taller.

"Jesus, Francine," I said as Abdul reached for her.

I shook Ryan off and kicked the back of Abdul's right knee. His leg bent but did not buckle. I jumped onto his broad back, but he casually shrugged me off and tossed me aside. I almost fell into the water, saved myself by grabbing onto the gunwale of Maggie Urquhart's Boston Whaler. Some hero. Francine was on her own.

Then Harvey came bounding down the dock, jowls flopping and slobber flying, to join the fun, with Maggie chasing after him. With a loud, joyful woof, he launched himself at Abdul. At last, here was someone his size to play with. Planting his huge paws in the middle of Abdul's chest, Harvey woofed again, spraying dog slobber into Abdul face. But Abdul didn't want to play. With a snarl, he grabbed Harvey and tossed him off the dock as easily as if he'd been Mr. Oliphant's Yorkshire. Harvey hit the water with a huge splash and an indignant yawp.

But while Abdul's back was to her, Francine kicked him hard in the kidneys with the side of her foot. He grunted and turned ponderously toward her. She stepped back, spun and leapt and kicked. Abdul's head rotated almost one hundred and eighty degrees on his thick neck. His bulky body followed more slowly. He toppled to the dock and did not move.

"Aw, Christ," Ryan said. He looked at Abdul then at Francine. "All right," he said, raising his hands. "I give up. Jesus, you fucking killed him. It's going to take a goddamned forklift to get him out of here." He prodded Abdul with the toe of his shoe. Abdul did not move. "Well, your problem, not mine. See ya." He headed toward the gate.

Bobbi and Hilly came out onto the dock. Maggie Urquhart knelt on the edge of the dock, holding Harvey's collar, trying to pull him out of the water.

"Is he dead?" Hilly asked, looking at Abdul.

"No," Francine said.

"Where'd you learn that stuff?" I asked her.

"Working some of the places I have, you learn how to take care of yourself. Are you all right?"

"Yeah, sure," I said. And I was having a tough time dealing with her being stronger than me. "What are we going to do with him?"

"I'll call the police," Bobbi said and took Hilly inside.

Francine and I helped Maggie drag Harvey onto the dock. His dignity was damaged, but he was otherwise unharmed. Abdul moaned and tried to sit up. There was blood on his lips and his jaw was already starting to swell. Harvey and his mistress watched as Francine and I tied Abdul's hands and feet with rope from Maggie's Whaler.

"I've got to go," I said to Francine. "Maybe you should lock yourselves in the house until the police get here."

"We'll be all right," she replied. "But what about the other guy?"

"I don't think I have anything to worry about from him."

I was wrong. When I got to the parking lot the limo was still there, nosed up against the boardwalk and blocking a number of parked cars. Ryan was standing by the Porsche.

"I can't drive," he said.

"Tough," I said to him. "Take a cab." I unlocked the Porsche.

"Listen, I'm sorry about that. But I didn't know what else to do. Is Abdul dead?"

"No."

"Too bad. He's not going to be much fun to be around after getting the shit kicked out of him by a girl. It was a girl, wasn't it? Or do you swing both ways?"

"You really are an unpleasant son of a bitch, Ryan," I said. "I hope I've seen the last of you." I started the Porsche.

"McCall, don't do this." He took out a small automatic pistol, held it so that no one could see it but us. If anyone else were looking. Where was Francine when I really needed her? Or Harvey? "I'm a desperate man, McCall. Tell me where she is."

"And if I don't, what are you going to do, shoot me?"

"If I have to," he said. He looked as if he meant it. "Don't be an idiot," he added. "I've never actually killed anyone, but I'm always open to new experiences. No woman's worth dying for."

He was right. About Carla, at least. She wasn't worth getting killed over. "Get in," I said.

As he passed behind the car I thought about slipping the shift lever into reverse, popping the clutch and knocking him down, but before I could make up my mind he was around the car and settling into the passenger seat. A man of action shouldn't think too much.

Twenty minutes later I stopped the Porsche in front of the Bridgepoint Yacht Sales office, set the emergency brake and turned off the engine. I sat, without opening the door, looking straight ahead, hands at ten past ten on the steering wheel.

"Let's go," Ryan said.

I turned to him.

"Listen," I said. "I don't know what we're walking into here, but I don't want you waving a bloody gun around. Someone could get hurt. Me, for example."

"No one's going to get hurt if they do what they're told. Get out of the car."

"Carla doesn't have the tape," I said. "I delivered it to MacIlroy."

"I don't care about that," Ryan said, waggling the gun back and forth, but keeping it pointed at my chest.

"Don't give me that 'I love her' routine again." I said. "It's wearing thin."

"So what? C'mon, move it." He gestured with the gun for me to get out of the car.

I reached for the keys but he snatched them out of the ignition. We got out of the car. He slipped the gun into his jacket pocket, kept his hand in the pocket. He looked just like a man holding a gun in his pocket.

The security gate at the top of the ramp leading down to the docks was similar to the one at Sea Village, but it was not locked. Ryan stayed behind me as we walked down the ramp to the main dock. Slip 23 was on the middle of the three finger docks, third from the end on the right. The *Moon Spinner* was moored bow in, a big, sleek, aerodynamic cruiser, looking more like a spaceship than a boat. We walked along the narrow dock separating the slips and stepped through the gate-like hatch in the gunwale onto the afterdeck. The wide upholstered bench at the stern looked more comfortable than my sofa.

"Hello," I called.

Ryan said, "I think you're supposed to ask permission to board."

"Sure," I said.

Frank Poole's bulky form appeared in the hatchway of the pilothouse. He pointed a gun at us. I recognized it as the same gun Carla had pointed at me on Hastings's boat. I wondered when I would get used to people pointing guns at me.

"Shit," Poole said, waving the gun back and forth between Ryan and me. "Why'd you have to bring him?" He stayed in the hatchway, under the overhang of the flying bridge, out of sight of anyone on the docks or the other boats. His wide face looked flushed and shiny and his rug was mussed.

"He insisted," I said. Ryan was standing to my left and slightly behind me. I was uncomfortably aware of the pistol in his jacket pocket, fervently hoped he wouldn't do anything stupid, like start shooting.

"Did you bring the money?" Poole asked.

"What money?" Ryan asked over my shoulder.

I ignored him and said, "Where's Carla?"

"Never mind her," Poole said. "Where's the money?"

"What money?" Ryan asked again.

Poole said, "The two hundred thousand the lawyer is paying her to get back the videotape of him balling his clients, that money."

The pocket of my shirt seemed to suddenly grow warm. I'd never bothered to look in the envelope.

"That plus the fifty grand he paid me to make sure she doesn't bother him again," Poole added. "I've got a nice little grubstake to set me up in business in Mexico." He moved the muzzle of his pistol slightly to my left and pointed it at Ryan, who was still hanging back and standing slightly behind me, keeping me between himself and Poole. And Poole's gun. "Now you shut the fuck up, all right? McCall, stop wasting my time. Did you bring it or not?"

"MacIlroy paid you to kill her?" I said.

"Who said anything about killing her?" Poole said. "That would be an awful waste. No, we're going to take a little trip to Mexico."

"You're going to turn her over to Alvarez's friends," I said.

"Why would I do that?"

"She killed him," I said.

"Is that right? Then she did everyone a favour, saved them the trouble of doing it themselves. He was using a little too much of the product and becoming unpredictable. No, I'm going to introduce her to some people I know who will find a nice position for her in one of their establishments. Carla's always wanted to break into show business. Now's her chance."

Did he think I was just going to hand over the money and let him sail away with Carla and sell her into white slavery or whatever he had in mind? Surely not.

I asked him.

"That was the plan," he said.

"Then you're as stupid as you look," Ryan said.

Poole said, "Hey, pally, who're you calling stupid? I'm the one with the gun here."

"Ryan's right," I said. "The only way you're going to get the money is to turn Carla loose."

"Yeah, well, I sorta figured that was the way it was gonna go. I gave it a shot, right? Sure, I'll trade Carla for the money. It doesn't matter to me one way or the other. If she wants to go after the lawyer again, it's fine with me. What's he gonna do, sue me?"

"Where is she?" I asked.

"Where's the money?"

I shook my head. "I want to see her," I said. "I want to make sure she's all right."

Poole shrugged. "Sure, why not?" Over his shoulder, he called, "Bring her up here."

Carla stumbled up the companionway into the pilothouse, in the grip of a burly man with a surgical patch covering one eye. Her arms were bound in front of her with duct tape, a couple of turns around each wrist and a couple of longer loops between them, like flexible manacles, so her hands were two or three inches apart. Another strip of tape covered her mouth. She breathed with difficulty, bloody mucous bubbling from her nostrils and dripping onto the front of her T-shirt. Her right eye was swollen almost shut and beginning to blacken. She struggled weakly, but the man maintained a tight grip on her upper arms.

Where was the other one, I wondered, the one she'd said she'd kicked in the kneecap?

"Let her go," I said.

Poole shook his head. "Not until I get the money. Now where the fuck is it?"

"She can't breathe," I said. "Take the tape off."

"Fuck that," Poole said. "And fuck this, too. I'm tired of talking. Where's the goddamned money?"

"McCall," Ryan said. "Give him the bloody money."

"All right," I said, and I put my hand inside my jacket to undo the flap of my shirt pocket.

Suddenly, Carla twisted and almost wrenched free of One-Eye's grip. Poole lashed out and hit her in the face with the side of the pistol. Blood sprang from a gash on her cheek and she thrashed in One-Eye's grip.

There was a sound from behind and beside me, a harsh crack remarkably like the sound of a bat striking a baseball. A chunk of hatchway combing splintered next to Poole's face. Another crack and a red flower of blood blossomed on his left chest. He looked momentarily surprised, then all expression went out of his face and he sagged, as if someone had yanked out his plug.

Acting on sheer reflex, I spun and lashed out with my right arm, catching Ryan on the cheek with the back of my closed fist. My mind registered the pain in my hand, but I didn't really feel it. Ryan staggered, eyes unfocussed. His gun went off and blew a thumb-sized hole in the deck carpeting, a little too close to my foot. He slumped to his knees, tried to get up, sat down with a thump, eyes refocussing but still stunned. I reached down and took the gun out of his limp hand. The metal was warm. I tossed it over the stern into the water. Too late, I realized I'd just left my fingerprints on a murder weapon.

The man with the eye-patch darted out of the pilothouse, vaulted over the side onto the dock, and ran away.

Frank Poole lay on his back halfway through the pilothouse hatchway. There was a bloody patch on his chest, over his heart, but he didn't seem to be bleeding. Dead men don't bleed, I supposed, and there was no doubt in my mind that he was dead. Poor bastard, I thought, filled with a sadness that surprised me. The gun lay on the deck beside him. Hooking my little finger through the trigger guard like they do on television, I picked it up and tossed it overboard as well. Ryan watched it arc past him and splash into the water.

An elderly pot-bellied man appeared on the deck of the sailboat in the slip next to the *Moon Spinner*. He wore baggy green bathing trunks that reached to his knobbly knees.

"What's going on over there?" he demanded.

"Call the police," I said to him. "A man's been shot."

He disappeared below.

"Fuck," Ryan said. "Where's Carla?" He tried to get past me into the pilothouse.

I put my hand on his chest. "Let it go," I said.

"Yeah?" He pushed against me.

I held my ground. "Yes."

He continued to press for a few heartbeats, but he did not raise his hands. Then he backed off, head down, shoulders slumped, deflated.

"Well, hell," he said. He took a breath, raised his head and squared his shoulders, re-inflating himself. I readied myself, knowing that if this bull of a man wanted to get past me, he would, but he just said, "See you around, McCall."

"I hope not," I said to his back.

I watched Ryan's retreat for a moment, until I was certain he wasn't going to change his mind and come back, then, stepping carefully past Poole's body, I went into the pilothouse. There was blood on the deck and on the steps of the companionway leading down to the main salon. I went down the steps. The salon was almost as big as my living room, a third of the below-decks area at least, and better furnished.

"Tommy," Carla said from behind me.

I turned. She was sitting at the breakfast nook in the galley, leaning on her elbows, right hand clamped over her eye, left hand clenched into a fist. Blood streaked her face, dripping onto her white T-shirt and the table-top. Her hands were still taped together, but she'd removed the piece of tape that had covered her mouth.

"Fucking Vince," she said. Her voice was strained and flat. "He tried to kill me." Had he? I wondered. "Where is he?" she asked.

"He's gone," I said. "Are you hurt?"

"Something is sticking in my eye. I think it's a piece of the hatchway combing. It hurts like hell, Tommy, like there's a red-hot needle through my eyeball." Tears ran from her swollen left eye, diluting the blood on her cheek.

"The police are on the way. An ambulance too, probably."

I found a pair of scissors in the galley and removed the tape from her hands. I did it as gently as I could, but she winced and went rigid as I peeled the cuff of tape from her right wrist.

"Did you bring the money, Tommy?"

I took the envelope containing the cashier's cheque out of my shirt pocket, held it out to her. She took the envelope in her left hand and jammed it into her jeans pocket. "What are you going to tell the cops, Tommy?" she asked.

"I don't know, Carla. I haven't thought about it. Maybe I'll tell them the truth."

"Listen, Tommy, you don't have to tell them everything, do you? It'll just complicate things."

"I'll tell you what, Carla," I said. "I won't mention MacIlroy or the money. Ryan and I came here to get you away from an abusive ex-boyfriend. Ryan freaked and things just got out of hand. You're a victim. The police will have no reason to take you into custody, so you won't have to explain the cheque."

"Thanks, Tommy," she said. "I really appreciate it."

"But there's something you have to do for me in return," I said.

She looked at me with her undamaged eye. "Ah, there's always a catch, isn't there? All right, what?"

"Go home. Finish your business degree. Take singing lessons. Teach sailing. Open a coffee bar. Anything but what you've been doing. Before you end up dead."

"I've been thinking about finding another line of work," she said. "Maybe I'll even settle down. What do you think, Tommy? Do you think you could love a one-time thief, drug smuggler, killer, blackmailer?"

"Not to mention stripper, whore, con artist, and pirate. Yes, I suppose I could. But I don't. Not any more."

Jack Thompson came down the companionway.

"Looks like I'm late for the party," he said.

"Who the hell are you?" Carla said.

"I could be a friend," Thompson said.

"I don't need any more friends," she said.

"Is she all right?" he asked me.

"She's got a splinter of plastic or fibreglass in her eye," I said. "From the hatchway combing."

"Who's the dead guy upstairs?"

"His name's Frank Poole," I said. "Ryan killed him," I added.

"I saw Ryan driving your Porsche," Thompson said. "If you can call what he was doing driving. Don't expect to have a clutch or a gearbox if you ever get it back. He was grinding the gears and laying rubber all over the place."

Heavy footfalls on the deck over our heads signalled the arrival of the paramedics or the police. I helped Carla to her feet. Thompson stood aside as I guided her up the companionway.

A paramedic was hunched over Poole's body. He spoke into a microphone clipped to his collar, but I couldn't hear what he was saying. Another paramedic helped Carla to the upholstered bench at the stern.

"Let's take a look at you," she said, gently taking Carla's right wrist and slowly removing her hand from over her eye. Thompson hovered nearby.

A few minutes later, a pair of Richmond cops came aboard and for the next half hour I answered a lot of questions, most of them more than once, some of them three times, many of them silly. They weren't happy that I'd thrown the guns overboard. I told them it was my personal form of gun control.

I stuck to my story. Who was going to tell them anything different? Not Carla, that was certain.

In the middle of the interrogation, Carla called me over as the paramedics strapped her into a gurney. She had a huge patch of gauze covering her right eye. Her left eye was bright, pupil dilated. The gash on her cheek was held closed by tiny butterflies of adhesive tape.

"Tommy?"

"Yes?"

"I'm sorry I ever got you into this," she said.

"Me, too," I said.

"You really know how to fuck things up, don't you?"

"Yes, I guess I do."

"Y'know, maybe I will go home. Will you come and visit me?"

"No, I don't think so."

The paramedics lifted the gurney onto the dock and locked the wheels down.

"'Bye, Tommy."

"Goodbye, Carla."

Thompson followed the gurney, not wanting to lose sight of her. I went back to answering questions.

39

On Monday morning I was at the studio bright and early. I packed Ron's collection of girlie magazines and any personal items I could find into a couple of file cartons and shipped them, along with a cheque for three months' pay, to his home. I then called a company that specialized in on-site disposal of sensitive documents and told them I had a file cabinet full of photographs and negatives I wanted destroyed. They said they'd send a man with a portable shredding machine first thing Tuesday morning. That night I lit a fire in the woodstove in the living room and burned Ron's photos of Carla. I kept mine.

"Do I have to?" Hilly asked.

"Yes," I said. "You have to. It's only for a couple of weeks, then you'll be back here until the end of the summer."

"They're not going to fight all the time?"

"No. I told you. They're seeing a counsellor."

"Grandma doesn't like Beatrix," Hilly said.

"She agreed to let you take her with you, though." I scratched the ferret behind the ear. She seemed to like it.

"And you'll bring Courtney for a visit next weekend?"

"Yes, Grandma said it was all right."

"I dunno . . ."

"Let's put it this way," I said. "You spend a couple of weeks with your grandparents and I'll help you smuggle Beatrix onto the plane when you go home. Your mother is your problem."

"All right," she said. "Deal."

As I've said, you just have to be creative when it comes to raising kids.

"Boss?"

"What do I have to do to get you to stop calling me that?"

"Give me a raise."

"So call me boss. What is it?"

"Do you want the good or the bad news first?"

"The bad."

"West Coast Hotels pulled the plug."

"That's no surprise. What's the good news?"

"Meg and Peg have a couple of new girls and they want comps done."

"That's good news?" In addition to his hard-core sideline, Ron had also been using our equipment and facilities to do publicity photos for exotic dancers and photographers' models and to produce comps for Meg and Peg's escort service girls. "Oh, well," I said. "We can use the business."

"If you want, I can take care of it."

"No, I can handle it."

"You sure?"

"Yeah, I think I can squeeze it in."

"Well, if you're sure it's no trouble."

"No trouble at all."

"Have you heard anything from Francine?" she asked.

"Yeah, I got a postcard day before yesterday." To change the subject, I said, "How's the new apartment working out?"

"My upstairs neighbour is Bigfoot's sister, I think, walks around like she's wearing deep-sea diving boots. And she feeds pigeons from her balcony. Other than that, it's okay, I guess. I miss Hilly, though."

"So do I, but she'll be back from Victoria this weekend. Why don't you come to dinner Sunday?"

"Uh, Sunday? Can't. I've got a previous engagement. Remember Clint, the car-rental guy in Whistler? He called. Rain check, though."

"Too roight."

Toward the end of July, Jack Thompson called. He told me to keep an eye on the mail and on the news. The next day Brian MacIlroy accepted nomination as a candidate in the upcoming provincial by-election. That same afternoon two of his former clients held a press conference, at which they screened a videotape. The quality was not very good – it was a copy of a copy – but the actors were easily identifiable. The following day MacIlroy withdrew from the race.

A few days later an envelope arrived at the studio, postmarked Toronto and bearing the return address of J.A. Thompson, Investigations. Inside was a certified cheque for ten thousand dollars and a handwritten note that read: "Just to show there are no hard feelings. Carla. P.S.: Jack thinks I'd make a good private eye. Speaking of which, the doctors say mine will be good as new."

The envelope also contained a newspaper clipping, a grainy black-and-white file photo of Vince Ryan. The article accompanying the photograph said that he was wanted by the police for questioning regarding the death of his wife. Swell. He was still out there somewhere. Not a cheery thought.

Two weeks later I was sitting on my roof deck trying to catch up on my reading, but I couldn't concentrate. My eyes automatically scanned each line, but my brain seemed incapable of absorbing anything. I'd find myself at the end of a paragraph without any memory of what I had read. I finally gave up and just sat, heels up on the railing, head against the back of the chair, letting my thoughts drift where they may.

I'd received another postcard from Francine the day before, in which she'd written that the job in San Diego was working out fine and she hoped to get back to Vancouver someday soon, for a visit at least.

I'd spoken briefly to Reeny Lindsey a couple of days earlier and she'd told me she was doing all right, working again, but there was still no word from Chris. She was thinking about filing a missing person's report.

The police had found the Porsche, at least what was left of it after Ryan had got through with it. He'd ditched it near the airport. Miraculously, the insurance company hadn't given me a hard time with the claim, in spite of the car's age. As for the house insurance, the bankruptcy trustees had evidently recovered a little – very little – of the money the Pacific Casualty officers had absconded with and, according to Wally Hoag, I might actually get enough to cover the rental of the little purple pump.

And Linda had called. She and Jack were cutting short the Asian leg of their vacation – Jack had broken his arm falling out of a pedicab – and were going to be stopping over in Vancouver for a couple of days on their way home. Hilly, who had been on the extension, surprised me by asking if Jack was okay.

"Ask him yourself," Linda had said.

"I'm fine, short stuff," Jack had said, coming on the line. "Feel a bit stupid, though." Lowering his voice to barely a whisper, he had then asked, "Beatrix behaving herself?"

"Uh, yeah."

"I miss you," Jack had said.

"Me too," Hilly had replied.

I closed my eyes and Frank Poole's face materialized on the inside of my eyelids, so I opened my eyes and it went away.

The gate bell rang. Not really caring who it was, just glad of the company, I went down to the dock to answer it.

I almost didn't recognize her. She wore snug-fitting black Spandex riding shorts and a bright orange top that showed her flat, tanned midriff. Iridescent Oakley wraparound sunglasses dangled around her neck. She was wheeling a purple mountain bike, a teardrop-shaped helmet slung from one of the hand grips. Her riding shoes clicked on the surface of the dock.

"I was out for a ride, so thought I'd take the chance and drop by. You wouldn't by chance have any club soda in your fridge, would you?" Bright beads of perspiration glistened on her upper lip and a vein pulsed slowly in her throat.

"I think I might be able to find some," I said.

She leaned her bike on the kickstand and followed me inside.

"How's Colin?" I asked as I took a big two-litre bottle of club soda from the fridge and poured a tall glass. "It's gone a little flat, I'm afraid," I said, handing her the glass.

"Easier to drink," she said, gulping down half the glass. "Colin is history," she said when she came up for air.

"Sorry to hear that."

"Thanks," she said. "But don't waste your sympathy. I don't think I've ever known anyone quite so self-absorbed. He wasn't a total loss, though. He turned me on to cycling."

"I wondered." I looked her up and down. "You look pretty good in that outfit."

She smiled, brightening the room. I'd missed that smile.

"You know I left Chez François," she said.

"Yes, I'd heard. What are you going to do?"

"I'm going to open my own restaurant."

"That's terrific," I said. "I hope you haven't come to me for advice on how to run your own business, though."

327

She cocked her head and gave me a look of disbelief that said it all. I got a Kokanee out of the fridge and suggested we take our drinks up to the roof deck. As we started up the stairs, Susan stopped, looked around and said:

"Is it my imagination or is your house still tilted?"